GW00499715

The Beta and his Mate

By B E Wakeford

ISBN: 9798367280487

Cover design by: everaftercoverdesign
Library of Congress Control Number: 2018675309
Printed in the United States of America

For all those who don't believe they can…
You can.

Prologue
Xavier's POV

I've always loved running.

Ever since I shifted almost two years ago, all I seemed to want to *do* was run.

Every chance I got I was out in the forest, either running laps around the border of our territory or chasing small rabbits and other creatures for some light entertainment between my lessons and duties. I couldn't seem to get enough of it. It helped to clear my head whenever I started to feel suffocated, after dad and I had another argument or the ache from my mate bond got too much, I came out here and I ran.

That's what I was doing when it happened.

I was currently out here, running laps because my dad and I had got into yet another fight, about me not taking my Beta position seriously. I honestly didn't understand what the big fuss was about, I mean yes at one point the pack was going to have to rely on me a little more than they did right now as I'd become second in command, but it wasn't like I was Jax or anything. He was the one who always had to act responsible and take things seriously, not me. That was the perk of not being the Alpha.

I internally rolled my eyes again at my dad's words as they floated around in my head.

He had caught me with one of the pack girls as I tried to sneak her out of my room after a drunken night out. Safe to say he wasn't amused, and I'd run out of the house before I could feel the full weight of my parents' disapproval and disappointment. I could still feel my mum poking around in my brain, trying to open up the mind link so that she could talk to me about it, but I continued to block her out and focused on my run.

I loved my mum, deeply, but sometimes she could be a bit much. She was the peacekeeper between my dad and me, she never took sides and she never yelled, but you could always tell there was more she wanted to say. She wasn't one to step on toes though, so she just stood between the two of us as we yelled in each other's faces, acting more as a referee than a mother and a wife.

It wasn't like I didn't get along with my dad, he was probably one of my best friends, it was more the fact that we were *too* similar. We both always had to be right, and we both hated being wrong.

We had some good times though. Being so alike also meant that we had the same hobbies. We both loved to practise our fighting techniques, we both loved to watch and play football and we both enjoyed camping. Every year my whole family, my little sister Louise included, would head out into another packs territory and spend a week out in the woods and living off the land.

Of course, we'd ask the Alpha's permission first, and we never interfered with their pack's life, but we always enjoyed our quiet time together. With dad working so much with Alpha Jackson and mum was constantly helping Luna Emily as the Beta female, it was rare that the family had more than one night uninterrupted. But when we did, it was amazing.

We hadn't gone on our annual holiday yet, but we were looking to leave in the next few weeks. The place we usually stayed at was having issues with rogues and so didn't feel comfortable with four relative strangers staying on their land, so we were currently looking for another place to visit. Not that I blamed the Alpha, rogues were serious business.

I smiled at the memories and sighed as I felt the wind ruffle my fur. I couldn't wait until we were back out there, away from the pack for a while and away from the distractions. My pack was my home, and I knew that, but it was nice for us to get away for a while and just let our hair down.

I couldn't wait to go fishing with dad, usually unsuccessfully, as we spoke about the recent football games. Laugh at Louise as we watched her eat her sixth toasted marshmallow dipped in chocolate sauce, the sauce dripping down her chin as she tried to shove the huge chocolate treat into her mouth in one go. Smile as I watched my parents, still as in love as ever, dance in the light of the fire, dancing to some music that was obviously going on silently in their heads.

It was bliss.

I hated my family sometimes, but damn did I love them.

Just then I heard the snap of a twig not too far behind me. I instantly froze and went into a crouched, defensive position, the training I've recently had with my dad surfacing into the forefront of my mind, until it was all I could think about. I was upwind and so couldn't get a smell of the wolf, but if they were crouched behind a bush and not announcing themselves, it couldn't be good.

I bided my time, waiting until it got a little closer to me, and right when it was about to break through a nearby hedge and pounce, I made my move. I leaped in the air and landed on the wolf's back intent on sinking my claws and teeth into its neck, but when I finally got a look at the jet-black wolf that was now under me, I sighed and stood up.

"Jesus Jax I nearly took your head off," I laughed as I rolled my eyes at him. Only he would find it hilarious to sneak up on someone who was doing border patrol.

"In your dreams Xavier, there is no chance in hell that you could take me on and win," he laughed as he shook out his fur, dislodging the few leaves that had tangled their way into his fur after being on the ground. *"What are you doing out here anyway? It's not your turn to patrol,"* he asked as he came and stood next to me.

I waited until he had sorted himself out before turning around and carried on running, I was the only one on patrol and so I couldn't sit and chat, that would leave the rest of the borderline unguarded and unprotected from potential threats.

"I wanted to go for a run, clear my head a little, so I thought I may as well do something useful whilst I'm at it."

"What happened this time?" Jax laughed as he easily kept up with my pace, not that it was hard as I was only doing a light jog.

I stayed silent, hoping he would drop the subject if I showed no interest in carrying it on, but unfortunately it seemed to only spur him on further.

"Let me guess." he laughed. *"You went out to that party last night, got steaming drunk and came home with*

4

some random girl, and then got caught by either your mum or dad as they saw her sneak out of the house this morning?"

Damn it he knew me so well. Let's just say this wasn't the first time I had done something like this, and it probably wouldn't be the last either.

I sighed as I hung my head slightly, was I really that obvious?

"It's all right man, we've all been there," Jax muttered as he tried to make me feel better. He knew how painful it was for me the next morning, the guilt of sleeping with someone who wasn't my mate. It was always the same, after I get a few drinks in me it's like the world is a better place and every girl I see is my mate, a potential person to help fill the void that constantly ached in my chest at the pain of an incomplete blood bond.

"You haven't," I grumbled, feeling a little annoyed at how much self-control he had over himself. I mean sure he'd caved once or twice, it was only natural with the amount of hormones racing through a teenage wolf's blood, but he didn't mess up nearly as much as I did. *"I just find it so hard sometimes,"* I mumbled. *"Sometimes I feel so lonely, even though I'm surrounded by people. I look at my parents and the other mated couples around the pack and I get so jealous I feel like I just have to... fill the void with anything I can find... any*one *I can find."* I know it sounded sad, and a little soppy, but I was really struggling not having my mate by my side.

Being mate less can affect people in different ways. Some, like Jax, didn't struggle with the separation at all. Sure, he wished he had her by his side and was doing everything in his power to find her, but he didn't feel the

5

gaping hole in his chest at not having her around like I did. Whereas for me, I was a rare case, a rare bond that wasn't common due to the side effects and stress it could have on the wolf.

I had read about them in one of my mum's old history books. That a blood bond, even though it was extremely rare, *could* happen, and that *I* happened to be one of the lucky few who seemed to suffer from one. No one was really sure why the Goddess chooses to make someone suffer the blood bond whilst others could happily wait until their mate turns up, but it was thought that it was because the people who had one needed a strong link with their mate later in life. Something that would tie them together so completely they could never reject each other and never live without the other once the initial meeting happened. I don't know what that meant for me, why the Goddess thought I was someone who needed a bond like that, but I always chose to just ignore it and cross that bridge when I came to it.

"So was it your mum or your dad?" Jax suddenly asked and I frowned as I thought about his question. He must've seen the confused and blank look in my eyes because he sighed in exasperation before explaining. *"Who saw the girl leave your room, was it your mum or your dad?'*

"Oh, my dad," I cringed, the argument we'd had earlier resurfacing in my mind once again.

"Ouch," Jax cringed, knowing what my dad was like.

"Tell me about it," I grumbled. *"It's not like he knows what it's like to go without his mate, my mum was in the same pack as him. As soon as they both turned*

sixteen bam! *they were together,"* I grumbled, angry at the unfairness of it all.

"I hear you man; I can't imagine what you must be feeling when you have to watch mated couples all day. Its not fun me, so it must be torture for you. If letting loose with a random girl keeps you sain then who am I to judge," Jax replied.

And that's why he's my best friend.

"I just hate the fact that he thinks I'm going to be a bad Beta because of it, just because I sleep with a girl every now and then doesn't mean I'm bad at my job. It's not like we're taking over anytime soon anyway, we have a few years yet." We ran in silence after that, both of us just enjoying each other's company as we let off some steam.

It wasn't till about twenty minutes later when I picked up the scent, a scent that makes every wolf's blood run cold with dread.

Jax and I both looked at each other for a split second before we both unanimously said the dreaded word. *"Rogue."*

Within a flash we both sprinted off to track the scent, making sure we didn't lose the owner. This was it; this was my moment to shine and prove to my father that I could be trusted with the Beta position, and he would finally get off my back and trust me.

"Jax," I linked as we continued our pursuit. *"What if we don't tell your dad what we suspect and deal with this ourselves,"* I muttered, hesitant with my suggestion as I knew it was technically breaking the rules of border patrol. If you suspected anything, no matter how small, you always had to inform both the Alpha and the Beta through the pack link. Always.

He surprised me though as he smiled a wolfish grin, *"way ahead of you',"* he linked as he picked up his speed. *"You aren't the only one who needs to prove themselves to their father."*

And with that we were off.

We followed the trail for a good five minutes, darting and weaving as we followed the scent of the lone rogue. I had to hand it to the wolf, this person could run.

We froze when we got to the clearing, both with our muscles coiled and ready for anything as we surveyed the area.

"I don't understand," I muttered as we stood with our backs to each other, keeping each other's six's safe. *"The scent trail ends here... so where are they?"*

"They must've shifted back into their human form to weaken their scent or something," Jax replied as he continued to scout the area.

We broke apart from our position and started sniffing around the place, hoping that we could maybe pick up the scent of the rogue who had passed through. *"This doesn't make any sense, why willingly enter a pack's territory if you're only going to shift out of your wolf and retreat. That is the least tactical thing you could do."*

"Umm Xav... I think we should link our fathers now," Jax linked as he continued to stare at something at his feet.

I frowned as I walked over to him and froze when I saw what he was staring at. It was a t-shirt, not one of ours, that had been soaked in animals' blood. I leant down and took a sniff of the fabric and cringed as the smell of rust filled my nostrils, but it wasn't just animals' blood I had picked up, it was the stench of rogue.

"This must've been what we were tracking," I growled as I kicked the top away. *"Whoever did this must've drowned the fabric in the blood to kill the scent after they lead us here."*

"But why did they lead us here?" Jax asked as his eyes fogged over.

I did the same, tapping into the packs link to try and contact anyone I could. What I received was a shambles, it seemed that everyone was shouting through the link at once, asking for help and trying to find their loved ones.

One thing was clear, we were under attack... and we had fallen right for their trap.

As if a gunshot had gone off, signalling the start of a race, both Jax and I shot off into the forest, intent on getting to the centre of our pack as fast as possible. *This could not be happening* I muttered as I felt my muscles burn as I pushed them to run faster and faster. *This could not be happening!*

We made it to where most of the fight was taking place and I instantly got stuck in, killing rogues wherever I could and helping out pack members who needed it. There weren't that many rogues, and with any luck we could make it through this attack virtually unscathed, with just my pride as its only casualty.

I spotted my dad in the distance, fighting a particularly strong looking rogue and I cringed as I saw its paw connect with his head. The rogue didn't draw blood thankfully, but that would definitely give him a headache in the morning.

"DAD!" I yelled through the link as I made my way over to give him a hand, if something happened to him, I don't know if I could ever forgive myself.

"I'm fine son, go to the house and help protect your mother and sister," he linked back, not breaking his focus from the rogue in front of him.

I nodded, even though he couldn't see me, and turned to make my way back to the house, whispering a quick *"I'm sorry,"* to him as I ran. I hope he knew I was saying sorry for more than just letting the rogue attack happen. I was saying sorry for everything that I had said to him today, and for every argument before that.

I didn't turn around to see if he had gotten the message as I ran the short distance to my house, I had to make sure I was fully aware of my surroundings and that no one could spring a surprise attack on me.

I breathed a sigh of relief as the air cleared of the stench of blood that was thick in the air. I had never liked the smell of blood, but the smell of rogue blood? That was so much worse.

I took in another breath as I ran, calming and focusing my mind as the cold air cleared my thoughts, but when I picked up on the scent of pack blood I froze. I knew that smell anywhere, it had been ingrained into my brain ever since Louise was a little girl and had fallen off a rope swing and broken her leg. Her bone had broken the skin and I had to carry her all the way to the hospital as she cried in pain . Her blood had soaked through my shirt, and it was a constant reminder of what had happened as I sat in the waiting room for hours, waiting for her to get out of surgery and for the doctors to tell me she would be okay.

What I smelt in that second was Louise's blood.

If possible, I ran even faster, and what I saw when I rounded the corner would forever be burned into my skull. My sister, lifeless, with her throat ripped out and a rogue standing over her, her blood dripping down his face. He had shifted back into his human form, and as he stared down at her, I saw a type of fire in his eyes that made my blood run cold.

My eyes were suddenly drawn to movement at the other side of our house, where a little alleyway led down to our back garden.

"*MUM*!" I screamed through the link as I ran towards her, hoping to get to her in time before the rogue holding her captive killed her too.

"Xavier, get out of here!" My mum screeched in panic as she saw me running towards her, tears running down her face as her eyes clocked onto her cold and lifeless daughter. "Xavier *please* run," she begged but I ignored her, no way was I going to abandon her.

"Who's this little wolf?" The rogue holding my mother by the throat asked, his lips brushing her ear as he spoke.

I growled at how close he was to her but skipped to a halt when the other rogue blocked my path, my sister's blood dribbling down his chin and onto his chest as he grinned, flashing his teeth at me.

I crouched into a defensive stance as I opened the pack link up, hoping someone would see what was happening and come to help us. Please let someone come and help us.

"Here little puppy," the rogue in front of me mocked, and with that I pounced.

The rogue quickly shifted as he dodged my claws, smirking at my attempt, toying with me. I growled as he danced from foot to foot, dodging left and right as I stood there and stared, one eye on the rogue in front of me and one on my mother. She was doing what she could to get out of the guy's hold, but with his claws digging into her neck, threatening to rip it open at any second, there was little she could do.

One of the first things dad had taught me to do was assess my opponent, find out if they had any weak spots and track their attacking style, and after a few seconds of watching this rogue dance from foot to foot I noticed something. It wasn't much, but he was favouring his front right leg ever so slightly, it wasn't much but at least it was something.

With my focus zeroed in on the rogues' leg I lunged, faking going left before quickly spinning and slamming my head into the rogues' weak upper leg. The rogue went down with a whine as I heard a sickening snap and as I looked back, I saw that the leg had been shattered, broken in two different places, making the limb look disfigured and caused my stomach to churn slightly.

I quickly clamped my jaws around the wolf's neck, ending its life, and when I was sure he was dead I rounded on the rogue holding my mother with a growl. She was staring at me wide eyed, her fear scenting the air, but I tried to ignore it as I focused in on the last rogue male.

"I'm coming Xavier, just hold him off for a little longer," Jax yelled at me through the link, and I sighed in relief as I realised that help was coming.

"Stand down boy, you don't know who you're up against," the rogue warned as he shifted so that he'd put my mum in front of him, using her as a human shield between us.

I just growled back in response, blood and saliva dripping from my teeth as my hackles rose.

"You're going to pay for killing my brother, you hear me?!" The rogue suddenly yelled, sinking his extended claws into my mother's neck.

I growled as I watched her blood trickle down his dirty fingers before dripping onto the grass below. The grass my dad had obviously been halfway through cutting before running off to the rouge fight.

Everything after that moment was blurry. During our fight I'd somehow managed to separate my mum from the rogue, long enough for me to pounce on him and rip his throat out as I sank my teeth into his delicate human skin. He'd never shifted back into his wolf, so it was easy for me to tear into his skin and sever his carotid artery, ending his life before the fight could go on.

I growled at him for a second longer as I watched the life drain from his shocked eyes, feeling no remorse at taking another wolf's life. He had deserved it, they both did.

I turned around, intent on taking my mum in my arms and assess her injuries, but when she wasn't where I thought she'd be I panicked, had another rogue come and taken her?

I frantically looked around for her, frowning when I noticed a small blood trail leading its way out of the alleyway and back up towards our front garden. I hesitantly followed it, preparing myself for any surprise attacks that could happen, but what I saw when I rounded the corner of our house broke my heart more than I ever thought it possibly could.

My mum had used the last of her strength to crawl towards Louise and hold her in her arms with her head bowed into her hair.

I sobbed as I walked over towards my sister and my mum, shifting in the process so that I could take both of them in my arms and cry, for the loss of my baby sister. But as I got closer, I noticed something that almost brought me to my knees.

My mum, with her lifeless daughter in her arms, had stopped breathing.

I screamed as I ran over to her, skidding to the floor as I took her in my arms and held my hand against her neck, hoping to stop the flow of blood from leaking out of her skin.

The rogue had done more damage than I had originally thought, sinking deep enough into her neck to hit her vein and cause serious damage. I cried as I held firm on her neck with one hand whilst trying to perform CPR with my other, hoping and praying that my efforts would help in some way until the doctors could get here.

"Don't leave me mum... please," I begged as I repeatedly pushed down on her chest, trying to keep her heart beating and oxygen going through her veins. My vision blurred until I could no longer see anything, but I carried on pushing, praying that a miracle would happen, and her heart would magically start beating again on its own.

Jax was still on his way, fighting his way through as best he could, but it seemed that whenever he was finished with one, another would take its place. As if his black Alpha coat was a beacon to all that he was our future and he needed to be taken out.

As I performed CPR the best I could I cried, staring into Louise's lifeless eyes, as she stared back at me, empty and black. How could this have happened? How was it only this morning the worst thing I was suffering with was a mild hangover and another pointless fight with my dad. Now I had lost my mum and my sister all in the space of an hour.

My CPR attempts became weaker and weaker as my muscles grew shaky and numb. I had been running for hours on patrol before any of this even started, and with the attack and the strain of CPR they were finally starting to give up.

I had failed them.

I collapsed into a heap on the floor, sweat beading on my forehead as it mingled with the countless smears of blood that coated my body. Some of it was the rogues, but most was my mothers and sisters. Their blood was quite literally on my hands, and I could never forgive myself for it.

It felt like hours before someone finally arrived at my house, the blood that soaked my skin now dry, causing my skin to feel tight and crack every time I moved. My tears had stopped as I held my mothers and sisters' hands, refusing to let them go as I felt their bodies become cold. If I let them go then they were gone, for real, and I don't think I could survive if they were gone.

"Xavier I'm... I'm so sorry," I heard someone sob as they came and sat in front of me, draping a blanket around my shivering form. I hadn't even realised I was cold.

"I did this," I muttered to nobody in particular, not finding the strength to even raise my head and look at the people who stood in front of me. Too worried to look up and see the disappointment that undoubtedly clouded my friends and packs members faces, too cowardly to look into my father's eyes and see his broken expression as he looked down at his dead mate and daughter.

"You didn't do this," the voice continued as she crouched down until she was eye level with me.

I looked up slightly and came face to face with Emily as she looked at me with her own watery eyes. My mum was her best friend, and to see her like this must be killing her.

"I *did*," I cried as I held on tight to my family's hands. "I'm…I'm so sorry dad," I sobbed as I built up the courage to look up.

I noticed a lot of faces around me, all looking worse for wear as they stared down at me in sorrow, but as I continued to look I noticed one face was missing, one that definitely should be here and looking down at me in anguish and disgust.

"Where's dad?" I asked as I continued to take in the few faces around me. They all looked back at me with sympathetic eyes as they shared small glances with each other. I frowned as I continued to stare... something had happened.

"Where's my father?" I asked a little more forcefully this time, but with one look at Emily who was still crouching in front of me, I knew. My dad was no longer with us.

With one simple mistake, one decision I had made in the moment of anger and ignorance, I had gone from having a happy family to becoming an orphan.

Chapter One
Blaine's POV

EIGHT YEARS LATER

Crap, they were gaining on me.

These suckers were fast, I'd give them that.

It wasn't often that a rogue male could keep up with me, let alone one that had already gotten a taste of what my sharp claws were capable of. I don't even know why they're chasing me. I was only minding my own business, doing a bit of hunting, when these three idiots jumped out of the bushes and started a fight with me.

Thank goodness I could shift quickly. I'd managed to shift into my wolf mid pounce and slashed one of the three in the throat before any of them could even blink.

I was kind of used to this by now. Being a lone rogue she wolf *did* draw a lot of unwanted attention, particularly of the male variety, if you catch my drift. They just couldn't seem to take *'no'* for an answer, always seemingly thinking I'd secretly meant *'yes'* with the non-existent eye flutter I'd given them; or so I've been told by other male rogues I'd turned down in the past.

Slime balls, the lot of them.

After I'd quickly disposed of the first attacker, the other two had pounced towards me in unison, noticing I wasn't going to be the easy target they'd probably planned and hoped for. I'd quickly dodged and jumped backwards and out of their reach, before turning and making a run for it. I'd managed to get away from them nearly unscathed, just a few cuts and bruises here and there, but they were all from sharp branches that would definitely be healed by tomorrow morning.

I continued ducking and weaving through the trees and shrubbery, trying to make it as tricky for them to follow me as I possibly could through the undergrowth. There was only so much I could do that wouldn't result in me slowing myself down in the process though and in the end, I had no choice. If I wanted to stand a chance at getting away from them, I had to ditch my plan of losing them and just go for distance.

Most rogues couldn't run for long periods of time, due to their poor diet and lack of food they had to hand, but my parents had taught me how to survive even the harshest conditions, so I was never short on supplies.

I just hoped and prayed that these two wolves were too hungry to care about me for much longer. They'll see that they were wasting all their precious energy on me and decide to save it to catch their next meal rather than waste it on a hopeless chance of catching me for a bit of fun.

As I continued to run as fast as I could through the forest I could feel the air uncomfortably shift around me, causing me to unwillingly slow down and trip on an old tree stump hidden beneath the tall grass, and I cursed. *Damn it*. It was all the opportunity they needed for the two asshats to catch up with me and swipe at my back legs with their claws, trying to get me to stumble further and become vulnerable.

I knew exactly why the atmosphere in the forest had changed, and my hackles rose as the realisation washed over me like ice water.

We were in a pack's territory.

I could feel the crackle of their Alpha's power as it tingled through my veins, warning me that I was trespassing and should turn around before their border patrol found me and taught me a lesson on why a rogue should *never* enter pack lands without permission.

I quickly turned around, intending to run before I was caught by any pack members, but before I could I was met with the two furious rogues who had been chasing me. Furious I'd killed their buddy and ran from them. Furious I'd made them expend so much precious energy in the chase for something they believed they deserved and were somehow entitled to.

Their teeth were showing, saliva dripping from their gums, and I couldn't help but cringe at the sight of it. Lovely, I was stuck between a rock and a hard place.

How could they not tell that we were in pack territory right now? It was rule number one living as a rogue to stay away from all border lines unless you wanted to die a slow and painful death.

Packs did not react well to rogues, never even letting us plead our cases before we were either captured and tortured or just plain killed on the spot, and I honestly couldn't figure out which was worse. It was unfair if you asked me, not even asking what we were doing on their land before they attacked, but there was little I could do about it. It wasn't like the Alpha would allow a rogue like me onto their land for a discussion on the off chance that we were dangerous.

If you were a wolf without a pack, it was always for a reason. You were a rogue for a reason, and that was something an Alpha couldn't risk allowing onto his land and near his people.

The wolf on my left lunged at me, pulling me from my thoughts, his teeth and claws extended as he aimed for my jugular, but I quickly dodged out of the way, not wanting to get on the receiving end of those canines.

My my grandma, what big teeth you have I chuckled to myself as I dodged his teeth once more, his buddy staying back and watching the show, trying to assess how I moved and find an opening of his own.

I inwardly rolled my eyes at our little dance we were having. The wolf had no skill, and I was honestly starting to get a little bored and dizzy from all the spinning he was doing trying and failing to catch me off guard.

I acted quickly, and before either of them could figure out what I was planning, I lunged at the more aggressive of the two wolves, taking out the biggest threat first in the hopes that it might scare the last one off, so I wouldn't have to deal with that one too.

I quickly pinning my target down with my paws, making sure I kept an eye on the other wolf, before I used all my strength and weight to crush his windpipe with my claws, feeling his warm blood seep under my claws and onto my skin.

I hated taking another wolf's life, no one ever deserved to die the way they did, but I was always taught that if it was a life-or-death situation you had to do the unsettling tasks to survive. Being a rogue was a tough life, and if you didn't have the stomach to defend yourself when the time came you were as good as dead.

20

After I was convinced the second rogue was no longer a threat, I turned to face the last of the three wolves but whined as I felt his front teeth sink into the muscle around my back leg. Damn that hurt, he was faster than most rogues I'd encountered. I'd give him that. Seemed I was wrong in my initial assessment on who was more of a threat out of the two, a mistake that could well cost me my life.

I tried to shake him off as I reached around and swiped at him with my front claws, but I couldn't reach. He was too far behind me, and my wolf's spine didn't bend the way I needed it to no matter how much I tried.

I growled at him, in both anger and frustration, before quickly shifting back into human form and harshly smacking him over the head with the first rock I could blindly get my hands on. The attacker released my thigh with a whimper and took a step back as he moaned in pain and shook his head to help clear it. My wolf body may have been helpless in that situation, but my human body wasn't. *Thank you opposable thumbs.*

Now that problem was solved, I was now onto the next one. The issue with shifting into my human form was it left my delicate skin exposed and without the protection of fur that my wolf self could provide.

I quickly started to shift back into my wolf form, knowing that I was vulnerable in my current form, but before I could complete the shift the rogue's front claws dug into my unguarded skin and left four ugly gouges across my upper thigh, not too far from where his bite marks were.

I screamed in agony as I fought through the pain, finally managed to shift back into my wolf and lunged forward, determined to kill him before he could do any further damage. I had lived a long time as a rogue, longer still if you counted living with my family, and I'd be damned if I let a wolf like him be the end of me. No way was I going down like that.

But before I could take even a step in my defence, another wolf appeared out of nowhere, slamming my attacker out of the way and me out of his line of fire. *What the-*.

I watched on in shock as the two male wolves circled each other, sizing each other up with their hackles raised and snarls leaving their throat. The rogue wolf made the first move and suddenly darted for the pack wolf's throat, but before he could do any damage the pack wolf dodged his attack and turned so his teeth bit into the rogue's neck, biting down hard on a particularly soft spot. Even I had to admit I was impressed at how easily he'd managed to deal with the rogue, and I wasn't easily impressed.

I stood there for a second, stunned at the fact that a pack wolf had willingly gotten in between two fighting rogues, alone and without backup, but as I took in a deep breath of fresh air to help ease the adrenaline from my veins, I realised why he'd done it.

He was my mate.

Crap.

I stared for a second in shock, taking in the huge grey wolf that was standing before me, before I turned tail and ran as fast as my injured leg would allow me. It had already started healing, but annoyingly not enough for me to be able to put my full weight on it or stop the blood from flowing freely from the wounds.

I quickly glanced over my shoulder, to make sure the guy wasn't gaining on me, but frowned slightly and stumbled when I saw that he hadn't moved an inch from where I'd left him. He just continued to stare at me wide eyed as he watched me leave.

That was weird, I thought pack wolves were all about finding their mates and being all *lovey dovey* with each other.

I mentally shrugged, happy with the fact that he seemed just as uninterested in having a mate as I was, and turned back around to focus on getting out of here. Being on pack territory always gave me the shivers, and not in a good way.

I sighed in relief as I made it to the outskirts of their land, but before I could cross the boundary line, I was suddenly surrounded by pack warriors.

Double crap.

Chapter Two
Xavier's POV

"Just get off my back would you?!" I growled at Jax as he explained to me yet again why I needed to dedicate more time to finding my mate. I mean it wasn't like I hadn't been *trying*. He knew full well how much it made me ache inside, knowing that I still didn't have my mate by my side.

I was one of the unfortunate few in our race to suffer from an incomplete blood bond, a kind of mate bond that was so strong, a person couldn't reject their destined mate even if they wanted to. You were bound together by spirit and by soul and not even the most powerful magic on earth could release you from the other.

It wasn't clear why the Goddess made some wolves endure this type of bond, it was near agony for the wolves who had one incomplete, like a part of your soul was missing, but it was believed she did it because she knew we'd be dealing with issues in our future. Issues that would test us and our bond to our limits, issues that we'd need each other to help us through and to survive.

God knows what that even meant. I felt like I'd already had enough drama to last me a lifetime over the past couple of years, but every time I watched a wolf live happily with their mate, it made my heart crack just that little bit further inside my chest.

I'd asked Anna if she could somehow ask the Goddess why she had given this to me, why she'd thought it was necessary that *I* was one of the unlucky few that needed a blood bond with my destined mate, but every time she tried to connect with her and ask, she came up empty handed.

"Watch your tone with me Xavier, you may be my best friend and Beta, but it doesn't give you the right to be disrespectful to me," Jax growled back, and my wolf flattened his ears, unhappy with the fact that we'd angered our Alpha.

I sighed as I rubbed my eyes with my hand. "I'm sorry, I know you're only trying to look out for me and make sure I'm happy and all, but I don't need to be told something I already know. I *know* I need to find her, but I just don't know where she is, where she could be hiding." At twenty-six it was pretty much unheard of for a Beta not to have found his mate by now, and it was taking its toll on both me and my wolf. I felt like I was going crazier by the day, losing my temper more frequently and finding it harder to want to stay in my human form the more I shifted. It was worrying, for both me and the pack, and I knew the only thing that could fix me was to find the one girl I couldn't.

I sighed again as I rested my head in my hands. It had been almost three years since Jax had found his mate and since then more and more pack members were finding their mates, seemingly daily. All but me.

Every year Anna and our pack hosted a ball of sorts and anyone who wanted to come, from all walks of life and all packs, were welcome. The idea was to help people find their mates, and it had been beyond successful the past two years. It has been successful for everyone... except for me.

Jax sighed as he took in my defeated expression and came round his desk to clap me on the shoulder. "You'll find her soon, just keep the faith that the Moon Goddess has picked someone amazing for you, the wait will be worth it in the end... trust me," he smiled with the same goofy smile he always had on his face whenever he thought about Anna.

I rolled my eyes before getting up, unable to be around his positive thinking for another minute without losing it again. "I'm going to go for a run, hopefully it'll help clear my head and stop me from being so on edge," I sighed.

Jax nodded as he made his way back around the desk, so he could carry on with his paperwork that seemed to be forever building on his desk. "Alright, just keep the faith, okay? You never know what's around the corner."

I nodded my head but didn't respond as I made my way out of Jax's house and into the woods surrounding his garden.

Just as I was about to shift, I heard running footsteps behind me and I quickly looked around to find Anna, Jax's mate, running to catch up with me.

"Xavier! Xavier, wait... are you okay?" She asked when she got close enough to me that she didn't have to shout.

I smiled before giving her the best convincing smile I could manage. "Yeah, Anna I'm fine, just a little antsy for some reason, so I thought a run would help clear my head," I explained as I gestured behind me to where I was planning to shift.

We'd had a rocky start to our relationship, after I'd all but threatened to kill her when she first showed up here a few years ago battered and bruised from her previous life. We'd quickly put it behind us though, after Anna had done the unthinkably selfless thing and gave herself over to a deranged wolf who'd stolen her parents from her and then threatened the lives of our pack members. It was all because of what she could do and who she was connected to, the Moon Goddess herself. She was the bravest person I knew, and I silently thanked her and the Goddess every single day for the person she was and the Luna she'd become.

She nodded as she shoved her hands into her hoodie's front pocket, "alright well be careful alright? I'm getting a weird vibe that something is going to happen... I'm just not sure what."

I frowned, she was never usually wrong about her feelings and since she was directly connected to the Goddess, we always took her gut instincts seriously. "Did you want me to call Jax to put out a red alert?" I asked, worried for the safety of the pack.

She smiled before shaking her head, "no it's nothing bad like that, just a feeling that something is going to change... soon," she muttered with a small frown.

I frowned, that didn't exactly convince me that everything was going to be okay. "Alright well... I'd still tell Jax if I were you, you know how he gets when we keep things from him," I chuckled as I rolled my eyes.

She nodded before gesturing back to the house, "well I better get in and see if JJ is awake for his afternoon feed. Do be careful Xavier and please just... keep an open mind."

I frowned down at her, "umm... okay?" I agreed before I watched her run back into the house.

Well, that wasn't weirdly cryptic at all.

I ran my fingers through my hair before turning around and continuing my walk into the shadows of the trees so that I could shift. I loved running, it always helped clear my head and ease the tension out of my muscles, making it easier for me to think.

. . .

I ran for a solid two hours, having no destination in mind, just enjoying the feel of the wind in my fur and the dirt under my paws as I dodged tree roots and jumped over fallen branches.

This was my happy place.

Just as I was about to turn back and head home, wanting to give myself enough time to get ready before I was due over at Anna and Jax's for dinner, I heard growls and scuffles coming from the pack border not too far from me. Was a pack member in trouble?

Usually if something like that happens they'd mind link Jax immediately for help. Then again, if it was a youngster in trouble who hadn't learnt to shift, then maybe they *couldn't* call for help.

You could only link another pack member once you'd met your wolf and shifted for the first time at the age of sixteen, and even then, it could take some time after that to gain control of it and get to grips with how it worked.

I quickly turned and ran towards where the fight was happening, just as a girl's scream pierced the otherwise silent woodland.

My wolf growled in my head as we made it into the clearing and what I saw had me momentarily frozen. Two rogues were fighting in our territory, one a female who hadn't shifted into her wolf and just had her thigh ripped into, and another a male who was staring at her waiting for his next opening to deal his fatal strike.

I quickly took in the scene around me, noticing she had already killed one of the rogues, but was starting to struggle with the other now that her leg had been badly damaged.

Before I could think, I flung myself at the male rogue who was getting ready to pounce at the woman, too distracted by the blood lust to take in its surroundings. We circled each other, each of us trying to find an opening in the others defences, but seeing as how I was a pack wolf and a Beta he was no match for me and I quickly pinned him down and clenched down on his jugular before he had a chance to do any more damage than he already had. Ugh I hated the taste of rogue blood; it always allowed unwanted memories to come flooding back to me from the first time I'd tasted their blood. It had this bitterness to it that made me want to wipe my tongue on some grass to get rid of the metallic taste.

I leapt off him and looked up at the girl who had now turned back into her wolf form and froze.

Mate.

No. No! How could my mate be a rogue? Was the Moon Goddess so cruel that she would pair me with the one thing I despised most?

Mate! My wolf continued, seemingly unconcerned with the fact that our mate was a rogue, the thing that had killed our entire family all those years ago.

We stared at each other for a few short seconds, neither of us believing what was happening, but before I could do anything or react in any way, the girl turned and ran as fast as she could... *away* from me. Even with her damaged leg she was making good time.

My wolf screamed at me to run after her, but I just couldn't bring myself to do it. Her kind were cold blooded killers, plain and simple, and there was no way I was going to be mated to someone like that.

Once she was out of sight, I reported the two dead wolves to the border patrol to be cleaned up and slowly made my way back to my house in a daze. The whole extended family were having dinner at Jax and Anna's this evening and I couldn't wait to see the look on their faces when I told them that the one person I'd been waiting just under a decade for was a rogue.

Just then Anna's words floated back into my mind and I cursed. She had seen this coming.

"Just promise me you'll keep an open mind."

Ugh great, now I'm going to have to experience the wrath of Annabelle.

Chapter Three
Blaine's POV

Today officially sucked.

After I had been surrounded by pack warriors, I had been forced to shift back into my human form before they cuffed me in silver chains and lead me straight down to their cells. At least one of them had the decency to throw me an oversized shirt so that I could cover up, but that was where my luck had ended with their chivalry. I'm just glad they gave me one long enough to reach past my thighs, I was not in the mood to parade around naked for everyone to see.

I had a strong limp thanks to the damage the rogue had done to my leg, but that didn't get me any sympathy from my escorts. They marched me at a fast pace, through the outskirts of their territory and down a flight of stairs and into a cement building.

At least this place was semi clean, I had seen and been in some cells in other packs where they didn't even bother hosing down the floors in between cell mates. Safe to say it had been less than sanitary, especially when they didn't even give you access to a toilet.

I swear, some pack wolves think all rogues live like savages. Just because we live in the woods and don't have a permanent home of our own doesn't mean we live in our own filth.

Blood was still free flowing from my thigh, causing me to become slightly woozy and lethargic. With the added effects of the silver chains slowing down my wolf's healing ability, there was little I could do as they led me to an empty cell and threw me in, not caring that my hands were still tied behind my back, meaning I landed face first onto the concrete floor.

Great. I had lived as a rogue all my life, managing to dodge all kinds of things trying to kill me, but the thing that finally succeeds in capturing me? My mates pack. Great. Just great.

I sighed as I shuffled into an upright sitting position, making it easier to get a better look at the damage on my leg.

Through the blood and dirt that caked my skin, I could see that the four claw marks on my outer thigh were deep but not particularly long, only a few inches, and the bite mark near them had already started to clot before the chains had been put around my wrists which was a good sign. It seemed I'd also somehow managed to injure my ankle if the purple colouring was anything to go by, but it wasn't bad, slightly bruised but not broken.

I sighed as I rested my head back against the concrete brick wall. "Well at least it could be worse," I muttered to myself as I closed my eyes. I wasn't sure how, but I'm sure if I thought hard enough, I could think of some awful situation that was worse than finding my mate then being captured by his pack as they left me to bleed out and die on the floor of their cells.

. . .

I sat there for a while, thinking about all the ways my situation could be worse, as my thigh continued to drip blood onto the concrete floor. I could be stuck with a cellmate, or have a rabid dog chained next to me who barked every five seconds for no apparent reason. Or maybe they'd get me to put on a stupid hat and get me to dance the funky chicken... I think I'm going delirious from the blood loss.

Just when I felt my eyes start to drift close, hoping for some much-needed sleep away from my crazy thoughts, my cell door burst open, causing my eyes to spring wide in shock, adrenaline spiking my blood stream from the noise of metal on metal.

I quickly went to stand up, not liking being vulnerable sitting on the ground, but all that achieved was my leg screaming in agony and giving out on me as more blood seeped from my cuts. I slammed back down onto the hard floor and groaned in pain as my butt took the impact. First my leg, then my face and now my tailbone. Looks like I've hit the trifecta.

I looked up to see a tall man blocking the doorway with two guards flanking him on either side, this must be the Alpha.

"Hi there," I greeted in an overly sweet voice as I tried to smile with a half-bruised face. "You must be the big bad Alpha. My name's Blaine, it's so lovely to meet you. I'd shake your hand, but as you can see, I'm a little tied up at the moment," I said as I rattled the silver chains behind me. They bit at my skin as I smelt the telling smell of burning flesh, but it was nothing I couldn't handle. I'd been trained to deal with pain like this. My parents liked to make sure we were all well prepared for survival in the rogue lands, and one of the key things was being able to handle and ignore pain.

The Alpha frowned before crouching down in front of me with his elbows resting in his knees, a scowl plastered on his face as he looked me up and down. "What were you doing on my territory?" He growled as he looked me dead in the eye.

Even as a rogue you could feel the power of an Alpha, and I couldn't help myself as I lowered my eyes slightly towards the ground.

"Look I wasn't trying to invade your land or anything I promise, I was just trying to get away from a few males who wouldn't take no for an answer, and I accidentally ran into your pack's territory. It won't happen again I promise," I explained. At least I was getting to tell my side of the story with this guy, I'd heard stories where captured rogues in some packs weren't even allowed to talk, let alone plead their case.

He sighed before standing up and looking at his two pack mates, "can we verify her story?" He asked in a low voice, but I could still hear what he was saying thanks to my wolf hearing.

"Yes Alpha, I'll head out now and scout the area. I'll also link the warriors on patrol, maybe they have some insight on the situation."

The Alpha nodded before looking back at me. "You will stay here whilst we look into your story. If you're telling the truth we'll let you go, but if I found out you were lying... you're going to wish those rogues finished you off," he growled as his eyes swirled gold.

I shrunk back slightly at the sight of him and I nodded my head in understanding. No matter who you were, unless you wanted to die, you never messed with an Alpha.

"JAX!" I suddenly heard a voice yell from the stairwell as they made their way down into the cells. Her voice echoed slightly off the walls, and I cringed at the pitch.

"JAX ARE YOU DOWN HERE?!"

I heard the Alpha swear quietly before heading over to the direction of the voice.

"Annabelle, what are you doing here? You know how unsafe it is in the cells," the Alpha, who's name I now know as Jax, said as he tried to convince the girl to leave.

"Oh be quiet, you know as well as I do that I'm perfectly safe down here, this place is guarded more than our house," she sighed. I could literally hear her rolling her eyes as she said that.

She must be Jax's mate and Luna to the pack, because there is no way anyone else would ever get away with talking to him like that, especially in front of someone like me,

Jax just sighed in response, I still couldn't see either of them, but I could tell he had given up trying to convince her to leave already.

"What do you need, little mate?"

"I just need a hand finishing dinner; everyone will be arriving soon and JJ is screaming his lungs out so hard I can barely hear myself think. Mum can't seem to calm him like you can, as much as she tries."

"Alright baby I'll be right there," he murmured affectionately as I heard him kiss her. "I'll just finish down here then I'll head up."

I shifted slightly, hoping to relieve some of the pain in my leg and the pins and needles that were threatening my lower half. If it hadn't been for the silver, I'd be halfway healed by now. I better not scar because of this, I had enough of those already, damn chains.

"Jax is someone down here?" The girl suddenly asked as she started walking towards me.

"Annabelle everything is under control, could you please just head on back home and trust that I have this?"

Apparently, Annabelle didn't listen to him because a second later I saw a head peak around the wall of my cell, my door still open and guarded by another pack member.

"Luna," the guy greeted as she came closer. She gave him a friendly smile before turning around and taking me in.

It took her a second to react, but her shock at seeing me quickly morphed into anger as her eyes continued to survey my injuries. "Jax what the hell is that poor girl doing in a *cell*!?" She yelled as she turned around to look at her mate.

"She's a rogue Annabelle, I need to make sure she isn't dangerous before I can release her," he explained.

Annabelle rolled her eyes before gesturing to me. "Look at her Jax, she's injured and needs help. Just because she's a rogue doesn't mean she's *dangerous*. I was technically a rogue when I turned up here and if it wasn't for you, I probably would have ended up in a worse state than her. Surely you would have learned from that and not judge someone before you know all the information?"

I liked this girl.

"Release her," Annabelle demanded as she gestured to me on the floor again.

"Umm Luna?" The guard questioned the same time as Jax said "release her? Are you serious!"

"Yes Jax I am deadly serious... look... I have a... a *good* feeling about her, okay?" She explained as she looked between the two men with her eyebrows raised, as if she was trying to tell them something without actually telling them.

It must have meant something to the two guys as they both looked at each other, probably having one of their stupid silent pack talks, before looking back at Annabelle.

"You're sure?" Jax pressed, still looking unconvinced.

Annabelle just sighed as she crossed her arms over her chest and popped her hip. "When have I ever been wrong Jax, just trust me on this. You know I wouldn't put our pack *or* our family in danger, so why would I suggest it if I wasn't sure."

Jax stared at his mate for a few seconds before sighing and looking over to the guard. "Release her," he sighed with a wave of his hand in my direction.

I stared open-mouthed at the girl. How the hell did she just convince an Alpha *and* a warrior to release a rogue she didn't even know? However she'd done it, she was definitely my new hero of the day.

The guard made his way over to me and I shrunk away slightly before realising he was just coming over to release the cuffs on my wrists. I sighed as the silver dropped from my skin and brought my wrists round to inspect the damage. They were red and slightly blotchy from where my skin had started to blister from the burns but overall, they didn't seem too bad. I'd had worse.

I looked up when I saw movement out of the corner of my eye and saw Annabelle slowly making her way towards me, shaking off her mate's hand on her elbow with an eye roll as he tried to hold her back.

"Hi, my name's Annabelle, but you can call me Anna if you'd prefer. Are you doing okay?"

She was talking to me as if I were a wild scared animal and I couldn't help but smile, trying to hold in a laugh. The last thing I wanted to do was insult the woman who'd just saved me hours if not days wrapped up in chains on a cold concrete floor. "Yeah I'm good," I nodded as I pushed myself up onto my good leg, using the wall behind me for support. "Nothing a bit of time won't heal." I smiled at the trio as they all took me in, Anna with a smile on her face and Jax and the guard with apprehension.

Anna nodded before taking my hand in hers causing Jax to shift uncomfortably. "That's good, I'm glad my mate over there didn't intimidate you too much," she laughed as she rolled her eyes.

I smiled again, the feeling a little bit easier now that the silver was off and my body could start to combat the swelling on my cheek. "Nahh they're alright, besides it wasn't even them that did this," I explained as I gestured to my leg. "I was in the middle of fighting some rogues when someone came and helped me out."

"Oh... well I'm glad someone did," she smiled as she lifted my arm over her shoulder, helping me hop out of the cell and back up the stairs. She was a few inches shorter than me, but the height difference didn't cause her help to be too awkward.

"Umm Annabelle, where are you taking her? The pack hospital is that way," Jax suddenly stated as he blocked our path and pointed to a direction behind us.

"I know where the hospital is Jax," Anna said as she rolled her eyes at him. "But that's not where I'm taking her, she needs a proper meal in her and a chance to rest. I know what the food is like in there and as much as you'd like to say otherwise, patient food sucks."

I laughed as Anna made a face at the mere thought of having to eat hospital food.

Jax frowned as he dropped his hand back to his side. "Then where are you taking her?"

"Home silly, I'm making enough food to feed an army anyway, one more won't hurt. Besides, I've already mind linked Doctor Tessler and she's on her way and meeting us at ours so that she can have a look at her leg... I'm sorry, what was your name again?" she asked me.

I smiled as I watched the showdown between these two, I was officially in love with this girl. She knew exactly how to handle an overbearing Alpha mate. "Blaine," I answered as I tried to shift slightly on my good leg, making sure I didn't lose balance and take out both me and the girl next to me that couldn't be more than 5'3.

Anna nodded before she looked back at her mate with determination. "Blaine is coming back to ours and that's the end of it. Now are you going to give me a hand getting her there or are you just going to stand there and sulk?"

I held back a laugh as I watched the big bad Alpha grumble before taking my other arm around his shoulder and helped me to their house. The height difference between the two made it a little awkward, but we made it work.

It didn't take long, even with me hobbling along, until a huge house came into view. It had a few cars parked on the cobblestone driveway and the building looked a cross between a small village cottage and a modern-day piece of architecture. It was surrounded by trees and had a beautiful floral scented garden filled with flowers of all colours of the rainbow and I couldn't help but stare at it in awe. Now this was the house of an Alpha. It put my little homemade den out in the woods to shame, that was for sure.

As we walked through the front door, the first thing I noticed was the smell of roast beef as it cooked in the oven, and my mouth couldn't help but water at the idea of what it would taste like. It had been so long since I had eaten a decent tasting meal. Usually, I just hunted what I could find in my wolf form and ate it raw. It didn't taste particularly great, but it got the job done.

We weren't alone in the house, and as I went to take a seat on one of the three comfy sofas in the living room, a woman came forward with a large leather bag clutched in her hand. I sat silently as the woman who'd introduced herself as Doctor Tessler rummaged through her bag before taking out a pair of white latex gloves and snapped them on.

Anna had left the room, explaining that she was going to quickly get me a pair of shorts for me to wear under the top, which meant I was left with her grumpy Alpha mate and the kind looking doctor as she knelt in front of me and took my bruised ankle delicately into her hands.

I hissed as she carefully twisted the joint from left right to see how much movement I had before placing it gently back on the ground.

"Nothing seems to be broken, which is good, but your ankle is sprained. Your wolf should heal it fairly quickly with no issues, but you'll be walking with a slightly limp for the next few days. Try to stay off it as much as possible and only put pressure on it when it feels comfortable to. As for these lacerations on your thigh, I'm afraid I'm going to have to stitch them up if you want to minimise the scarring. They will heal on their own if you'd prefer I leave it however," she offered.

I shook my head as I gripped the edge of the sofa, preparing myself for the pain I knew would come. This wasn't the first time I'd been stitched up without any anaesthetic. "Stitch it up doc, the last thing I want is a leg that looks like something out of a special effects horror movie," I laughed, trying to lighten the mood.

The doctor smiled at me before leaning down and getting everything out of her bag that she needed. "Alright, hold still then."

Seventeen stitches and a lot of grunts in pain later the doc was finally finished as she snapped her bag shut and stood up. "Take it easy and if you have any problems don't hesitate to get someone to contact me, okay?" She asked as she slowly started to make her way to the door.

I nodded as I shifted into a more comfortable position on the sofa. "Sure doc, thanks a lot," I thanked her as I sighed back into the cushions, thankful the pain and discomfort were now over with.

Just then the front door banged open as someone let themselves in, someone I'd hoped I'd never have to see again.

"Anna, you are never going to believe who I ran into on my run earlier."

Just perfect, my mate was here. So much for the pain and discomfort being over with.

Chapter Four
Xavier's POV

I'm pretty sure this was the most *uncomfortable* dinner since records began. We were all currently sitting around the dining room table, where the only noise being made was the sound of cutlery scratching on plates and the occasional babble for the one-year-old sitting in his highchair.

The awkwardness wasn't *my* fault though. *I* wasn't the one who'd invited a rogue to dinner, and I *also* wasn't the one who was currently staring daggers into my forehead as she dug into her food. Cutting the meat with a little more force than was necessary. Anna sure could hold a grudge, and after not listening to her about keeping an open mind about Blaine, I was number one on her *I am not a fan of you right now* list.

Walking into Jax and Anna's house, the last thing I expected to see was my runaway mate, making herself at home, on their living room sofa. Anna had done the introductions, knowing full well what we were to each other, but I wasn't interested. Why would I be interested in a rogue? Whether she was my mate or not, it was irrelevant.

"So… Anna, how are the preparations going for next year's ball? I heard even more packs are interested in coming following the success of last year," Hannah asked as she tried to fill the awkward silence.

Anna reluctantly dragged her eyes away from my forehead, before filling her in on all the preparations that were still needed for the ball in six months' time, but I didn't pay much attention to her. A few days ago, hell a few hours ago, I had been really into this ball, making sure the party went off without a hitch just in case my mate would be there. Now I'd met her and knew who she really was, all enthusiasm for it had gone out the window.

I stared at Blaine as I watched her eat her food. What was she even doing here anyway?

"Hey Xav, could you help me with something in the living room for a second please?" Jax asked as he threw his napkin down onto the table and made his way out of the kitchen/diner area and through the door into the downstairs corridor.

I sighed already knowing what this conversation was going to be about. As I followed him out of the room, I could feel the daggers of my loving mate piercing into my skull, and I couldn't help but feel just a little satisfaction in knowing that I made her just as uncomfortable as she was making me.

"What's up?" I asked as we stood in the middle of the room where I'd first spotted Blaine making herself at home on the sofa.

"You know exactly what Xavier; you're treating your mate like she's a damn criminal. You've been wanting and waiting for her for years and now that you finally have her you're going to throw it all away and because of what... because she's a rogue?"

I chuckled, but there was no humour in my laugh as I crossed my arms over my chest in a defensive manner. "Not that it is *any* of your business Jax," I stressed, "but yes. There is no way in *hell* that I will *ever* acknowledge a filthy rogue as my mate and you more than anyone should know why, blood bond or not." I couldn't believe Jax was taking her side on this, he used to hate rogues just as much as I did.

Jax sighed as he ran his hands through his hair. "Yes, usually I would take your side when it comes to rogues Xav, you know that. But not only is this girl your mate, someone the Moon Goddess paired you with, but Annabelle said she had a feeling about her. You know that's something we can't just ignore, whether she's a rogue or not she's a good person and someone we need to keep around. Annabelle's feelings about people's intentions are never wrong."

I sighed as my defence melted away slightly. I knew we could trust any instincts that Anna had about someone entering the pack, if the Goddess had told her something about Blaine, then she was obviously here for a reason, but it didn't change anything for me. "I know Jax. I know why we have to take any of Anna's instincts and premonitions into consideration, she gets from the Goddess we'd be blind not to, but it doesn't mean that I can just forget about my past and jump for joy at the idea of having a rogue mate. Rogues are rogues for a reason, remember."

"You know nothing about my life," a voice suddenly said from the doorway behind me and we both looked over to find Blaine standing there, using the door frame for support so she didn't have to put weight on her still injured leg. "You know *nothing* about me. Nothing about why I'm a rogue or what I've been through, so don't you *dare* pass judgement on me until you know the full story," she growled, her eyes wild with rage.

"Oh please," I laughed as I turned to her. "Don't try and play the innocent game here, we all know that an Alpha doesn't make the decision to outcast a pack member lightly and would need serious reason to do so," I said as I rolled my eyes at her.

She bristled at my words as I saw her clench her fists in anger. Damn she looked threatening and sexy with her fiery red hair all over the place and green eyes piercing into mine, as if she could drop me dead with just one look. She remained silent though, not retaliating to my words. "What was it anyway? Did you steal something, or maybe betray your pack? I mean that's definitely something that would get you kicked out," I mused.

Still I got nothing. I don't know why I was trying to get a reaction out of her, but for whatever reason, I couldn't stop myself. "Nah they're too simple, I bet it was a lovers triangle of some sorts. I bet your family was just heartbroken when they had to stand by and watch you get outcast all for the love of some guy that couldn't bring himself to love you back."

At the mention of her parents her right eye twitched slightly. It wasn't much, but it was enough of a reaction for me to know I was on the right lines to get under her skin. "Or maybe they were relieved when you left... maybe they were so fed up with having to deal with you day in and day out that they-"

"Shut the *hell* up about my family," she suddenly yelled as she limped over to me. "You will shut your mouth about my parents if you know what's good for you. If not I won't hesitate to cut off what little balls I'm assuming you have and force feed them to you in front of your entire pack, understand!?"

She was right up in my face at the end of her rant, and I couldn't help but smirk as I looked around at all the shocked faces of Jax's and Anna's family who'd also joined us for dinner. As if suddenly realising that we weren't alone, Blaine went bright red as she too looked around and took in the shocked expressions.

"I... umm... I'm sorry about that everyone, I don't know what came over me," she stuttered as she looked over to Anna. "Thank you for the dinner, it was wonderful. Would you mind maybe showing me where I'll be staying for the night? I-I think I need some time to myself, I've suddenly come over all tired."

Anna's eyes suddenly glazed over and I looked over at Jax to notice that his too were glassy and it didn't take a genius to figure out what they were arguing about, whether she'd stay at theirs or somewhere else. Eventually though Anna sighed in defeat as she made her way over to Blaine. "Come on, you'll stay in the pack house. It's not too far from here and if you need anything in the night you can get someone to link me okay?"

Blaine just nodded before taking Anna's outstretched hand as she hobbled out the front door.

"Well, I'd say that was a success," Hannah muttered sarcastically after the front door had closed, looking over at me with a scowl.

I just rolled my eyes back at her before I stalked through the back door and made my way home without a backwards glance.

Chapter Five
Blaine's POV

I woke up the next morning still fuming about Xavier and what he'd said. How *dare* he make assumptions about my family when he didn't even know me, when he couldn't even bring himself to say a single word to me all night.

I was embarrassed beyond belief after I had finished yelling at him, but Anna assured me that no one was mad or even surprised at the fact that I had snapped at Xavier. Apparently, according to her and her sister-in-law Hannah, he had it coming, and they were more surprised at the fact that I hadn't snapped at him sooner.

I sighed as I sat up in bed and pulled the duvet back to inspect my injured leg. Thanks to the doc stitching me up yesterday the claw marks were halfway healed already. I smiled as I gently ran my fingers over the raised cuts, grateful that I wasn't going to have any scars there like some other scraps I'd gotten into over the years. Battle scars were cool, don't get me wrong, but if I wasn't careful I'd have more scar tissue than skin by the time I hit middle age.

I sucked in a sharp breath as I flung my legs over the edge of the bed and slowly tested putting weight on my ankle. There was still a little pain there but overall it was liveable.

Just as I was about to sit back down there was a knock on my bedroom door and I frowned as I limped my way over to answer it. I wonder who it could be? There were only a handful of people who knew about me and where to find me and even fewer people who actually *wanted* to visit me.

I pulled the door open and smiled when I saw who was on the other side, Anna and Hannah. Well, that wasn't going to get confusing at all, maybe I should change my name to Alanna so I could fit in with the rhyming duo.

"Hey guys, what are you doing here?" I asked as I stepped aside so that they could come in.

The room that I was assigned to was small but comfortable. It had a single bed pushed up to the corner of the room by the window with a desk just opposite it. A small wardrobe and chest of draws were on the opposite side of the room where another door led to a little private en-suite bathroom.

Even though it was small I didn't mind, it was ten times better than anything I'd lived in in the past. Cleaner too. It wasn't that me and my family had lived in filth all our lives, it was just that we moved around so often to avoid becoming easy targets that we never saw the point in making anything too homey.

"We were wondering whether you would want to come out shopping with us today?" Anna asked as she came and sat on my unmade bed. "JJ has grown out of all of his clothes *again* and apparently there's this new dress that Hannah just *has* to get," Anna laughed as she looked over at Hannah in amusement.

"What! I Do! The people in Vogue were saying that this was the must-have dress of the season, so I *have* to go get it before the store runs out of stock," she explained in a *duh* tone of voice.

I laughed at her as I settled into the chair in front of my desk. Oh how the other half live.

"So you in?" Anna asked hopefully.

I sighed as I looked up into her hopeful face and nodded in agreement. "Sure," I smiled back at both of them. After all, I did kind of owe her for stopping her mate from keeping me locked up until I bleed to death.

Both the girls squealed slightly, "great, why don't you quickly have a shower while we go and find something for you to eat for breakfast," Hannah suggested as she got up off the bed and made her way out of my room, dragging Anna along with her.

I smiled at their retreating forms before turning around and making my way over to the bathroom. Anna had set me up with everything I would need, including clothes for the day, and it wasn't long before I was all ready to go. She had left me a few cosmetic products, but I left my face free from any makeup, not having really worn any in the past. I just ran a tiny bit of conditioner into my curls with my fingers to help try and tame the frizz.

The pack house was fairly large, with a lot of pack members living in it who either didn't want to live with their parents or hadn't found their mate yet and so didn't see the point in getting a house. Thankfully as it was a little later in the morning, everyone was already out, either having gone to work or the local school that I knew wouldn't be too far away. I had been into a few pack's territories in my life, all with permission of course, and they nearly always had the same set up. With a hospital so remote no human would ever accidentally stumble

50

onto it and a town just near enough to get any supplies that were needed.

I huffed at my reflection as I already started to notice some flyways detaching themselves from my curls and rolled my eyes at them in annoyance before turning and leaving to find where Anna and Hannah had gone. The curls never did what I wanted them to do so I don't even know why I bother.

As I made my way down the stairs and walked into the kitchen, the most amazing sugary smell hit my senses and I couldn't help but groan at the idea of being able to eat something that sweet. Sugar was a luxury I rarely had the opportunity to enjoy.

Anna was in the kitchen, cooking up a huge pile of chocolate pancakes with what seems like a whole pack of bacon grilling in the oven and I smiled as I took in the view. Now this was something I could get used to.

"I hope you're hungry Blaine, as you could probably guess from last night, my portion control is awful and I always end up making way too much," Anna laughed, not looking away from the pancake she was cooking.

I smiled as I took a free seat next to Hannah at the island in the middle of the kitchen. "Oh, I'm so hungry I could literally eat anything you put in front of me," I laughed as I took in the scent of Anna's cooking once again.

"You're in for a treat Blaine, Anna's cooking is literally *unbelievable*, when I first started eating her food I went up a whole dress size," she laughed.

I laughed along with her as I turned to face Anna as she placed the plate of food in front of me. "Really? How did you get into cooking?" I asked her as I took my first bite of chocolate pancakes with bacon and maple syrup. Hannah was right, Annas cooking was literally the best thing I had ever eaten. The pancakes were soft and fluffy with just the right amount of sweetness to them without being overpowering. Add in the saltiness of the bacon and this was a breakfast made for royalty.

Anna blushed as she took a seat on my left, not bothering to take the apron off she'd put on whilst she was cooking. "I... didn't have the best upbringing," she shrugged as she too took her first bite of food. "I had to learn quickly," was all she said as she slowly chewed her food.

I was curious as to what she meant, her parents seemed lovely when I met them last night, even if the dinner had been a little awkward. I wanted to pry, find out what had been so awful about it, but I could tell she wasn't in the mood to talk about it, so I left it alone and quickly changed the subject.

After we'd all finished eating, we quickly cleared up the kitchen and it wasn't long before we were on the road towards the closest shopping centre, with a few of Jax's warrior friends for company.

Chapter Six
Blaine's POV

"What about something like this?" Hannah asked as she held up a blue and white floral daisy dress with spaghetti straps and a small section cut out of the back. "It's really pretty and I think it would go really well with your complexion."

I internally cringed at the number of flowers that were on the print, it was safe to say that I was not a girly girl. "Umm... yes, it's very pretty," I agreed, not wanting to disagree with her. "But... don't you think something like that would look better on Anna?" *Please agree, please agree* I chanted in my head, the last thing I wanted to do was to walk around wearing that for the rest of the day.

I was still new to their group, and even though it sounded stupid, I really wanted them to like me. I had been alone for what felt like forever, and the idea of having someone to talk to and call a friend made a weird knot begin to form in my chest.

At the mention of her name, Anna looked up from the shirt she was admiring and came over to where we were standing. "Oh that *is* pretty," she agreed as she quickly forgot about the shirt in her hand, her full attention now on the dress. I sighed in relief at not having to try it on and silently crept my way over to a black and red flannel I had seen out of the corner of my eye. Now this was more my style.

After we had finished shopping, Hannah and Anna fighting over who was going to pay for my stuff, we made our way over to a small cafe. One of the guards that had come with us had gone to drop off the obscene amount of clothes the two of them had bought, so it was just us three and one other warrior who went to take a table that was vacant two tables over from us.

"So Blaine, tell us a little about yourself," Anna asked as she placed her vanilla latte onto the table in front of her.

I smiled at her as I too sat down with my drink, black coffee. I was grateful to finally be sitting down, my leg had started to feel uncomfortable about an hour ago, but I didn't want to say anything and ruin the day. The girls were obviously having so much fun picking out clothes for each other and little JJ that I didn't want to be the one to ruin it.

"I think you mean 'tell us about how you became a rogue'," I laughed as I looked pointedly between the two of them. I was honestly surprised the topic hadn't come up sooner, it was usually one of the first things that was asked when pack members got into a conversation with me.

"Well," Hannah cringed sheepishly as she joined us at the table. "We didn't want to be as forward as that, but sure now that you mention it, how *did* you become a rogue?" She laughed as Anna lightly smacked her on the arm.

"That is *not* what I meant, Blaine," Anna said as she tried to reassure me that I didn't have to talk about it if I didn't want to.

I shrugged, not bothered with the conversation topic nearly as much as I usually am. "No it's alright," I reassured them. "To be honest I'm surprised you hadn't asked me that before you let me join you for dinner last night," I chuckled. It had been weird, how trusting they'd all been about me being in their house without even asking one question about myself or why I was there. Maybe it was because they knew I was their Beta's mate? Even if we hadn't acknowledged each other more than that little rant we had last night. Maybe the connection we had meant something to this pack.

Anna just smiled as she took a sip from her drink, "I knew you weren't dangerous and had no intention of hurting us," she explained. "There was nothing else I really needed to know about you," she shrugged.

I smiled at her, grateful that she had taken my side yesterday. Today would have turned out very different if she hadn't. Who knows, maybe I'd still be chained up on that concrete floor, slowly bleeding out while they were all up in their warm house having a relaxing roast dinner.

"Well if you must know, I was actually born a rogue," I explained as I took a sip of my drink. It was a little bitter, but it definitely wasn't the worst cup of coffee I'd ever had.

When I didn't hear a response, I looked up in confusion, only to see both girls staring back at me in shock. "What?"

"You were *born* a rogue?" Hannah asked, her drink suddenly forgotten about as it hung in mid-air.

I nodded my head, a little taken aback by their reaction. "Yes… why?"

"You know… it explains a lot," Anna suddenly said as she rested her head on her hand. "All the rogues I have ever met, which isn't that many but still, they have always given off this vibe. They're always snappy, hate authority and are… well quite frankly… plain mean."

"Mean?" I asked with a smirk.

Anna just rolled her eyes as she took a sip from her drink. "Oh you know what I mean,” she sighed. “But you, you're actually *nice*."

"Thank you?" I replied, chuckling at her backwards way of saying she liked me.

She smiled before taking another sip, "you're welcome."

"So how come you were born a rogue? I didn't even know that was a thing," Hannah asked.

I shrugged, knowing this story by heart. It was my favourite one my parents used to tell us before we all went to sleep. "Well, when my mum and dad found out they were mates it didn't go down so well with either of their packs,” I explained. “See, my mum was the daughter of an Alpha and her dad decided that she was going to be forced into an arranged marriage with another packs Alpha to form an alliance."

"That's *horrible*," Anna suddenly exclaimed, her hand covering her mouth in embarrassment after she realised how loud she'd said it as a few heads turned our way.

I laughed, "horrible but apparently not unheard of."

"So what happened? I mean I'm guessing your mum didn't marry him," Hannah asked, clutching her drink tight in her hands.

I shook my head, "no she didn't. She actually did intend to go through with it at first. She went over to the pack to meet her future husband and everything, but as soon as she got out of the car, she could smell her mate, my dad, was there. She ran around the pack grounds looking for him like some crazy person and when they finally found each other they went over to her father and her fiancé to ask if the alliance could be formed with them instead. Well, long story short the news of their mating didn't go over so well, and they both ended up running away before my dad was killed and my mum was forced to marry someone who wasn't her mate."

The girls sat there in silence for a second, absorbing the information whilst I just drank my coffee.

"So what happened to them?" Hannah suddenly asked.

I frowned into my drink as I thought about my family. "We were happy for ages. I mean we had to move quite a lot to stay off their radar, but I had my mum and dad and my older brother and younger sister. Life was good," I shrugged. "But a few years ago, my brother and sister went hunting and didn't return," I mumbled as I felt the grief of their disappearance settle over me. "My parents decided to go out and look for them, hoping they could find them and bring them back. but they never did either. To this day I don't know where they are or what happened to them," I shrugged.

"Oh Blaine I am so sorry," Anna whispered as she reached over and took my hand in hers, doing what she could to comfort me. "No one should have to go through losing their parents, let alone losing their siblings as well."

I shrugged my shoulders as I took another sip of my coffee, hoping they would change the subject.

"It's okay, I've kind of come to terms with the fact that I may never see them again." I was trying to reassure them just as much as I was trying to reassure myself. God my life story was so depressing.

"Was it a while ago?" Hannah asked in a quiet voice, pity in her eyes which I hated seeing.

"About two and a half years ago."

We remained silent as we finished our drinks, none of us knowing what to say after the revelation of my possible dead family.

Chapter Seven
Xavier's POV

I sighed in frustration as I ran the perimeter once again. No matter how hard I tried, I still couldn't locate where Blaine was. It wasn't that I cared about her or anything, I just wanted to make sure I knew where the rogue was, just in case something happened and I wasn't around to help.

I sighed as my wolf rolled his eyes at my weak excuse for wanting to find her, *yeah right*.

My wolf and I were at peace with each other now. Ever since seeing Blaine yesterday in the woods it's been easier to shift back into my human form and my mind has cleared to the point I don't even remember how I was struggling before meeting her. It was frustrating, because I knew my wolf was now at ease because the blood bond latching itself onto Blaine, but I was torn in half on how I felt about it.

I hated the idea of even being in the same room as Blaine, the death of my family playing out in front of me every time I closed my eyes at the knowledge that a rogue and potential threat was waltzing around our land. But on the other hand she was my mate, my blood bound mate, and even I couldn't completely ignore the strong magic tying the two of us together.

I was in so much pain, and I had no idea how to relieve it.

I growled and shook my head, not allowing my wolf to put any more disturbing thoughts into my head. I was not going to let this girl get to me, I *couldn't* let this girl get to me.

I quickly shifted out of my wolf form and made my way over to Jax's house, he had to know where Blaine was. Once I knew, I could relax knowing she wasn't anywhere near me or putting my family in danger.

"Hello!" I shouted as I walked into their house. "Jax you around?"

All of a sudden, I heard JJ scream his lungs out from upstairs and I heard Jax groan from in the living room. I turned the corner and laughed as I saw Jax rolling off the sofa, still half asleep, at the high-pitched wail of his son.

"You alright there?" I chuckled as I took in his zombie-like state.

"Screw you man, it took me ages to get him down, and when I finally did you come barging in here and screaming at the top of your lungs," he grumbled.

I chuckled as I watched him rub his hands over his eyes. "So, are you going to get your son or just leave him up there to cry?" I laughed.

Jax just grumbled again before dragging his feet out of the room and up the stairs towards JJ's bedroom. Screw having kids, if this is what it turns you into then it's *definitely* not for me. I'll just stick to being the cool uncle who gives the kids sugar when the parents aren't watching.

I sat down on one of their sofas and laid back as I waited for Jax to come back down. It wasn't long before he emerged with JJ in his arms, wide awake and staring around the room. "What happened to getting him down for his nap?" I chuckled as I followed them into the kitchen.

"Shut up," he muttered as he sat JJ into his highchair.

"So... Where's Anna?" I asked as casually as I could. If I couldn't find Blaine and Anna was missing as well, it was a safe bet to say that they were out together somewhere.

Jax smirked as he sat opposite JJ to feed him some form of carrot mush. Eww. "You mean where's your mate?" He asked with a chuckle.

I growled slightly, "she is *not* my mate Jax."

All Jax responded with was a chuckle as he fed JJ another spoonful of mush. "*Sure* she's not, if Blaine isn't your mate then Annabelle isn't mine," he laughed.

"Whatever man," I grumbled as I leant against the kitchen counter, munching on one of Anna's cookies she had obviously baked this morning and left on the side to cool. "I was just wondering because she wasn't here to help you with JJ, that woman is like the baby whisperer."

Jax only responded with another chuckle as he continued to feed JJ. "Well if you're that curious about *my* mates where abouts then she's out shopping for new clothes for JJ, this little man is growing faster than we can keep up with," he laughed as he cleaned some carrot stuff off JJ's face.

The little guy was cute I had to admit. "So is she... alone?" Smooth Xavier, real smooth.

Jax looked over at me with a smirk, enjoying my discomfort way too much, probably because of all the crap I used to give him when he was obsessed with Anna's every move. Who was I kidding, he's still obsessed. "No she actually went with Hannah, you know that girl could never say no to a shopping trip."

"That's nice," I nodded. "... Anyone else?"

Jax sighed as he put the food down on the table and turned to me, giving me his full attention. "If you want to ask about Blaine, just ask. You have a right to know where she is seeing as she's *your* mate," he emphasised.

"That rogue is *not* my mate," I growled, suddenly getting all defensive.

Jax stood up and came to stand next to me as he clapped me on the shoulder. "Xavier... you can't let what happened to your family hold you back from something as wonderful as a mate bond. You've been struggling with your blood bond for years, are you really going to put you and your wolf through a lifetime of pain and misery because of something that happened years ago?"

"But Jax she's a rogue, I just... I don't know how to get over that," I sighed as I pressed the heels of my hands into my eyes. "Besides, it's not like she was jumping for joy at the thought of being mated to me either. If I remember correctly, *she* was the one who ran away from *me*."

Jax shrugs, "we can only guess what she's gone through to cause her to act the way she did Xav. Maybe she's gone through something traumatic, making it hard for her to trust others," he explained. "Take Annabelle for example, when we first met she was terrified of everyone and everything around her, but that was because she had a reason to be. After a lot of persuasion, time and patience on both of our parts, she was finally able to realise that not everyone was out to get her like that sorry excuse of a family she used to live with, and she finally managed to accept me and the pack. Now look at her, she's more badass than half of our warriors and she's not afraid to put someone in their place when they're being disrespectful to her, including me," he laughed.

I laughed at the memory of Anna ripping into Jax because he'd rolled his eyes at her one day when she was particularly tired. That girl sure had turned into a little spitfire.

"I still don't know if I can get over it Jax," I sighed as I ran my fingers through my hair and over my face, suddenly exhausted. "Every time I look at her all I can think of is my family and how it was a rogue who had taken them from me."

"You'll never know until you try," Jax said as he clapped me on the shoulder once again.

"What in the world happened here?" We suddenly heard from the kitchen door and looked over to see Anna, Hannah and Blaine standing there with shocked expressions on their faces and looking past us at JJ.

We turned around to see what had happened whilst we were talking and I couldn't help the laughter that escaped as I took in the little one year old covered from head to toe in orange mush. Not only that, but he had also managed to get it all over his highchair and the floor surrounding him.

"I leave you guys alone for one afternoon and this is what happens?" Anna tried to scold Jax with a slight frown in between her eyebrows, but I could tell that she was struggling trying not to find this just as cute as we were.

I took my phone out of my pocket and took a quick picture of him as he grinned at the camera with his cheeky chubby cheeks. "Now that is an eighteen-year-olds birthday card if I've ever seen one," I laughed.

Anna just rolled her eyes as she made her way over to JJ who proceeded to squeal at the sight of his mum. "Come on little man, let's get you all cleaned up so I can see if the new clothes I got for you fit," she smiled affectionately down at him.

I laughed as I watched Anna pick up the wriggling orange mess before her and Jax left the kitchen, leaving just me, Hannah and Blaine standing awkwardly in the silence of the kitchen. Before I could come up with an excuse to leave, not wanting to be in the same room as Blaine, Hannah beat me to it.

"Well, I need to get back home, mums just linked me and asked for my help with something so… I'll see you both later okay? Blaine, it was great hanging out with you, just let me know if you ever want any company." She smiled as she pulled a surprised Blaine into a hug. "Xavier I trust that you can take Blaine back to the pack house? She still hasn't quite got her bearings around here yet and still needs a bit of help getting around," she said before turning and swiftly leaving out the front door, both mine and Blaine's protests falling on deaf ears as the door slammed shut behind her.

Great, this won't be awkward at all.

Chapter Eight
Xavier's POV

We stared at each other in awkward silence, not knowing what to say or how to interact with each other. I mean what can you say to someone you were supposed to be mated with but couldn't stand being in the same room as them?

"Listen I'm sure I can figure out how to get back to my room from here," Blaine sighed, breaking the slight tension that had built up in the room. "There's really no need for you to escort me or whatever," she muttered.

I watched as she picked up the few shopping bags she'd had with her before slowly making her way towards the front door. The limp she had from her injuries yesterday was slightly more prominent than it should have been. It was probably because of all the walking she had done today, and I sighed in frustration as Anna's words from yesterday flickered through my mind. *Keep an open mind.* Yes, she was a rogue and yes, I hated everything rogues stood for, but does that really mean I should pass judgement on her purely for what she was?

"Wait," I sighed as I jogged after her reluctantly, moving before I had the chance to change my mind. I'd caught her just as she made it through the front door, a few seconds later and I would have been off the hook.

I took the bags from her hand, hoping to lighten her load so that the strain on her ankle and thigh lessened. "Just because we don't see eye to eye about... certain things... doesn't mean I should leave you to roam around the pack grounds lost. I mean for all we know you could get ambushed on your walk over there for not being part of our pack, you do stink of rogue after all," I muttered, trying to justify my desire to walk her to the pack house other than because I wanted to be around her, which so wasn't true.

Blaine frowned as we both turned and started walking the short distance to the pack house, taking it slightly slower than usual to stop her leg from worsening. The last thing I needed was a grilling from Anna or doctor Tessler because her stitches had ripped, or she'd twisted her ankle again trying to keep up with me.

"Umm thanks... I think?"

I smiled at her tightly before turning to look at where I was going. We were silent for a while, neither of us knowing what to say to the other as we walked through the long grass.

I had never been in a situation like this before, I was so torn it was driving me crazy. On the one hand, I had been waiting ten years for my mate, ten years of watching other wolves find their mates and living their happily ever after lives. It had made me crave mine more and more as the years went on. I was always so jealous of them, but now that I finally had her within touching distance, I didn't know how to handle it... all because she was a rogue.

After what happened to my parents and sister, I had promised myself that I would avenge them anyway that I could. I had already killed the rogue that had killed my mother and sister, but seeing as I wasn't with my dad when he'd died, I had no idea who had killed him. At their funeral I had promised my dad that I would kill the rogue that killed him, so if that meant hunting down every rogue that I could get my hands on then so be it.

I had been a very angry teenager, and it took me years to get over my grief and rage over what I had lost. It wasn't until Jax's dad threatened to take away my Beta title that I started to calm down. That title was the one thing my dad had wanted me to have. He always spoke about how proud he was of me, knowing that I was going to be the future Beta of his pack, and I couldn't disappoint him by going on a rogue hunt every other day and putting my pack and myself in danger.

That day was the day I stopped going out and looking for fights, but it didn't mean if a rogue crossed our borders, I would show it any mercy.

"Are you okay? You seem deep in thought," Blaine asked from beside me. If I was being honest, I'd half-forgotten she was even there.

I sighed, running a hand through my already messy hair before nodding my head. "Yeah, just thinking about some stuff," I muttered. *Nice Xavier, real intelligent answer that one.*

"You mean thinking about us," she stated, not needing to phrase it as a question.

"Amongst other things yeah," I sighed and I shrugged my shoulders, my brain already so tired with the million thoughts running through my head.

"I know what you mean," she laughed, although it lacked humour. "My wolf has been yelling at me nonstop to get over myself and just accept you already, but I just *can't*. I promised myself a long time ago that I was never going to be involved with a pack. Meeting you has kind of put a slight spanner in the works, but I'm working on it," she nodded, acting as if she'd already gotten over the fact that I was her mate.

I frowned, I wonder what her deal was with being tied to a pack? Maybe it has something to do with why she was cast out of her last pack. I turned to face her, intent on asking her, when we were suddenly interrupted.

"Xavier my man, what's up?"

Both Blaine and I looked to our left to find one of my pack members, Jason, running to catch up with us. Great, what did he want?

"Hey Jason, what can I do for you?" I asked, hoping he would just ask his question and leave. Don't get me wrong, Jason was a great guy, but I wasn't in the mood for any form of conversational pleasantries right now.

"Nothing really, I heard Anna allowed a rogue into the territory and I just wanted to make sure you are alright, you know considering everything-."

"Yeah I'm fine Jason, thank you," I quickly interrupted, not wanting him to say anything about my past in front of Blaine. I tried to subtly gesture with my head towards Blaine, hoping that he would get the hint that she was the rogue he was talking about, but he didn't get the hint as he carried on blabbering.

"Okay good, I mean we all know how you can get when a rogue gets near us," he joked but I didn't laugh with him. I don't know why but I really didn't want

Blaine knowing about my past, about how many rogues I had sought out and killed.

"Oh really?" Blaine asked next to me, seeming very interested in the conversation all of a sudden, "and how is that?" She asked with raised eyebrows and her arms crossed.

Chapter Nine
Blaine's POV

This Jason guy blinked several times, as if he was just now realising that I was standing there, and I couldn't help but grind my teeth together. Was I invisible or something?

"Oh hello beautiful, and who might you be?"

I rolled my eyes as he took my hand in his and kissed it, were people really still doing that?

"I'm Blaine, the rogue you were just talking about," I said with an overly sweet smile, hoping it would at least knock the guy down a peg and shut him up. Unfortunately, it did not.

"Wait... *you're* the rogue everyone's talking about? The one Luna saved from the dungeons and gave a room in the pack house?"

I shrugged with my arms slightly outstretched, "the one and only." Was it really that big of a deal that a rogue was spending a few days on their territory whilst they healed before going their separate ways?

"Well no wonder you're okay with her being here Xavier, she's blooming gorgeous."

Charming, talking about me as if I wasn't here. I rolled my eyes at the slightly cringy compliment but froze when I heard a low growl coming from beside me. Was Xavier... *jealous?*

Jason frowned as he too heard the warning growl that Xavier just made. "Are you sure you're okay? You're looking a little... tense."

"*Fine,*" Xavier replied through gritted teeth, obviously anything but.

"Oookay then... well Blaine if you ever need some company or someone to keep you... you know, entertained I'm more than happy to offer my services." I cringed again at his *very* obvious invitation, and was just about to put him back in his place when the continuing growl next to me gave me an idea. What's the point in having a mate that doesn't want you if you can't have a bit of fun with it right?

I fluttered my eyelashes at Jason and plastered an alluring smile on my face. I had gotten quite good at flirting over the years, it helped with getting simple things like if I would accidently 'forget' my purse to pay for food. I hated doing it and I only did it in an emergency, but it was always a good skill to fall back in.

"Well Jason, that's so kind of you to offer up your time for little old me, I may just have to take you up on that." I winked at him before subtly looking beside me to see Xavier grinding his teeth and glaring daggers at Jason, if looks could kill Jason would be 6 feet under by now. If I knew having a mate would be this much fun, I would have sort him out years ago.

"Jason," Xavier continued to growl next to me, and I looked over at him to see gold swirling in his eyes. For someone who claims he doesn't want me for a mate he was acting awfully protective over me.

"Are you sure you're alright man?" Jason asked as he took a step back from Xavier, obviously noticing how irritated he was. "Wait a second," he said as he looked between the two of us "you guys aren't... you both aren't mates, are you?"

I went to respond with a simple 'no' but before I could Xavier burst out in laughter. "*Mates...*with *her?* Of course not, you know me Jason, see a rogue kill a rogue. I'm only showing her to her room because I was asked to and no one else was around to do it."

I flinched back slightly at his hateful words and the venom that he spat them with, what an ass.

"You know what," I piped up as I reached down to take my bags from Xavier's hand, being extra careful not to touch him, I do not need to feel those stupid sparks right now. "I think I've got it from here, it was lovely to meet you Jason... and Xavier... bye," I said as I turned on my heel and started walking in the direction I hoped was the pack house. I must've been right because neither of the boys corrected me and thankfully it wasn't long before the pack house came into view.

I couldn't believe what an ass Xavier was being. I mean I know I kind of started it by flirting with Jason in front of him, but he didn't need to laugh in my face and insult me. I huffed in annoyance as I slammed my bedroom door shut like a moody teenage girl. Even though no one was around to hear it, it still made me feel better.

I don't even know what I was still doing here, it wasn't like I was wanted, not by anyone who really mattered anyway.

I stood there, in the middle of my room, as I took everything in. Yes I now had people to talk to, I had a roof over my head and food in my belly… but did that really matter if my own mate didn't want me? Couldn't even stand to look at me? I felt okay about it now, but what happens later down the line, when Xavier falls in love with someone else and makes a life with them, could I really stand by on the side-lines and watch it happen? I know I said I wasn't interested in Xavier, or anyone who was in a pack, but now that I'd met my mate and felt what it could be like could I really stick by that statement?

No, I don't think I could.

Not when the pain in my chest from losing my family, the feeling of my heart being ripped from my ribcage, had slowly started to diminish and extinguish the more time I spent with him. Not when my wolf had settled after what felt like years of searching and pacing.

I sighed as I realised what I had to do. I quickly packed everything up that I could carry, taking the few items of clothing that the girls had bought me earlier, and as much food and water as I could fit into a backpack before I strapped it onto my back and ran out the front door. I didn't know where I was going, but I knew I couldn't last much longer here. I am not willingly subjecting myself to the pain of being laughed at and openly rejected by my mate in front of his entire pack.

I ran through the woods as quickly as I could, which wasn't very fast considering my busted leg, as I paid attention to every noise and scent that surrounded me, making sure no one spotted me or attacked me.

It wasn't long before I was at the perimeter of the pack lands, and as I crossed over I offered one final glance over my shoulder at what could have been before turning back around.

Goodbye Xavier.

Chapter Ten
Xavier's POV

"I *told* you to keep an open mind Xavier, I told you! And what do you go and do... laugh in her face and deny the fact that you two were mates *in front* of a pack member. I mean do you know how hurtful that must have been for her to hear?" Anna yelled at me from across their living room, her face turning red from the rage bubbling away inside her.

After Blaine had walked off, I had excused myself from Jason and started the slow walk back to my place. I didn't know why I'd said the things I did to Jason, but I had instantly regretted it when I saw the look on her face.

I cringed when Anna continued yelling, but I was too much in my own head to pay attention to what she was saying.

Not long after I had left Blaine the alarm was set off by one of the wolves on border patrol, informing us that Blaine had crossed the boundary line and had disappeared into rogue territory or what we sometimes refer to as *'no man's land'*. I had run straight over to Jax and Anna's place in a panic, hoping that they had some form of plan on how to get her back, but so far all they've done is give me grief.

"I know Anna, I *know*. I was a jerk, but please just tell me how I can get her back here where it's safe," I pleaded as I rested my elbows on my knees and my head on my hands. My wolf was going mad in my head and it was giving me a raging headache. I guess it was what I deserved for denying her and our blood bond.

"Oh so *now* you want her? After successfully pushing her away you now realise who she is to you and want her back?" Anna laughed sarcastically as she continued to pace the living room, narrowly avoiding hitting her knee on the coffee table several times.

"I don't *know* what I want," I groaned as I tugged at the roots of my hair. "All I know is that my wolf is going *crazy* right now, thinking about Blaine being all alone in no man's land whilst being injured and vulnerable. Look, I promise to try with her but please... just help me get her back on our territory and away from danger. She's already faced off with three rogues and with the way she was walking earlier I don't think she'll be as successful if any more came after her."

Anna sighed as she sat on the coffee table in front of me. "I'll make some calls, maybe a neighbouring pack has seen her passing nearby or something."

I smiled up at her in thanks before getting up and stretching. "I'm going to go for a run and see if I can catch up to her, could you let the surrounding packs know that I may be passing through? Oh and if you hear anything please link me."

Anna smiled as she too stood up, "sure thing Xavier and *please* remember to be nice to her when you find her. She's been through a lot in her life and the last thing she needs is a jerk of a mate telling her she's not worth it."

75

I nodded in response before stepping outside and made my way over to the tree line to shift. I still couldn't believe that she'd run. I mean I knew I was a bit harsh on her, but it wasn't like she acted any better towards me. She must've known that flirting with some other guy in front of me was a sure-fire way for me to retaliate and get under my skin. Even if we didn't share the blood bond it'd still set off a mate's jealousy instincts.

I sighed as I followed her scent through the trees as quickly as I could. If anyone could follow her scent it would be me. Even though I hadn't known her very long, I already knew my mate's scent by memory. It wasn't fruity like most females, it was woodsier, like freshly cut grass and the way the ground smells after a fresh rainstorm, clean and fresh.

Thankfully Blaine hadn't shifted yet, making the possibility of me catching up to her that much more plausible seeing how slow she was moving earlier today. She was probably trying to hide her scent from us, it's always more intense when we're in our wolf form. It was also probably why the border patrol couldn't pick up where she was straight away and couldn't follow her for very long. She was a smart girl and knew how to survive undetected.

As I ran, I thought about my family. About what had happened to them and the promise I'd made to my father at his funeral. I felt so torn, on the one hand I wanted to honour that promise I'd made to him and get revenge on the rogue that killed him, but on the other hand I wanted my mate. I needed my mate. The more I thought about her the more I wanted... everything from her. She was so snarky and sarcastic, she had fire in her soul that matched the colour of her hair, and I couldn't help but admire her for it. One thing was for sure, the Moon Goddess gave me a challenge with this pairing, but was it a challenge I was willing to accept?

Blood mates couldn't reject each other, our only options were to live with each other as destined mates, the way the Moon Goddess intended, or live a life of misery that would slowly but surely turn you and your wolf mad. Wolves weren't designed to be alone, and the idea of being away from Blaine, even now, seemed to cause me physical pain.

I skipped to a stop as I took in my surroundings. Blaine knew how to confuse someone who was following her, her scent was all over the place with it going this way one minute and that way the next. So much so I was struggling trying to successfully track her. Thankfully I had a keen nose, and even though I wasn't a gifted tracker like Will, Jax's brother, my wolf was solely focused on finding our mate, so after a bit of sniffing around I managed to find the correct route that she'd taken and took off.

Her scent was getting stronger with every passing minute, and it wasn't long before I heard a noise in the distance, a noise that sounded an awful lot like a scuffle.

I pushed myself harder, panicked that she was in some form of danger. I knew she could handle herself, any wolf who had survived a significant amount of time as a rogue could, but she was injured and to other rogues in the area that could mean weakness. An easy target.

I skidded into the clearing and what I saw had my heart in my throat. Blaine was on the floor, the fabric covering her thigh completely saturated in her blood from the stitches being reopened, and a rogue male pinning her down by her shoulder blades and forcing her face into the dirt. Both were in their human forms, but I could tell Blaine was struggling to stay conscious. Whether it was from exhaustion or blood loss I wasn't sure, but all I knew was that I had to help her, I had to help my mate before I was too late to save her.

I growled towards the couple, resulting in gaining both of their attention, as I slowly stalked towards them with my hackles raised, assessing the stranger and looking for any weak spots that he may have that I could use to my advantage. I didn't shift, seeing as I didn't have any clothes with me, so I couldn't communicate with them, but I hoped Blaine could remember what I looked like in this form, could smell that it was me, and know that I'd come to help her.

"Who the hell are you?" The stranger snarled, not getting off my mate's back as he shoved her face further into the dirt, covering her skin and hair with grime and leaves.

Blaine suddenly looked up, realising that the wolf that had entered the clearing wasn't a friend of the stranger holding her down and I saw shock register on her face as she took me in. "Xavier?"

Chapter Eleven
Blaine's POV

I'd been walking for what felt like hours, my feet were aching and my ankle and thigh were both screaming at me to take a break, but I couldn't. I knew that Anna would have noticed that I was gone by now, and that she may even be looking for me as we speak. I couldn't stop on the off chance they caught up with me. There was no way I was spending one more day in that pack and with Xavier.

I was also in no man's land, rogue territory, and if I showed any sign of weakness out here, I was toast. The items in my backpack were reason enough for someone to come and challenge me. On any other day I would have laughed and told them to bring it, but I knew I wasn't in any state to fight, not with the way my body was screaming at me.

I wasn't sure why my leg hadn't healed yet; sure, I'd had the delayed effect of the silver from the cuffs but that should be long gone from my system by now. I should be getting to the stage where I could walk without issue, but with the rate I was healing you'd think I was an average human being.

I sighed as I swiped the small amount of sweat that had dotted across my forehead with the back of my sleeve before I tied my unruly lion's mane up into a loose bun. Having curly hair was sometimes a blessing and sometimes a curse. When the curls worked in my favour, I felt amazing, but when they didn't, boy was it a bad hair day.

I grumbled in defeat as I gave into my body's demands and took my backpack off my shoulders and sat down against a tree. It wasn't particularly warm out today, but for some reason I was sweating up a storm. I retrieved a bottle of water from the confines of my bag and took a huge gulp to try and help rehydrate myself, sighing in relief as I felt the water cool my throat. What was happening to me?

I cringed as I accidentally brushed my arm against my stitches, *damn rogue managing to sink his claws into me*.

Just when I was about to shimmy out of my jeans and take a look, I heard a rustle in the bushes and instantly froze. This was not good, I wasn't exactly the most popular wolf in the rogue community, not that there really was one. It was more of a dog-eat-dog world out here, if you could excuse the pun.

My family and I had killed a lot of rogues in our lifetime, and it had made a lot of wolves angry and resentful. Angry that we had killed their friends and 'pack mates' even if it was for self-defence. They didn't care, it was an eye for an eye out here.

I tensed up as I heard the footsteps coming closer and closer and remained perfectly still in the hopes that the stranger would walk right by me unnoticed. I mean maybe I would get lucky, maybe this was just one of Xavier's pack mates who had caught up with me? I mean it wasn't like I was moving fast enough to get too far, even if I was using every trick in the book to make tracking me difficult.

Unfortunately, luck wasn't on my side, and I felt the breath catch in my throat as I came face to face with someone I hoped I'd never have to see again. I hadn't seen or heard from him in years and to be honest I'd kind of forgotten all about him, but looking into his eyes I could tell he hadn't forgotten about me.

"Well well well, look what we have here..." the guy growled as he took me in, semi passed out and on the verge of delirium as I leant against the tree for support. I don't know what was wrong with me, but I felt like I was coming down with some sort of fever. I was sweating buckets, and my body had started violently shaking, as if I was being electrocuted by something low voltage. *Now was seriously not the time to give up on my body* I prayed.

"Who are you?" I managed to get out, hoping I could fake innocence, but I knew it was useless. He knew who I was.

"Oh you know very well who I am sweetheart," the guy sneered as he started to advance on me.

I stood up as quickly as I could, not liking the height advantage he had on me, but when I stood a huge wave of nausea hit me and I stumbled as I lost my footing.

"You don't look so good princess, let me help you take a seat," he laughed before he struck out and punched me in the stomach. Normally I would be able to shake a blow like that off no problem, or better yet block it entirely, but this time the hit felt so hard I staggered backwards, causing me to trip on a tree root and fall onto my side hard.

I cried out in pain as my thigh took the brunt of the fall and before I could blink, I felt the guy leap on my back and pin me down to the ground. This wasn't the way I was expecting to go, I thought I'd at least go down fighting and living up to the reputation of the redheads fiery nature, but I guess that wasn't in the cards for me.

I groaned as the guy twisted his hands into my hair before he smashed my face into the ground with enough force to bust my lip open. "This is for my brothers you piece of crap," he growled as he smashed my face into the mud again.

My brain started to drift out of consciousness as the shivers continued to wrack my body, causing me to violently shake. At least if I passed out, I wouldn't be awake for the pain he would undoubtedly cause.

I spat out the twigs and mud that managed to get into my mouth that was mixing with the blood from my cut-up lip. I must look like a treat right about now, at least no one was here to witness it.

Just as the guy started to put pressure on my neck, I heard frantic footsteps running towards our direction. Great, must be one of this guy's new friends not wanting to miss out on the action.

"Who the hell are you?" I heard him yell from above me and I quickly looked up, shocked that this guy didn't know the wolf that had just entered the scene.

When my eyes finally focused my heart lodged itself in my throat... it couldn't be.

"Xavier...?"

I don't know what happened after that, my brain started drifting in and out of consciousness, but when I suddenly felt myself being lifted into the air, I stirred enough to notice the tell-tale signs of the sparks that crackled beneath the surface of my skin. Xavier had come for me, and he'd saved me.

"Don't worry Blaine, I've got you," I heard him whisper in my ear. "Crap Blaine... you're burning up. Don't worry, Dr Tessler is ready and waiting for when we get you home, she can fix you up in no time." It was the last thing I heard as I drifted to sleep to the sound of Xavier's rapid heartbeat in my ear.

Chapter Twelve
Xavier's POV

I sighed as I stared at the heart rate monitor making its routine beeping sounds, hoping it would give me any indication as to when Blaine was going to wake up.

After she had passed out in my arms, I could tell something was seriously wrong with her. There was very little that could make a werewolf pass out, and none of them were good.

I ran as fast as I could back to the pack hospital where Dr Tessler and her team were already ready and waiting for us. I had stayed in constant contact with her through the pack link, telling her everything I knew so that when we got to her, she knew exactly what was needed.

It had turned out that Blaine had gotten some form of infection in her thigh which had caused her own blood and tissue to attack itself. It was uncommon for something like this to happen to one of us, but unfortunately not impossible.

With the help of some research, mainly on Jax and Anna's part as I refused to leave Blaine's side for fear that her infection would come back without me close, we found out that being away from a blood bound mate, especially a mate bond that hadn't been fully formed yet, could cause a wolf's healing ability to virtually stop if they weren't within close proximity to one other. It turns out there was a lot we still didn't know about the effects of a blood bond. To my knowledge we were the only ones, on record anyway, that had even attempted to part ways from one another after finding each other, and so the effects that parting could have on each other were unknown.

Apparently when blood bounded werewolves parted ways, their wolves became so laser focused on finding each other again that they became completely laser focused on their missing mate and ignored everything else around them, including mind link messages and healing themselves.

I had thankfully gotten to her in time, and thanks to the staff at the hospital quickly attaching her to a drip bag filled with antibiotics and fluids she was slowly starting to make a recovery; it was all just a waiting game now for when she'd eventually wake up. I had made myself comfortable in the corner of her room, making sure that I was nearby just in case she woke up and needed anything or her wolf needed me near to continue healing.

"Knock Knock," I heard from the doorway and looked over to see Anna and Jax entering with a sleeping baby JJ in her arms. "We just wanted to stop by and see if there had been any changes," Anna smiled as she adjusted the sleeping baby in her arms.

I sighed as I looked over at a sleeping Blaine. "Nothing's changed since you guys last came by a few hours ago," I shrugged.

Anna looked at me sympathetically as she instinctively leant against Jax who was standing behind her, with his arms wrapped around both her and his child.

Seeing someone else's mate harmed or in pain always pulled on the heart strings of others who had already found their mate, it was as if they were imagining themselves in our situation. That kind of pain always made you want to reach out for your mate for reassurance, assurance that *their* mate was okay and unharmed.

It tugged at my heart as I watched the two of them being able to interact with each other. I mean it wasn't like I *deserved* anything like what Jax and Anna had, I had thrown the right away to feel sorry for myself the moment I drove my mate to run away from me and into the arms of danger.

"It wasn't your fault man," Jax sighed as he came over and placed his hand on my shoulder, as if he was somehow reading my mind.

"Yes it was," I exhaled as I ran my hand down my face, having not slept since I had brought Blaine in yesterday afternoon. "It's *all* my fault, she wouldn't have run away and put herself in danger if I had just manned up and not acted like a total jerk to her."

"You're right," Anna nodded as she came and took a seat next to me. "It *is* partly your fault, but you have a chance to now make it right, so don't waste it," she explained as she smiled over at me.

"But how do you know she'd even want me back," I muttered in defeat as I pushed my fingers into my temples, hoping to relieve the ache and pressure there.

"You just have to ask yourself whether she is worth the effort," Anna smiled as she stood back up. "You can make this right Xavier; you just have to try."

"But where do I even begin?" I asked them both, not even knowing how to start apologising for all the crap I've said to her over the last few days.

"Well, you can always start with an apology, you'd be surprised how far that can actually get you," Anna suggested with a shrug.

"That and food, more specifically junk food and chocolate," Jax piped up as he smirked over at Anna. "Food always seems to work with this one," he laughed.

Anna just rolled her eyes before looking back at me, not bothering to warrant that comment with a response knowing that it was one hundred percent true.

I smiled as I watched the two of them interact, hoping that I could have something like that one day.

. . .

It had been several hours since Anna, Jax and JJ had come to visit me and Blaine, and the stream of visitors hadn't lightened up. It seemed the whole pack had heard about the rogue girl I'd saved and were curious to see who she was.

I mean I couldn't blame them; the whole pack has known for years that I hated every rogue that even came close to our border and it seemed almost impossible for the Rogue Killer to even be seen saving a rogue... and yet I did. If anyone told me a week ago that I would go out of my way to save a rogue on more than one occasion I would have laughed in their face and told them to stop day drinking. Yet here I was, willingly sitting in a hospital room and waiting for my rogue mate to wake up.

After a while I'd eventually had enough of all these people coming in and out of Blaine's room, scared that they were going to wake her up before her body was ready, and so I'd asked Jax to politely ban anyone from entering this room that wasn't needed. Thankfully people had respected their Alphas wishes without resistance and I hadn't seen a soul in well over an hour.

Just when I was about to doze off, I couldn't even remember the last time I'd slept, the heart monitor spiked and I shot up in alarm to find Blaine lying there with her eyes semi open taking in her surroundings.

"Hi," I whispered, not wanting to startle her any more than she probably already was. Her eyes snapped over to me and she quickly assessed me as I stood over her, not really knowing what to do or say.

"Would you like some water?" I suddenly blurted as I went over to the corner of the room and filled up a small cup with some water from the neighbouring pitcher before placing a straw in so that she could drink it easier. "Your body is probably still a little dehydrated, so the doctor said to offer you this as soon as you woke up." I carried on rambling as I walked over to her, offering the cup to her with an outstretched hand.

Blaine assessed it for a second, debating whether to take it or not, but I guess her thirst won out as she reached out with one of her hands, still attached to a drip, and took the cup from me. She took a long thirst-quenching sip before sighing in relief and handing the empty cup back to me.

"Did you want anymore?" I asked as I went back over to the pitcher, hoping to help her out in any way that I could. It wasn't until this moment that I realised just why Jax had been so crazy after he'd first met Anna.

Seeing your mate injured and in a hospital bed was hell. I still wasn't even sure if I was allowed to call her that, my mate, after the way we'd both acted towards each other, but seeing as we shared a blood bond and our connection to each other was never going to dwindle, I guess we had to talk about us accepting the bond.

She quickly shook her head as she found the button to raise the back of her bed slightly, trying to get comfortable. "What happened?" She croaked out as she snuggled into the many blankets surrounding her. After her fever had broken her body started to rapidly cool down, making her shiver violent shakes, so I quickly covered her with a few blankets to try and keep her body at a more comfortable temperature.

"What's the last thing you remember?" I asked as I made myself comfortable on my hospital chair, thankful Jax had switched them up to a much more comfortable type last year.

"Well... I was running... and then I was sitting... or lying down... was someone holding me down? I don't remember too much of anything to be perfectly honest with you," Blaine sighed, cringing every now and then from her scratchy throat.

"After you ran, I decided to go after you. You didn't make it easy for me, I'll give you that," I chuckled. "But when I finally found you, you were lying on the ground with your face all banged up and your leg covered in blood. After you spotted me, you passed out. I was so worried that the rogue holding you down had done something to you I didn't think and just went for him," I explained as I tried to stay calm. Just the thought of that rogue forcing her face into the dirt made my blood boil.

"I remember," Blaine whispered with a nod as she brought her hand up to her forehead, as if the sudden flood of memories was causing her to have a headache. "Did you kill him?"

I frowned but shook my head. "No, I didn't know whether he was someone you knew, so I just made sure he was off and away from you without causing too much damage. After I ripped him off you though he ran, probably realising he was no match for me," I explained.

Blaine groaned at the news, "you should have killed him," she sighed.

"I'm sorry but it was either going after him or getting you the help you needed, you weren't in good shape Blaine," I muttered, not liking the memories that surfaced of her passed out in my arms and covered in blood. "Who was he anyway? Did you know him?"

She snorted slightly as she laughed before shaking her head. "Not really no, I bumped into him and his *'rogue brothers'* a few years ago. Safe to say their intentions weren't pure and his friends died as a result of crossing us, he's held a grudge against me ever since. I've bumped into him a few times, but I've always managed to avoid him. I guess I was a little too out of it to keep track of my whereabouts and surroundings this time."

I didn't respond to that bit of information, not wanting to overstep my place and demand more information than she was willing to give. "Well, I'm glad I managed to get to you in time," I whispered, mainly to myself than to her.

She sighed but otherwise didn't respond.

We stayed in that semi awkward silence for a long while before I finally decided to break it, not enjoying the awkward quiet between us. "Did you want me to get you some food or something? I mean the doctor hasn't technically okayed you for solid foods yet, but I'm sure I could sneak something in for you. Jax used to do it for Anna before she was allowed solid food and she turned out okay."

She smiled slightly at me in thanks before shaking her head. "Thank you but no, I'm honestly still feeling a little sick and the last thing I want to do right now is throw up all over myself after everything else I've been through already," she laughed. "Just give me a day or two's rest and then I'll be out of your hair, you won't have to see my face ever again," she sighed as she closed her eyes.

I frowned at her words, not liking the sound of them at all, "why would I want you to leave?" I questioned.

She looked at me with this *are you kidding me* look, her hair wild and her eyebrow raised, and I stared back with just as much confusion.

"Last time I checked you wanted nothing to do with me and the idea of me being your mate was laughable to you. Excuse me for thinking that meant you didn't want me around."

My shoulders slumped in defeat as I rubbed the back of my neck "look I'm sorry about... all of that. I know I can be a-."

"Asshat, dickwad, buttheat, douchebag-."

"Yeah I get it," I laughed slightly as I looked at her smug face. "I can be a bit... unfair sometimes, but if you're interested, I'd like to get to know you a little better. I mean you are my mate after all, and it seems the

Mood Goddess would rather us die than not be together so…"

Blaine stroked her chin with her thumb and forefinger with a slight smirk on her face. "You know I'm not going to make it easy for you to get back into my good books right?" She laughed.

I smirked back as I relaxed further into my chair "I'd be offended if you did."

Chapter Thirteen
Blaine's POV

It had been a week since I had been admitted into hospital and thankfully, I'd managed to make a near full recovery. Dr Tessler had decided to do a thorough examination of my thigh wound after my fever had broken and had found a small grain of dirt that had been embedded under my skin. No one knew for sure whether that was the thing that triggered the infection, but Xavier was still under the impression it was because I left him and his wolf... or something like that. After it had been removed, I'd made a rapid recovery, just in time to because I don't think I could deal with another day of hospital food. Anna was right, that stuff was awful.

When I was released, I expected I'd be heading straight back to my old room in the pack house, but when we started going in the complete opposite direction I had to question where we were going.

"Umm... Xavier the pack house is that way," I said confused as I pointed to somewhere behind me.

I heard him chuckle as he carried on driving up the tree enclosed driveway that led to where all the individual houses were situated. "Do you really think I would let you stay all the way over there in the pack house when you're still in no fit state to walk or look after yourself?"

"I umm… okay… so am I staying in Anna and Jax's house?" I questioned. After all, we were heading in that direction, from what I could remember from my short stay in the Crescent Moon territory.

Xavier was quiet for a second, so quiet I had to question whether he'd even heard me.

"No," he eventually answered. "You'll be staying with me in my house," he explained, saying it more as a statement than a request.

My initial reaction was to object, I mean did he really think that after everything he had said to me that I would just roll over and let him dictate where I would be staying? But then again, he had done everything he possibly could to make sure that I was happy and comfortable this past week. Making sure nobody overcrowded me or overstayed their welcome. Making sure the nurses didn't wake me up every half hour whilst they checked over my vitals. Checking I wasn't too hot or too cold. The least *I* could do was try a little to make things better between us.

"Okay," I nodded, looking through the front windscreen, hoping to catch a glimpse of Xavier's house.

"Wait really? You aren't going to fight me on this?" He asked, bewildered at my response.

I couldn't help but laugh at his reaction. "Yes really, you've done a lot for me over the past week, making sure that I had everything I needed. I'd be a hypocritical bitch if I just threw all of that back in your face and acted like a complete ass to you in return," I shrugged.

"Well, that's very... unexpected of you," he replied, and I couldn't help but smile. Was it just me or had we made some progress just now?

I relaxed into my seat for the rest of the journey, and it wasn't long before we were passing the house I knew Anna and Jax lived in. "Is it common for all packs to have their Alpha and Beta houses living so close together?" I asked, wanting to fill the silence. It wasn't that it was awkward or anything, but I always felt more comfortable when someone was talking, whether it was me or somebody else.

"Fairly yeah," he said as we drove past their house. "This is me."

We had stopped in front of a modest looking house, a little smaller than the Alphas, but nonetheless impressive. I was never really into the picket white fence look, but looking at Xavier's house I could definitely say I could get used to it.

"It's nice," I nodded as I opened the passenger door and waited for Xavier to bring around the crutches we'd brought back with us from the hospital. I mean you couldn't really call it stealing from the hospital if your best friend owned it and you helped run it could you?

"I'm glad you like it," he smiled, trying not to look so happy that I liked his house, but failing miserably.

He helped me up the brick walkway and through the front door, being careful with the small step that got you onto the front porch.

The layout was very similar to Anna and Jax's, with a short corridor leading to the living room on the left and the kitchen/diner on the right. The only difference was where the Alphas house ended in the living room the Beta house had a conservatory that extended from the living room, making the whole place seem more open and inviting. I wonder if Anna had ever thought of doing the same to her house, it obviously worked and gave them another living space to use for when they had people over.

"So this is it," he muttered as he rubbed the back of his neck, obviously feeling apprehensive about the whole situation with me and him under the same roof... alone... in his house. "Unfortunately, all of the bedrooms are on the second floor, but if you feel like you can't manage the steps one of the sofas is a pull out and I'm more than happy to set it up for you," he explained as he pointed towards the living room.

I smiled at how awkward he was being before shaking my head at his kind offer. "I'm sure I can manage, thank you though."

"Okay well I'm going to make us some chicken soup, I'm sick of that hospital food and it's light enough on your stomach so you shouldn't feel too sick afterwards," he said as he gestured towards the kitchen.

"You know how to make chicken soup?" I asked with raised eyebrows, a little surprised. He doesn't strike me as the cooking type.

"Well... Anna may have made a batch and sent me home with a few tupperware's to freeze in case of emergencies," he muttered, a sheepish look on his face.

I chuckled, that sounded more likely. "Well if it was made by Anna then I'll definitely have some please," I smiled. I'd only had a few of her meals but I was definitely already addicted to her cooking.

He just smiled back with a nod before disappearing into the kitchen to heat up some soup, banging pots and pans as he went. As he was in the kitchen, I decided to explore the place where I would be living for the foreseeable future.

. . .

I hobbled my way back into the living room after doing my quick exploration of the downstairs and got myself comfy on the sofa. It was weird, on the one hand this whole place was like a shrine, with photos and knick knacks scattered all over the place of him with whom I'm guessing are his family. But on the other hand, it was like this place was empty, there was very little of Xavier in the house and it definitely didn't look like his kind of decorating at all. Less bachelor pad and more American style family home.

"Here we go, reheated homemade chicken soup," he announced as he entered the room with two bowls of steaming soup with sliced up bread resting on the side, ready to be dunked in and enjoyed.

I smiled as I reached up to relieve him of one of his bowls, "thanks."

We ate in silence for a while, both of us too engrossed in the food to carry on a decent conversation and too hungry to really care.

Xavier had finished quickly though, obviously hungrier than me, and set his bowl down onto the nearby side table, but didn't make a move to get up, content with just sitting here and enjoying each other's company to break the silence.

Me being me, I couldn't deal with the silence, broken by only the ticking clock, so with a little encouragement from me to me I asked him a question. "Can I ask you something?"

"Shoot," he said, an easy smile on his face.

"Who *actually* lives here? I mean I know *you* do, but who else?"

He frowned at me slightly, confused at my question. "No one, just me... why?"

"Oh, well I was just wondering because there's all these family photos around and the place doesn't exactly scream you, so I just assumed someone else lived here with you," I shrugged.

Xavier's easy demeanour rapidly shifted, and his shoulders set in a rigid position with his fists clenched and his jaw set. Wherever they were, whatever happened to the people who lived here, it definitely wasn't good.

Chapter Fourteen
Blaine's POV

"They aren't here," he replied as he leant forward, resting his elbows on his knees, his posture drastically different from five seconds ago.

"I kind of guessed that," I chuckled awkwardly as I fidgeted with the end of my top. "That's why I asked where they were." Was he really not going to tell me anything about himself?

"I just..." he started before sighing and running his fingers through his hair. "I don't like talking about my family, it's a sensitive subject for me."

I nodded my head in understanding. "I get it, if anyone understands a complicated home life it's me," I chuckled sadly as I thought about my own lack of family life.

"I can imagine," he nodded. "Being made a Rogue would put a serious strain on any relationship."

I sighed, well it was now or never, right? "I wasn't actually *made* a rogue," I explained, not looking him in the eye. Partly because I was scared of what I was going to see, knowing how he felt about rogues, but also in case I lose my nerve and stop talking.

He frowned as he looked over at me in confusion, "did you willingly leave your pack or something? I mean it's rare for a wolf to *willingly* leave the safety of a pack, but I guess if anyone could survive the life of a rogue it would be you," he shrugged with a soft smile.

"Thanks?" I laughed as I looked back up at him, not really knowing if it was meant to be a compliment but deciding to take it as one. "But no, I didn't willingly leave either. I was born a rogue. I lived with my parents, older brother and younger sister," I explained.

He stared at me for a second, obviously baffled by the information. I could understand his confusion, it was hard living the life of a rogue when it was just you to look out for, let alone when you had to fend for yourself and a young family. I had heard of a few other rogues who had tried to start families outside a pack, trying to start a new pack with just their little family, but unfortunately it was extremely rare for the baby to survive the lifestyle without help.

"But how...?"

"My Mum has a brother that used to help us out any way he could. When he took over for her father and became Alpha of his pack, he set up a bank account for us and transferred small amounts of money any time he could," I explained. "He obviously couldn't lift his father's ban and allow us back into the pack, but he did what he could without getting found out," I shrugged.

"I... Blaine I'm..." he stuttered but couldn't quite find the right words for what he wanted to say.

I shrugged again, knowing what he was trying to get across, "no apologies needed Xavier, I mean something must've happened in *your* life for you to hate my kind so much, I just hope that one day you'll trust me enough to tell me," I smiled.

We were silent for a moment, the both of us taking in what the other had said. It was nice, having Xavier know a bit about my past and it was even nicer getting some form of apology from him in return.

"So... where are they now?" He suddenly asked, breaking the silence between us.

I looked up to see him looking back at me, a mixture of sadness and sympathy on his face and I sighed as the memory of my family was brought up. "I honestly don't know," I shrugged. "My siblings hadn't come back from a hunt and my parents decided to try and find them, but they never came back either. I waited for a few months for them to return, but after a while I kind of had to face the fact that they weren't coming back. It was becoming dangerous for me to stay in one place for so long and I knew they'd be so angry with me if they found out I'd stayed behind in the hopes that they'd come back, so I had to leave. I... had to face the fact that I was alone," I shrugged.

I hated bringing up the memory of my family. Even though we didn't have the safest or most secure childhood out there, it was still my childhood, and they were still my family, and I was still going to miss them, deeply.

"They died," Xavier suddenly said as he looked down at his intertwined hands. "My family I mean, they were killed in a rogue attack a few years ago," he sighed. "I tried to help, but I was too late. My sister and mum died right outside the front door and my dad close to the pack house after he felt the bond with my Mum break."

"I-I'm sorry," I stuttered as I stared at him in shock. "No one should have to go through something like that."

He shrugged but otherwise didn't respond.

"You make a whole lot more sense now though," I chuckled quietly. "Why you hated me so much when we first met, and why you couldn't get over the fact that I was a rogue, I'd hate me too if that had happened to me."

Xavier smiled at me in gratitude with a slight nod, "don't take it too personally, I wasn't a fan of Anna when she first stumbled onto our territory either. In fact if it wasn't for Jax I'm not sure what would've happened," he sighed as he shook his head. "Jax was so mad at me for yelling at her when we found her, I thought he was going to rip my head off," he laughed.

I frowned as I took in the new information. "Anna isn't from this pack?"

"No," he shook his head as he leant back in his seat, obviously feeling easier since the change in subject. "She's from a few towns over actually, she hasn't had the best life... but I think I should let her tell you all about that when she's ready, it's not my story to tell," he explained.

I nodded my head in understanding as we fell once again into a comfortable silence. We sat like this for a while, both of us just sitting on his sofa and enjoying each other's company. After the conversation we'd just had I somehow felt closer to him, as if opening ourselves up to the other allowed us to be more comfortable in each other's presence.

I smiled as I rested my head on the back of the sofa, perfectly content in the moment, and before I knew it, we were both slowly drifting off to sleep.

Chapter Fifteen
Xavier's POV

I stirred awake to the sound of a door slamming shut. Who the hell could that be and why the hell were they making so much noise?

"Is this a bad time?" I suddenly heard a voice ask; obvious humour laced in the person's question.

I looked up to see Jax standing in the doorway to my living room with his arms folded and a smirk on his face, what was he laughing at anyway? This wasn't the first time he had caught me having a nap on my sofa. "What do you want Jax?" I grumbled, not in the best mood from being woken up before I was ready.

"I just came by to make sure you two hadn't ended up killing each other, but I can see you've more than worked things out," he laughed with his hands in the air in a surrender pose.

"What are you talking about," I continued to groan, the sleep that laced my voice still audible. I went to sit up, finding it weird to be lying down with someone else in the room, but stalled in my movements when I felt an arm tighten around my waist, what the-.

"I have to say, I didn't peg you as being the little spoon kind of guy, but if it's comfy I'm not judging," Jax laughed as he went off into the kitchen, most likely in search of food or a beer or something.

I sighed as I looked behind me and took in Blaine's sleeping appearance. She looked different when she slept, without the constant presence of her slight frown she always carries in between her eyebrows she almost looked content, peaceful even.

She had always looked beautiful before, with her out of control red hair and freckles that covered her complexion, but without her fiery personality and her *I can do anything I want* attitude, I felt like I was seeing a different side to her. A more personal side that was just as beautiful, but more her. As if the person I had gotten to know over the last few weeks was just a facade, a way of pushing people away. Looking at her face now I was excited about getting to know the real her.

"Once you've finished creeping on your mate in there, I have some news," Jax yelled from the kitchen and I cringed at the volume he spoke. I looked behind me again, worried that his yelling had woken Blaine up, but when I took in her sleeping state I relaxed slightly. It turns out Blaine was a heavy sleeper.

I moved her arm from around my stomach and slowly got up, not wanting to disturb her. She hadn't gotten much sleep during her week's stay at the hospital; she says it was because the smell of it was keeping her up, but I just think she doesn't like hospitals and big crowds in general. I guess if you've lived your whole life blending into the shadows and staying out of the spotlight and not drawing attention to yourself it must be pretty weird to have a team of nurses and a pack of people wanting you to live to become their Beta Female.

I walked into the kitchen once I was sure Blaine was still sound asleep and found Jax with half a beer in his hand as he leant against the counter.

"So what's up?" I yawned as I took a seat at the dining room table, accepting the unopened beer he held out to me.

"Annabelle's been warned about another pack of rogues planning to attack us and try to kidnap her," Jax sighed as he ran his hand along the back of his neck. "The Goddess hasn't given her too much information on them, but I don't think they're much of a threat. Apparently, they've already attacked a few neighbouring packs and all they do is try to kidnap a warrior or two and then retreat."

I frowned, why would they infiltrate a pack and risk their lives just to take a warrior? "So why are they not a threat if they still manage to trespass and capture pack members?" I asked.

"We're a lot stronger than most of the other packs out there, since Annabelle has arrived, we spend longer training and more members have been voluntarily recruited than ever, everyone wants to be able to protect our Luna and the Goddess' Messenger," he shrugged, seeming unfazed by the threat. "I've called a pack meeting tomorrow to make sure everyone is aware of the threat and are ready for when they arrive," Jax continued as he took another sip of his beer.

I hadn't noticed it before, but he looked tired, more so than he usually did. I knew that he had been stressed lately, with the baby arriving and then us getting attacked left right and centre for their chance at getting Annabelle. He couldn't have been getting much sleep.

"When was the last time you slept man?" I asked, worried for my friend, but he just shrugged me off as he drained the rest of his beer.

"I sleep enough," was all he said as he went to get a glass of water, having finished his beer and needing something to do.

I sighed as I looked at him. Jax was the most stubborn man I'd ever met, being an Alpha you kind of needed to be, but it didn't mean that he wasn't allowed a break every now and then.

"Why don't you let me have JJ tonight? You could take Anna out on a fancy date and just spend time with her. When was the last time you were able to have a quiet meal with just the two of you?" I asked.

Jax stayed silent as he looked off into the distance.

"Think of it as a thank you, for letting me have the week off to make sure Blaine was doing okay in the hospital."

Jax smiled as he shook his head slightly, "you are so whipped for her and you don't even know it yet," he laughed.

"Oh *I'm* the one who's whipped? Lest we forget the time you met *your* mate? You were so lovesick you couldn't be away from her for ten minutes without freaking out," I laughed.

Jax just rolled his eyes as he chuckled along, not having a leg to stand on in his defence. "Yeah whatever," he laughed. "Just you wait."

I was about to come up with another response when a voice from the doorway stopped me in my tracks.

"Hey Jax."

I looked over and saw Blaine leaning against the frame of the door, still looking half asleep and I scowled.

"What are you doing up? You shouldn't be walking around yet," I scolded her as I walked over to her, wanting to be nearby just in case she lost her balance.

"Chill Xavier, I just came in for a glass of water," she mumbled as she rolled her eyes at my overprotectiveness.

"Well why don't you let me get it for you and you go back into the living room and sit back down," I said as I watched her roll her eyes again before making her way back into the living room.

"Yeah and *I'm* the one who's whipped," Jax laughed as I went to get the glass of water she wanted.

. . .

After Jax had gone back to his place it was just me and Blaine again. I don't know how she would feel about us looking after JJ, but if she felt like she wasn't up for it for whatever reason I could always take him out to the park or something whilst she relaxed. Jax and Anna had done so much for me over the years, and I wanted to repay them in some way, even if it was just looking after their kid for the night.

"So I offered to take JJ for the night," I said as I walked back into the living room. "I hope that's okay with you?" I asked as I went and sat next to Blaine who was watching some mindless TV program.

Blaine shrugged as she looked over at me, "why wouldn't I be okay with it?"

"I don't know, I just wanted to make sure I guess," I shrugged. *This living with another person thing was going to take some getting used to,* I thought to myself as I linked both Anna and Jax that they could bring him over whenever they were ready.

"Are you sure you're okay with looking after him Xavier? We don't mind cancelling our reservations," Anna responded almost instantly, sounding almost nervous about leaving him with us for the entire night. *"Or I could always just ask mine or Jax's parents if they wouldn't mind taking him?"*

"Don't worry about us Anna, just go and enjoy yourself," I reassured her with an internal eye roll. I don't know why they were so nervous, that boy was a poster child, and I was the best uncle a kid could ask for.

"If you're sure... we'll be around in a minute to drop him off," she said before she cut the link.

"They'll be here in a bit," I told Blaine as we focused back on the television. If Anna told me they would be two minutes they would more than likely be twenty, she's never been very good at time management.

Just as predicted, twenty-five minutes later, there was a knock on the door and Blaine went to pause the TV so I could go and answer the door without missing anything.

"Hi guys, we have to run because we're running late but here's everything that you're going to need for him this evening," Anna explained as she burst through the front door, looking more dressed up then I have seen her in a long time. "He's had his evening feed so there's no need to do that, but I've packed some snacks and other bits and pieces for him in case he does get hungry. There are plenty of nappies and clothes in there for when he needs changing, his blanket is in the back pocket of that bag, make sure you don't lose it as he will not sleep without it. He usually falls asleep around-."

"I've got it Anna," I laughed as I interrupted her babbling. "You are aware I've looked after him before, right?"

"Yes yes I know that," she said with an eye roll. "But this is the first time you or *anyone* will be taking him overnight and I just want to make sure that everything is in order before I leave you with him," she explained as she kissed the top of her baby's head and smoothed his hair down with her hand.

"We'll be fine Anna," I promised as I took both the baby bag and JJ from her outstretched hands. "We're all just going to have a quiet night in watching movies and sleeping. Now go and have a well-deserved evening with your mate and we'll be right here when you come and pick him up tomorrow morning," I reassured her as I looked down at JJ who had gotten himself comfy and snuggled into my arms.

I smiled down at him as Anna turned to leave but just as she was about to shut the door behind her she swung the door back open with wide eyes.

"A cot! How could I forget something as obvious as a cot!" She exclaimed as she looked around, as if expecting one to magically appear out of thin air right before her very eyes.

"Anna, just relax okay? I've got a pop up one in the attic that I can bring down and set up in the living room. I think we're all going to be sleeping down there tonight anyway seeing as Blaine still can't do stairs very well," I explained as I tried to reassure her that her baby was fine here with us.

"Anna you better get going before Jax starts honking the horn. He'll be fine here with us, and you can just link Xavier if you want an update, and we can do the same for you!" Blaine shouted from the living room, and I couldn't help but chuckle slightly.

"Okay, okay I'm going," she shouted back with her hands outstretched in surrender. "Like Blaine said, if you need anything at all just link me," Anna said one last time, sighing in defeat. She kissed her son on the head before smiling up at me and then ran to the car where Jax had been patiently waiting for her.

"I love that girl, but she sure knows how to fuss," I laughed as I sat the both of us back down on the living room sofa.

"She has a right to be nervous," Blaine shrugged as she looked over at me with a cheeky grin. "I'd be worried if I was leaving my kid here with you all night as well," she laughed as she leant over and played with JJ's feet. I just rolled my eyes at her before settling back into the sofa with a nearly asleep JJ in my lap.

"Are you going to press play or what?" I asked as I stroked JJ's back, hoping that it'll keep him calm and get him fully off to sleep.

"Sure," Blaine chuckled before she turned back around and hit the play button. Unfortunately for us, at that exact moment, the TV show we'd been watching decided to play a shrill fire alarm sound effect, waking JJ up with a startle and causing him to scream the house down.

"Crap," I muttered at the exact same moment Baine muttered "and so the fun begins."

Chapter Sixteen
Blaine's POV

"Please just make him stop already!" I begged Xavier as I watched him walk around the living room with a still crying baby JJ in his arms.

"Well what do you suggest I do!" He yelled back over the noise of the wailing baby. "I've tried to feed him, but he doesn't want any of that, he won't burp, and he doesn't smell like he needs a change," he exclaimed.

I groaned as I buried my head into a nearby pillow. "I don't *know* but *please* do something before we have your whole pack banging on our door and demanding why we are torturing their future Alpha."

"I don't know what to do Blaine! This baby is usually the chilliest baby in the world, I don't think he's ever cried this much," Xavier groaned as he cringed at another screech JJ released.

I huffed before getting up and limping over to Xavier's phone. Maybe Google has some answers that could help us.

"Hey where are you going?" Xavier suddenly demanded as he walked after me, "don't leave me here with him!" He exclaimed and I couldn't help but laugh at the fearful look on his face.

"Relax, I'm just getting your phone," I laughed as I handed it over to him so that he could put his passcode in.

"It's 1 2 3 4," Xavier said as he looked at my outstretched hand with his phone in it. "I am *not* taking my hands off this baby just in case he wriggles and I drop him."

I raised my eyebrows in amusement and couldn't contain my laughter, "your passcode is 1 2 3 4? Are you serious?"

"Hey don't judge me, it's not my fault I have a bad memory and can't remember a simple number sequence," he defended, but he couldn't help but laugh along with me slightly. "Why do you think Jax never trusts me with any of the numbers for their safe room? He knows I'd have to write it down and in his head that means someone could get their hands on it," he shrugged.

I just rolled my eyes at him as I opened up Google and typed in '*why is my one-year-old crying*'.

A bunch of websites popped up and after rifling through some of them, I finally found something. "Okay this site says that if we have tried all of the obvious reasons like him being wet, cold, hot, hungry etc the next thing would be teething," I stated as I looked up at a confused Xavier.

"What?" He asked, as he looked down at JJ as if looking for the answer.

"The website said that he might be teething, apparently that can be really painful for babies as their teeth are literally getting pushed through their gums," I continued to explain.

"Great, I have some whisky in that cupboard over there," he said as he gestured to a closed cabinet behind me.

I frowned as I looked over my shoulder before turning back around to stare at Xavier, hoping he could clarify why we needed alcohol in a situation like this.

"To rub on his gums," he explained in a *duh* tone.

I stared at him shocked before I burst out laughing, "we aren't living in the 1950's Xav! You can't just go and get a baby drunk in the hopes that you'll get a good night's sleep, especially when that baby isn't even yours," I continued to laugh over the noise of JJ.

Xavier just rolled his eyes as he continued to bounce JJ up and down in his arms whilst gently rubbing his back. "Well, what does the website suggest then?" He asked as he kissed JJ on the head.

"It says here a milk pop, whatever the hell that is, or a cold teething ring will help," I read off before looking up at him from the phone screen. "Do you have any of those?" I asked, hoping like hell he did.

"Do I look like someone who has teething rings stored away in their fridge for a rainy day?" He asked bewildered as he made his way over to the kitchen with me slowly limping behind him. On the plus side, at least the baby had stopped him fussing about me, I could now get up and walk around without being told off.

"Well what do you have that's cold?" I asked as I sat down on the kitchen table with my leg outstretched.

"Umm... beer...frozen peas... chicken... steak…"

"Well they're not going to help," I rolled my eyes at him as he carried on listing things he had off the top of his head.

He rolled his eyes at my sarcastic remark before carrying on, "I mean I have frozen chips, surely that could help right?" He said as he kicked the bottom of his freezer, signalling where they were.

I thought about it for a second before shrugging, I mean it couldn't hurt to try. I got up and limped over to the freezer before fishing out a frozen chip to hand off to Xavier. Please let this work, because if not, I don't know how much more of his shrill screams I could take.

Xavier took the chip off of me before waving it in front of JJs face, hoping to gain his attention, but when he didn't take any notice of it I sighed in frustration as I snatched the chip out of Xavier's hand and all but shoved it into JJ's open mouth.

He cried for a little longer and struggled a bit but when he realised that the coldness from the chip was helping ease his discomfort slightly, he took it from my hand and started to chew away at it, becoming the quietest he had been since he had gotten here.

We both stood there in the kitchen as we held our breath, waiting to see if JJ would pick up with the screaming again, but when he stayed silent and just continued to munch away at the frozen chip, we both let out a sigh in relief. He was quiet.

"Nice thinking with the chip," I sighed as I looked up at Xavier with a smile.

"Nice thinking with the phone," he said back as we both laughed quietly at each other, not wanting to startle the now silent and content baby.

It was then that I realised how close we had gotten to each other. We were both so focused on the fussing baby in Xavier's arms that we weren't paying attention to our proximity to each other, but now he was happy, our attention had suddenly shifted. He was so close to me I could feel the heat radiating off him, his scent completely intoxicating me as he looked down at me with his deep chocolate brown eyes.

I sucked in a sharp breath as I suddenly remembered to breathe, my eyes still entranced with his as we stared back at one another. What was happening to me? I had never felt something like this before, I felt all hot and fluttery and every time Xavier shifted slightly it released another wave of his scent and I was knocked backwards all over again. The butterflies were whirling around my stomach, and I closed my eyes as my vision became funny and my breathing became laboured.

I looked up as I heard Xavier's breath catch in his throat and before I realised what was happening, we were both leaning towards each other, closing the gap between us inch by inch. My eyes involuntarily shut on their own accord and I held my breath as I felt Xavier's breath against my face. This was it, we were going to kiss.

I was finally going to kiss my mate.

"AAAHHH," JJ suddenly screamed in between us and we both sprang apart at the loud noise in the quiet room.

We looked around, both blushing slightly at what had just happened, before we focused on the again crying baby in his arms. "It looks like we need another chip," Xavier said, his voice slightly raspier than usual.

This was going to be a long night.

...

I thought once we had found the chip trick with JJ's teething we were safe for the night, but unfortunately after ingesting a few frozen chips, JJ had managed to throw up everywhere. Not only was he now covered in baby vomit, but so was Xavier and the whole front of his shirt. At first I had laughed, finding his disgusted facial expression hilarious, but when he had given JJ to me to look after while he changed, JJ decided to give me the same treatment and threw up all over my back.

"That's what you get for laughing at me," Xavier chuckled, a satisfied smirk on his face as he looked over at my disgusted face. "Gotta love karma," he laughed.

I rolled my eyes at him as I held the heavy baby out to him, "yeah yeah whatever, can you please just take him back so that I can change as well? We also need to change him, I don't think Anna and Jax would be too pleased if they came back to pick him up tomorrow and he's covered in his own vomit," I said.

Xavier just smiled at me as he took JJ from my arms and walked back into the living room where his changing bag was.

I walked behind him, albeit a bit slower thanks to my stupid leg, and went over to my own bag so that I could find a clean shirt to change into. "I'll change in the kitchen; I won't be two seconds," I told Xavier as he continued to wrestle the wiggling baby into another pair of clothes.

I laughed at the sight before leaving them to it and shut the kitchen door so that I could change in privacy.

As soon as I was alone, I let out a breath that I hadn't realised I'd been holding. We had almost kissed. Xavier and I had almost *kissed!* I couldn't believe it, after everything that we had been through and all the hateful words that had been thrown back and forth between the two of us, I never thought we'd ever get close to that stage in our relationship.

My heart stuttered as I carried on thinking about it, getting more nervous the more the butterflies swarmed around my stomach. Don't get me wrong I wasn't a prude or anything, I'd hooked up with people before, but it was *never* as intense as what we had just shared, and we hadn't even done anything. God knows what would happen if we did, if that was how it felt just to be close to him.

"Blaine are you alright in there?" Xavier suddenly asked through the door.

I jerked out of my dazed state at his voice and quickly took a shaky breath to calm my heartbeat. "Yeah I'm good, just sitting down for a second."

"Well stop sitting and get in here, this is definitely a two-man job getting this little man back into some clean clothes," he laughed.

I smiled back, even if he couldn't see me, and quickly went about changing into a different T-shirt so that I could help Xav out.

When I walked back into the living room, I laughed at the sight of JJ crawling around the carpeted floor with only a top and a nappy on with one sock semi off his left foot. "Looks like dressing him was a success then," I laughed as I bent down to pick him up and bring him back over to where his clothes were.

"Yeah I kind of just gave up in the end," Xavier shrugged as he looked at me in amusement.

"What?" I asked as Xavier continued to stare at me "Do I have something on my face?"

"No it's just... your T-shirt is kind of inside out," he laughed as he pointed to the new top I'd put on in a hurry.

I blushed slightly as I went about finishing dressing JJ, "yeah well you can't even dress a baby," I defended as I finished putting on his last sock.

"Yeah but at least I can dress myself," he laughed and I couldn't help but laugh back as I smacked him in the stomach. "Oh and by the way, when I was going through his bag for another set of clothes I found this," Xav said and I looked over at him to find a bright blue and green teething ring in his hand.

"Oh my god are you serious? We had one here the whole time and instead of looking we just gave him frozen chips," I groaned as I put JJ back down on the floor.

"Yeah... maybe leave the fact that we fed their baby frozen chips out of the nightly report when they come to collect him," Xavier chuckled as he rubbed the back of his neck.

"Agreed" I nodded as I went and sat over on the sofa with a sigh, glad that I could get the weight off my leg.

"How's it going by the way? Your leg I mean," Xavier asked as he came and sat next to me.

I shrugged as I settled back into the cushions, making sure I still had an eye on JJ as he played with one of his many annoying musical toys. "It's fine, pulls every now and then when I've been on my feet for a while but other than that I can't complain" I shrugged. I kind of just wanted the whole thing to be healed now, that way not only will I be able to get around easier, but I will also stop being a nuisance to everyone. "Hopefully it'll heal

118

soon and I'll be out of your hair," I smiled as I looked over at JJ again.

I personally wasn't fussed about being around Xavier, sure I felt it was a little early for us to be living together, but it was nice being in such close proximity to your mate and him not hating your guts. I mean I now understood why he did, it was a similar reason as to why I hated pack wolves so much, but it still hurt slightly to be rejected by the one person who was made to love you unconditionally.

"I umm... I was actually going to talk to you about that," Xavier muttered quietly, as if he wanted to say it and bring up the subject but also hoped that I didn't hear him so that he had an excuse to drop it.

"Oh yeah? Are you wanting me out sooner or something?" I laughed but I couldn't help the little tickle of fear I got at the base of my neck when I realised that that could actually *be* a possibility.

"What? No I just... if you didn't want to move back into the pack house after you were better you can always just... stay here," he shrugged, as he shook his knee in nerves.

I froze as his words registered in my brain and stared at him open mouthed. Did he...?

"I mean I totally understand if you don't want to," he hurried on, taking my silence as a bad sign. "I didn't exactly make the best first impression... or second... or even third for that matter, but I hope we can at least you know... try to be civil with each other or something," he shrugged.

My heart stuttered as I continued to stare at him open mouthed, he was asking me to move in with him... wasn't he?

I cleared my throat, hoping my voice didn't come out as a squeal as I said the word that I'm sure will change the dynamic of our relationship for good. "Sure."

...

We sat in a semi awkward silence for a while after that, just watching a now happy JJ playing with his toys as he continued to munch down on his teething ring, that thing really was a godsend... or goddess send I should say. I hated the fact that we were feeling so awkward around each other, like neither of us knew what to say, after we'd been doing so well with communication lately, but I kind of understood it. We would now be living together, after only a few short days of tolerating each other, and we both didn't really know where to go from here. This was completely new territory for me, I only hoped that we could make this work.

"Are you hungry?" Xavier suddenly asked me, breaking the silence as he looked over at me expectantly, obviously hoping for something to do.

If I was honest, I wasn't in the slightest, I was more tired than anything as it was nearly ten thirty at night. I didn't want to upset him though, so I just nodded as I stood up, "sure I could eat, maybe a sandwich? Just something light and easy works for me," I smiled as I limped over and hauled JJ into my arms.

"You start on the food, and I'll start on getting this little one to bed, it is definitely *way* past his bedtime," I said as I smiled down at the sleepy baby in my arms.

"Okay cool, I still have to get the cot out of the attic though so just get him ready and when I've finished up in the kitchen I'll go and get it down for you."

He and I both knew that we were being overly polite to each other, but neither of us acknowledged it and just went about doing our respective jobs. Hopefully, with time, we can act more ourselves around each other.

I quickly went about getting JJ ready for bed, including changing his nappy, which was not a fun experience I have to say, and before long he was all dressed in his pyjamas and ready for bed.

When I brought him back into the kitchen Xavier was putting the finishing touches to some omelettes he had made for us, sprinkling something green on top before he plated them up and placed them on the already made up table. It looked like he had really made an effort with the place settings, using mats and napkins as well as the usual cutlery and drinks. I did like this new side to him, the one that cared for me and wanted to impress me with simple things like an omelette, but on the other hand I missed the old him. I missed what he was like when I was in hospital, the way he would banter with me and make me laugh about random things, things that were so funny I would choke on my water and the nurse would frown disapprovingly at him.

"You know you don't have to do all this for me Xav," I said as I gestured to the table. "I've lived as a rogue my whole life, so I don't need fancy things to keep me happy, just a roof over my head and I'm set," I explained as I rocked back and forth slightly. JJ was definitely asleep in my arms and the last thing I wanted to do was wake the little guy up by staying still.

Xavier just shrugged as he looked down at the food with a smile. "I know I don't have to, but I want to," he explained. "The fact that you've grown up as a rogue just makes me want to do stuff like this ten times more for you."

I smiled up at him and that's when I realised how close we had gotten to each other again. Somehow, within the space of our conversation, we had moved closer and closer together and I was now standing directly in front of him, so close that I could reach out and touch him if I wanted to.

My breath hitched as I stared up into his chocolate brown eyes and as I continued to stare the world around me just seemed to evaporate. I suddenly couldn't remember where I was or what I was supposed to be doing or anything apart from the person standing in front of me. Wasn't there something I needed to do?

As I continued to gaze up, I realised that Xavier's eyes started to change colour. They were still the chocolate brown colour that I was growing to love, but there was also a gold glimmer to them that wasn't there earlier. I smiled coyly as I looked up at him and I instantly knew that my eyes were doing the same thing.

MATE! MATE! MATE!

The mate bond was suddenly at the forefront of my mind and our wolves were so present that we didn't have much say in what happened next. Both him and myself, more wolf than human. A low humming growl escaped Xavier lips, telling me he liked what he saw, but before I could reciprocate, I felt something wiggle and whine in my arms and I looked down to find a now awake JJ wriggling and trying to get out of my grasp.

I sighed as I looked back up at Xavier and noticed that the gold swirl had vanished from his irises, and he was now staring down at the baby with a frown. I knew exactly what was running through his head and I couldn't help but laugh, this was now the second time he had butted in.

"Why don't you go and get the cot down from the attic and then we can put this wriggle pot down for the night," I suggested as I continued to hold onto JJ, if I let him down now he'd probably start crawling all over the place and wake himself back up even more than he already had.

Xavier sighed again as he rubbed the back of his neck, "sure I'll be two seconds, feel free to start without me," he said as he gestured to the now cool food on the table.

I shook my head as I readjusted JJ on my hip. "I don't mind waiting, just hurry up, I don't know how much longer I can hold onto this little guy," I laughed.

I watched Xavier leave the room and once I was sure he was out of ear short I turned down to JJ and sighed as I kissed him on the forehead. "You really know how to ruin the mood don't you little man."

...

We were now sitting at the table in silence as we ate our cold omelettes. Thankfully JJ went down pretty easily, and it wasn't long before he was passed out asleep with all of his soft toys and blankets surrounding him.

It seems like we had reverted back to our awkward silence status, and I sighed as the quiet filled the room.

"So what was Jax doing here earlier?" I asked, hoping the question would lead to a conversation.

"Oh you know," he shrugged as he shovelled another mouth full of food into his mouth. "Pack stuff".

I sighed as silence again fell and I put my fork down, hoping that if I seemed interested he would elaborate... he did not. "What kind of pack stuff?"

"Oh you know," he shrugged, "... stuff."

Why was he being so cryptic? Was the meeting some massive secret? I mean I know I wasn't pack, but Xavier has asked me to move in with him, surely that meant he was interested in me becoming pack and eventually the Beta female?

"What kind of stuff?" I repeated, asking more out of curiosity now than just trying to start a conversation.

Chapter Seventeen
Xavier's POV

It was nice to see Blaine taking an interest in our pack life. I'd been slightly worried that she wouldn't want anything to do with it after being a rogue her whole life. As a Beta I had responsibilities, and when Blaine eventually became Beta female it would be no different for her.

I honestly wouldn't know what to do if Blaine didn't want to become Beta female. By pack law there had to be one, and that would mean that I either had to hand my title off to someone else or reject Blaine to keep my title. It would be an impossible situation and a decision I knew I couldn't make. Giving up the one thing my dad had wanted for me, becoming the pack Beta, or rejecting my blood mate, something that was impossible and would cause both her and me intense pain and suffering.

I wanted to tell her all about our pack and what it would be like for her when she became one of us, but I had to be careful about giving up information to her. It wasn't that I didn't trust her, which I knew that's what she was currently thinking, but it was more about what the meeting with Jax was about.

Anna... and rogues.

I knew Blaine wasn't fussed about us needing to kill rogues, heck I even know she'd killed one herself on the first day we met, but what if part of the rogue pack was her family? I know she would hesitate, anyone sane would, but I couldn't have her hesitate with my packs lives on the line.

Then there was Anna. I definitely couldn't tell Blaine about her, not yet and not without Anna's permission. Yes, there were a few people, rogues and pack wolves alike, that knew about her, but the whereabouts of her and what pack she belonged to were virtually unknown.

If word got out that the messenger to the Goddess was amongst our pack, we'd be inundated with people, both wanting to meet her and wanting to harm her.

It was sad when you think about it. The reason the Goddess created Anna's line was to feel connected to her creations and to give us a direct line to be able to talk to her directly, but all it seemed to have done is cause more harm and chaos than good. We were just thankful that Matthew, the last wolf who was successful in taking her, and the pack members that the witch had enslaved, couldn't remember a thing of what happened, and even if they did, they had no idea which pack Anna was from or how to reach her. It had been our little silver lining in all the madness that had happened. All we had to worry about was the occasional wandering rogue bumped into our pack and recognised her wolf. She was pretty hard to miss, with her moonstone eyes and golden coat.

"So?" Blaine pressed; her food forgotten about as she folded her hands in front of her on the table.

I sighed as I looked down at my food, I *had* promised to be more open with her, but no one said about having to disclose the whole truth. "Jax said he'd heard rumours of a rogue attack on our pack, we aren't quite sure on the timing, but he wanted to inform me so that we can get prepared. I didn't tell you because-."

"Because you were worried about how I would take it," Blaine jumped in and I looked up at her, trying to gauge her reaction.

I nodded as I looked back down and I played with the leftover food on my plate, not really interested in it anymore. "Yeah."

I looked back up at her to see her shrugging her shoulders, "I honestly don't care what you do to them, they aren't my people. They shouldn't have been stupid enough to come onto your land," she said with finality as she took another bite of her food, seeming less than bothered with the whole situation.

I sighed in relief. I was still worried about the possibility of her family being involved, but now that I'd told her and she knew what was going on, well partially anyway, I felt the pressure of the *what if* situations lift from my shoulders.

"Let me know if there's anything I can do to help," she smiled at me after she had finished a mouthful of cheese and chorizo omelette. Thank God Anna had taught me how to do basic cooking a while ago, all part of her *'you need to be fully prepared for when you meet your mate to impress her'* training.

"Thanks," I nodded as I went back to my omelette, getting my appetite back. "We're actually pretty set, but if you wanted to come along and see our training fields with me tomorrow, you're more than welcome to," I smiled. Even if she didn't understand the gesture I had just offered her, I knew the pack would. It was almost unheard of for outsiders to be invited into the packs training grounds and even more uncommon for that outsider to watch whilst training was in progress.

Packs were notoriously private about how they defend their territory and people, and we were no different. If someone knew all of our moves and defence strategies, we were basically sitting ducks, an easy target for someone to waltz in and take our land.

Me bringing Blaine to the defence training tomorrow is my way of showing the pack who she is to me and what she is, or will become, to the pack. The Beta, helping run the pack alongside me and right under Anna and Jax.

She smiled at me from across the table as she put her knife and fork together on her empty plate, finished with her food. "I'd really like that, thanks," she nodded as she slowly got up to put her plate in the dishwasher.

I don't think she'd noticed, but I could tell she was really starting to slow down. Her leg was probably causing her more pain than she was ready to admit after all the walking about with JJ. Dr Tessler would have my head if she knew how much Blaine had been doing since she got home.

I jumped to my feet and quickly took the plate from her fingers. The last thing I needed was her stumbling and falling into broken shards of crockery or something. A bit excessive and over dramatic I know, but still. "Why don't I do that, and you go get ready for bed, you know where the downstairs bathroom is. Once I've put this all away, I'll pull out the sofa bed for you so you don't have to go up the stairs, your leg must be killing you after the evening we've had."

She smiled and muttered a quiet "thanks" before turning around and exiting the kitchen.

As I put our plates and the frying pan into the dishwasher, I thought about everything Blaine and I had been through in the past two weeks. We had gone through so much, from both of us hating each other to nearly kissing twice in the span of one evening, but there was so much more to come, and I don't know how she was going to take it.

For starters I don't even know if she knows anything about the blood bond we share, it's such an intense bond between two people it's hard to imagine her not knowing, but I still didn't want to assume. From the history books I'd read it can be pretty daunting for some pairs, causing them to become obsessed to the point of insanity with each other, and I just wanted to make sure we didn't get to that level. If we couldn't deal with being apart from each other, then we were going to have to find a way to coexist with each other until we were both comfortable in taking our relationship to the next level.

But it wasn't just the blood bond that was worrying me. She had been alone, with her family, for most of her life, and I knew that living with a pack would be an adjustment for her. I just hoped it was something she could deal with. Being a Beta came with responsibilities and I just hoped she could keep up.

...

And keep up she did. It had been two weeks since Blaine had moved in with me and since then she has shown both myself and the pack that she was a fine Beta. It was only a few short days after she'd moved in that her leg had completely healed and since then she has done everything she could to help both me and Jax out. She mainly helped with taking over our training lessons to help free us up to plan our defence for the oncoming attack, but she would also take a few voluntary shifts at the hospital, answering phones and filing paperwork, and also helping Anna with the day-to-day running of the pack.

I was amazed by her and the fact that she had settled into both the pack life and the position of power so easily. Not everyone was able to do it, but she acted as if she was born for the role, which I guess she technically had been.

"So, what's on the agenda for you today then?" I asked as I handed her a fried egg sandwich. After Blaine's first encounter with my kitchen, we both had decided early on that I would be the one to cook our food. She had tried her hardest, but after she had destroyed several of my pans with burnt food and set off the smoke alarm more times than I could count, she was banned from cooking anything in our kitchen. Not that I minded, I enjoyed cooking, and it also meant I could look after my mate, she was so independent that I often felt useless around her, but knowing that I was feeding her soothed that irrational part of me.

"Jax has asked me to head down to the training grounds again, he wants to make sure the warriors are fully trained before the invasion. He thinks that because I was a rogue, I have an insight into the attacker's mindset meaning I can guess their favoured moves… or something like that," she shrugged as she tucked into her food.

I nodded as I sat across from her, digging into my own fried egg sandwich. "He's not wrong, you know; a pack wolf's mindset is completely different to a rogues.

"With us it's all about the others around us and making sure that we have each other's backs. With rogues it's nearly always about themselves, and if they have to throw someone else under the bus to protect themselves, they will," I explained. We were lucky to have Blaine on our side and give us insight into how the rouges fought out of a wolf's territory. It has given us a definite tactical advantage and we had learnt stuff from her that we had never even thought of.

"Yeah I guess," she nodded with a shrug before taking a sip of her coffee, having finished with her breakfast. "I've got to get going anyway, I'm running late and the last thing I need is Jax breathing down my neck for not taking it seriously," she chuckled. It was true that Jax had been a bit on edge the last two weeks, but I guess it was understandable with the threat that loomed over his mate and family.

"If you can wait two seconds I'll come with you," I said as I darted across the kitchen and put my dirty plate in the dishwasher. "I don't have that much going on today, so it'll be good for me to actually get some training in for once," I chuckled. I quickly ran up the stairs to change into my workout gear, not waiting to hear a response from her, as I knew she would wait for me.

After quickly lacing up my trainers, I ran back down the stairs where I found Blaine by the front door tying up her hair into a high ponytail, making sure it was nice and secure for today's activities. I would never admit it out loud, but I secretly loved my mate's hair. It represented her perfectly. It looked fiery and out of control from a distance, but when you got up close you could see just how soft it was and the uniformed ringlets that it held. It was just perfect.

"Are you ready to go?" She asked as she caught my eye in the mirror.

"You know it," I nodded before I grabbed my front door keys and opened the door, ushering Blaine out in front of me. "So what have you got planned for us today then teacher?" I teased as we walked side by side towards the training ground. We very rarely took the car when travelling from one part of the pack to the other, much preferring the outdoors and feeling the wind as it brushed against our skin.

Blaine laughed as she shook her head, before she reached up to fiddle with the ends of her ponytail. "I honestly have no idea, I mean Jax could have given me a little more warning," she muttered with an eye roll. "Now I have to stand in front of a pack of warriors, all staring at me expectantly, whilst I just stand there like a stuttering idiot," she sighed.

I smirked at her nervousness before taking her hand in mine and pulled her to a stop. "There is no need to be nervous about today alright? You know these guys; you've trained with these guys, and I know that you are going to smash today. Don't let the fear of who's in the audience stop you from giving an amazing kickass lesson." My hand was still holding onto hers tightly and I stared down at her with a soft smile on my face, hoping the mate bond would calm her nerves down in some way.

I was standing so close to her; her scent was the only thing I could smell. I loved the fact that she didn't smell all fruity like most she wolves, it gave her more of a unique edge, and told everyone around her that she was not someone to be messed with. I was standing so close to her that I could see the slight spatter of freckles that dotted across her face, I could see the different colours of red and blond streaking through her hair, and I could see the gold swirl in her eyes as her wolf started to make itself known.

This time we had no JJ and no injuries to distract us, we had nothing to stop us as we slowly leant in towards each other. With my one hand still lightly grasping Blaine's, my other hand made its way towards her cheek, where it rested as I took in her features. She was the most gorgeous creature to grace this planet and I could not believe that she was all mine.

Her breath hitched as I took a small step forward, closing what little distance we had between us, and I growled as I felt her body become flush with mine. This girl was driving me crazy, and we hadn't even done anything yet.

I looked into her eyes one last time, looking for any sign that she wanted me to stop, but when I found nothing but want swirling in her eyes, I closed what little distance we had between us and pressed my lips firmly against hers.

Finally.

Chapter Eighteen
Blaine's POV

"You looked awfully happy with yourself walking into the clearing earlier," Anna commented with a smirk, looking at me as if she knew exactly why I had walked into my lesson with a huge grin on my face.

A slight blush appeared on my cheeks as they warmed at the memory of the most amazing kiss I'd ever experienced. I honestly hadn't seen it coming, but when Xavier took that final step towards me, making him my sole focus, I couldn't help but lean into him. My lips started to buzz again at the memory, and I brought my fingers up to touch my lips, confirming that they were still there and hadn't melted off from the sheer heat that was coming off my skin.

"I know that look!" Anna squealed as she happily jumped up and down, causing the warriors around us to look over, confused as to what their Alpha and Beta females were so excited about.

"Shh would you? I don't need the whole pack knowing about my business," I hissed as I grabbed her hand to stop her continuously happy dancing.

"I'm sorry I am just way too excited; I have been praying to the Moon Goddess for *weeks* now for you two to get together and now it's finally happened. You know people were starting to question whether Xavier would ever man up and acknowledge you as his mate. I mean I know he's introduced you as his and for all intents and purposes you are already a member of this pack and the Beta female, but you know as well as I do that we can never make it one hundred percent official until you mark each other."

I rolled my eyes and ran my hand over my hair. No matter how many times I re-tied it or how many hair products I used, the curls and frizz would always find a way to break free and run wild, springing up in ten different directions. "You know it was just as much me as it was him, I could have easily made the first move," I shrugged as I smiled down at the grinning girl in front of me, her smile too infectious not to share.

She rolled her eyes at me and playfully shoved my shoulder with a grunt. "We all know it was going to have to be Xavier who made the first move, he was the one with the problem, not you."

We walked up to a sparring mat and waited for our turn. Once I'd arrived in the clearing Jax had asked me to train Anna specifically today, making sure she was well prepared for whatever would be thrown at us. "True," I replied with a nod. "But I wasn't exactly all for it in the beginning either," I reminded her. After all, I had run off as soon as I realised who Xavier was to me.

"Yeah yeah whatever," Anna sighed as she waved her hand in my direction, having no other response.

"Girls you're up!" A warrior yelled and when I looked up, I saw that the mat we had been queueing for was now vacant.

I signalled that we had heard him and gestured for Anna to lead on as we both took the two steps up and into the boxing style ring. There were loads of them spread out across the field, at least twenty, and they were a great training platform to teach. It gave the fighters enough room to move around each other without having to worry about people accidentally stumbling into the ring and getting in the middle of the fight and being a distraction. The flooring was made with a slight spring to it so it wouldn't bruise as much when you were thrown to the floor and the height advantage meant spectators could watch and learn without getting in the way.

I turned and faced Anna, who was bouncing on the balls of her feet on the opposite end of the ring. We had both taken our shoes off and without the extra inch the soles of her shoes gave her she looked tiny. I would have second guessed fighting her if I hadn't already seen what she was capable of, she may be small, but she definitely knew her way around the ring.

"Now remember what I told you earlier. Rogues fight dirty, and they will exploit any and every weakness they find so the trick is to always keep them moving and distracted. The more time they have to observe you, the more chance they have of finding your weak spots," I explained as I bent my knees slightly into a fighting stance. "It could be something as simple as which foot you lead with, for example for me my weak spot would be my left knee, I injured it a few years back and it never quite healed right. You can tell it's my weak leg because I have placed it ever so slightly behind me, making sure your eye is drawn to my dominant leg, my right one" I explained as I pointed to each knee in turn.

Anna nodded as she took in my words, her eye zeroing in on first my dominant right leg and then shifting to my left, seeing if she could see the slight differences I was talking about. "Rogues are also weak and tire easily due to their poor diet and lack of nutrition. If you keep them moving and make sure you never give them a minute to stop and catch their breath and observe you, you have a significant advantage on them. They'll tire easier than you and that's when you make your final move."

Anna nodded again as she continued to bounce on the balls of her feet, making sure her muscles stayed warm and loose from the warm up we just did.

"So are you ready to have a round or two?" I asked, shaking my hands out before balling them up into fists again. We were wearing fingerless gloves so that our knuckles were padded over slightly, both for our protection as well as our opponents. The objective wasn't to harm each other, just to learn and improve on our weaknesses. We would pull our punches and never hit with the intention to injure the other, but with the way these fights sometimes went, you always wanted to be over cautious rather than under cautious.

As an answer Anna just gave one swift nod, signalling she was ready as her eyes zeroed in on me. I took a deep breath to steady myself and with one last look towards Anna to double check and make sure she was ready I ran towards her and the fight began.

About half an hour and three rounds later we were both panting on our respective sides of the ring. Anna was not an easy opponent that was for sure, and she was not one to be underestimated, which was made very clear to me after the first five minutes of our first round where she had me flat on my back. She was fast and even though she had only been training for just over a year she was a quick study and a force to be reckoned with.

Everything I had taught her and everything I had shown her had been absorbed into her like a sponge, making her have killer instincts and even quicker reflexes.

We had started to gain a slight audience after about fifteen minutes into our session, when we were both going at each other with neither of us gaining the upper hand. After she had taken me down the first time I seriously upped my game and quickly pinned her on her back, making it one all. After that we both gave it everything we had, neither one of us wanted to give in and lose to the other.

That's where we were now, we were still in the middle of round three, both of us too exhausted to carry on but also too stubborn to quit and give our opponent the point they needed to win.

"Alright girls break it up, break it up, you've made your point that you can hold your own in a fight so why don't you give the ring up to someone who still needs a turn and you both take a well-deserved break?" Jax asked as he stepped into the ring and made his way over to his mate. If I was being honest, I was secretly glad he had stepped in, I wasn't sure how much more I could have taken. I was still a little weak, and my body was screaming at me to sit down and get some desperately needed water before collapsing into a heap on the grass.

I smiled over at Anna as she brushed some hair from off her forehead, stuck there with sweat. We both gave a small wave and a smile to each other before I stepped out of the ring and down the stairs, toward the water dispenser where I took a huge gulp of refreshing water before pouring the rest over my face and neck in the hopes that it would cool me down.

"You were seriously hot up there" Xavier whispered from behind me and I couldn't help but snort as I felt my fly aways tickle the inside of my ear, damn baby hairs.

"Oh yeah?" I smirked as I turned around so that I was standing face to face with him, well face to mouth with our height difference, causing me to blush slightly at the memories of our kiss earlier. I just hoped the heat and sweat from my workout earlier hid the blush from him.

He had also been working out, which was made clear from the sweat that was lining his hairline and trickling down the sides of his face. I watched as it continued its descent down his sculpted jawline and down his jugular before disappearing into the collar of his shirt.

"You know if you continue to look at me like that, we're going to have to find somewhere more private," Xavier smirked as he wrapped his hands around my waist, pulling me close enough so that I could feel his breath on my face.

I flushed but otherwise didn't move, entranced with the way the sun shone off his skin and the gold that swirled in his eyes. I watched as another droplet of sweat rolled down his neck before landing at the base of his throat, right where my mark would eventually sit. I licked my lips at the thought of him finally wearing my mark and finally being completely mine, but before either of us could do anything about the obvious sexual tension between us we were interrupted by multiple pack members whistled and hollered in our direction.

I snapped out of it just as Anna and Jax appeared next to us, both of them with huge smirks across their faces, "get a room, would you?" Jax laughed as he wrapped Anna in his arms from behind.

I was just about to mutter an apology, a little embarrassed at having been caught in such a compromising position, but before I could Xavier laughed next to me. "Oh please, you have no right to say that to me after the number of times I have found you two in positions ten times worse than this," he exclaimed.

I looked over at Anna with raised eyebrows but all I got was a smug shrug in return. "What can I say, my mans a hottie."

I laughed as I looked over at her, "never would I have thought I'd hear words like that coming out of your mouth."

She just shrugged again in response before looking up at her mate, her blue eyes swirling and mixing with the colour of her wolves. But something was different about them, they weren't swirling with the usual gold, there was something almost transparent about them. I frowned, confused about what I was seeing, but before I could get a better look at them, I froze as I heard a white noise ringing in my ears.

I looked around to see if anyone else was hearing it but when I took in the faces of every pack member in the training grounds it was clear that something was going on. They were all frozen in their place, each with their own expression of fear plastered on their faces, and I instantly knew that they were all talking through the pack link. Even though I was doing the duties and taking on the responsibilities of the Beta, I still hadn't been sworn into the pack yet and without being sworn in I couldn't hear what was being said.

All at once the pack members unfroze and it was like a blanket of calm had spread across the grounds. I looked up at Xavier, hoping he could give me some insight into what was going on, but it was all made clear to me when Jax uttered two words that made my blood pump hot and run cold all at the same time.

"They're coming."

Chapter Nineteen
Blaine's POV

At first nothing happened, it was as if the pack had been frozen to the spot they were standing, but then in a blink of an eye, everyone was moving. One minute it was quiet enough to hear a cricket chirp in the background, the next it was so noisy with people barking orders left, right and centre that I couldn't figure out what any of them were saying. They all seemed to know what was happening, probably because of the mind link, because they all suddenly broke off in unison into their own respective parts of the forest.

I debated who to follow, seeing as no one had verbally told me what the plan was, before quickly deciding to follow Xavier. Anna would be fine without me, I concluded, as I saw her being escorted out of the training field by a group of fifteen warriors, blanketing her from view with their size. I watched her leave with a trickle of fear lacing its way through my spine. *She would be fine* I told myself again, before I turned in the opposite direction and followed Xav who had shifted into his grey wolf.

I paused for a second, debating whether or not I should change out of my clothes before shifting. They weren't mine after all, and the last thing I wanted to do was destroy some of Hanna's clothes. That and the fact that I wouldn't have any clothes available to me if I needed to shift back into my human form before heading home. I rolled my eyes at the stupid thought process and quickly shifted before running to catch up with everyone else. They were just clothes, if she was really that fussed about them I could just buy her some more. It would have to be with Xavier's money but at least the offer was there.

Thankfully I still was linked to the pack through Xavier, us being mates meant we could communicate without the need of me being officially introduced into the pack. If there was anything that I needed to know, he would tell me.

"What's the plan?" I asked Xavier through the link as I ran along beside him, easily keeping up with the speed he'd set.

He growled slightly as he looked over at me, clearly not happy that I had followed him. *"Blaine what the hell are you doing? You were supposed to follow Anna so that you don't get hurt"*.

I scoffed at his words, was that really what he was thinking about at a time like this? *"And what... watch helplessly from the side-lines whilst everyone else gets to fight for their pack? Hell no! There is no way I am going to let this pack, my home, go down just because I'm supposed to sit back and let others fight for me all because I'm a Beta,"* I growled.

"It's not because you're the packs Beta-," he started to explain but I cut him off.

"So is it because I'm a female then? Is that it? Just because I'm a girl it does not *mean that-,"*

"NO!" he growled in my head before skidding to a stop, the rest of the warriors carrying on without us. *"It's*

not because of your gender or your status I just... you were supposed to follow Anna so that you had some line of defence. I-I've lost my sister and my parents to these rogue attacks and there is no way I am going to lose you too."

His voice got softer in my head as his speech went on, almost as if he was breaking at the mere thought of losing me. I whined and slowly closed the distance between us until my nose was touching the side of his snout, hoping the contact would bring him some form of comfort. *"You're not going to lose me Xav, not anytime soon,"* I reassured him as I took a step back so that I could look into his bright golden eyes. *"Just let me know the plan next time, yeah?"* I laughed. *"Besides I'm too good to let anyone near enough to touch me,"* I grinned before turning around and started trotting in the direction we were originally heading.

I heard Xav chuckle slightly in my mind before running after me. I wasn't quite sure where I was going as I didn't know the plan, but Xav didn't correct me, so I was guessing we were heading in the right direction.

And headed in the right direction we did, because it wasn't long before my ears started to pick up the sound of growls and whines and my nose started to pick up the tell-tale smell of blood. I looked at Xavier with wide, alarmed eyes before sprinting the rest of the way and into a clearing where I saw a sight I had never seen before.

We had made it into a semi clearing in the woods where nearly seventy-five wolves were battling it out. You could tell who the pack wolves were and who the rogues were based on the condition of their coats and the scent they gave off. Thankfully we outnumbered the rogues, but it didn't make me any less nervous about the scene. If even one of our guys died it counted as a loss in my eyes.

I charged into the frenzy of the battle, picking off the odd rogue here and there that was unaware of my presence, as I assessed the individual battles that were going on around me. We were doing well all things considered, their bodies were piling up and from what I could see, not even one of ours had dropped, and I was going to try my damned hardest to make sure it stayed that way.

I spotted a lone pack wolf on the outskirts of the clearing being surrounded by three rogue wolves and quickly leapt over to offer my help.

Thankfully the first rogue went down easily. It was too distracted by the wolf in front of him to notice me behind him as I jumped onto his back and crushed his neck, quickly ending his life before he even knew he was in danger. The other two were a bit trickier to take down, but thankfully it was now one on one and with the help of the pack wolf next to me the battle didn't last long.

I nodded to the wolf next to me before we went our separate ways, both looking for our next target.

I carried on with that tactic, jumping into outnumbered battles, until the rogue numbers started to dwindle. At this point it was clear to the rogues that they were losing, and some started to make a run for it, trying to save themselves before they were met with the same ugly end as the others they'd attacked with. Unfortunately for them I was a fast runner and tracked down any loose rogue who'd decided to try and make a break for it. The last thing we needed was to leave survivors, it could tell other rogues or packs in the area that we were weak and ripe for the taking.

I sighed in exhaustion as I killed another rogue before looking up and taking in my surroundings. This rogue had been a fast one, and it had taken me way out of the way from the clearing where all the other wolves currently were. I thankfully wasn't out of the pack lands, but I was certainly far enough away for it to be deemed unsafe.

Xavier's words rang back through my head and I cringed as I started to make my way back to the clearing. If he knew how far out I'd gone he'd kill me.

I was about fifty yards from the break in the trees when I was tackled side on by a huge force that knocked the wind right out of my chest.

What the hell was that?

I looked up from my position on the floor, still unable to get up from the hit I'd just received, and stared into a pair of golden eyes, eyes that were so cold and calculating I couldn't believe they were real. I had never described the colour gold as being cold before, but looking into these eyes it was the only description I could think of. They were cold and menacing and I cringed away at the mere sight of them.

My vision swirled from the impact as I slowly stood up, not liking the higher ground this rogue had on me. I must've hit my head if my blurred vision was anything to go by.

As soon as I made it to my feet the wolf knocked me back down with a blow from his sharp claws onto my rib cage. My skin split with the impact, and I cried out in pain as I collapsed back onto the floor.

I quickly stood back up again, refusing to go down without a fight. I took a defensive position, but it was all in vain as the rogue quickly sidestepped my sluggish attempt of an attack and knocked me back to the ground for the third time. I was exhausted from the fighting, not just with the rogues but also from Anna when we'd been training, and I couldn't help but kick myself for using up all my energy on a stupid training session. All because I was short sighted and egotistical and wanted to show Xavier that I didn't give up and that I was a worthy asset to their pack. Now look at me, I was woozy and broken from only three hits from a rogue.

After the third hit the rogue didn't give me time to get back up, seemingly bored with my feeble attempt of self-defence, and placed his bloody paw on the side of my head. The pressure he was using was unbearable, just enough for it to be excruciating without actually breaking my skull open.

I writhed around as much as I possibly could, trying to find anything that would help me escape, but saw nothing. I was too far out for others to see me and too far gone to do anything about it myself.

"Xavier," I whimpered through our mind link, hoping that my jumbled up concussed brain could still figure out how to get a message across to him.

"Blaine? Blaine where are you," Xavier messaged back frantically as I felt his worry trickle through the link and into my own head.

"H-help," I managed to get out before my eyes rolled into the back of my head and I passed out.

I must've been out for only a second, seeing as the rogue was still using his unique form of torture on me, but it was enough for me to lose a grip on my wolf and before I could do anything about it my body started to shift. I screamed as I tried to fight it, which is something we are warned to never do from a young age for fear of damaging our bodies, but it was no use, within a matter of seconds I was back to my human form with my vulnerable skin exposed for the rogue to slice.

I lay there for a second, with the wolf still on top of me, mortified at the fact that I was naked in front of him. I know, not the thing I should be worrying about at a time like this, but what can I say. I screwed my eyes shut, ready for the rogue wolfs final blow, when all of a sudden, the weight disappeared.

I sighed in relief as my vision started to unblur and I looked up, expecting to see Xavier or another pack member fighting the rogue, but instead I came face to face with a human face, a stranger's face.

"Well well well... if it isn't little miss Blaine," the stranger taunted as he leaned over me.

The stranger's voice rattled around in my head, and I cringed at the volume, did he really have to be so loud?

"You're the last person I expected to see here, and in a pack of all things," he laughed. "I thought Isaac was joking when he said he'd found you here a few weeks ago with a pack wolf protecting you, but now I see he was telling the truth," the rogue mussed as he continued to stare down at me.

I tried to say something, anything to this person, but as soon as I opened my mouth the stranger wrapped one of his hands around my neck and pinned me to the ground, obviously not wanting to be interrupted.

"Do you know how long we've been looking for you?" He continued to question me as he brought my face close to his, close enough that I could smell the vile stench of his breath. It smelt of rot and decay, probably from a recent kill he'd just eaten, and the mixture of it made me gag.

148

I clawed at the hand that was gripping my neck tightly, enough to restrict my airflow but not enough to kill me.

"XAVIER!"

"Your mum and dad are going to be so happy that we've found you," he muttered with an evil grin as he looked into my panicked eyes.

My what?!

That was that moment I felt myself slip into unconsciousness, but not before I heard the stranger mutter one final thing...

"I'll tell the family you said hi."

Chapter Twenty
Xavier's POV

My blood ran cold as I heard Jax utter those two words we'd all been anticipating for weeks now.

They're coming.

Not only did I have a pack to look out for and protect, I also had a mate to worry about. I knew Blaine could look after herself, that she knew how to hold her own in a fight, but it didn't ease my nerves any less, especially when I saw her running alongside us towards the battle ground. Blaine was stubborn, and fiercely protective of the ones she cared about, so I knew trying to talk her out of running into battle was not an option. She was not one to cower in the corner and let others do all the dirty work for her.

That was why I didn't fight her on going back and staying with Anna. I had to remind myself that this was Blaine, and even if her stubbornness and lack of listening ability stressed me out to the max, I still wouldn't change anything about her. Blaine was my little firecracker, the crazy to my calm, and I'd be stupid to try and change that about her.

The battle was basically over before it'd even began, the rogues not having the ability and skill to last long against our freshly trained warriors. With Blaine's instruction and the amount of extra training sessions and warriors we had taken on board, it was an easy fight. Still, no matter how easy a fight seemed, you could never relax until way after the last rogue was dealt with and everyone had been accounted for. We learnt that the hard way when a neighbouring pack of ours had been hit with wave after wave of rogues. Unfortunately, the pack hadn't seen it coming and had suffered severely because of it.

I looked around the clearing as I killed one of the last rogues who'd been idiotic enough to enter our land. Just a few more rouges remained, but thanks to our increased stamina, they were being quickly picked off by warriors, making sure that not one escaped as the chaos eased.

I spotted Blaine run after an injured rogue and smiled as I watched her rust-coloured fur glint in the light, I sure was one lucky guy.

"Xavier get your head out of your ass, we still have stuff to do," Jax smirked as he made his way over to me.

Jax had already shifted back into his human form and slipped on a pair of old, worn out track suit bottoms that we had dotted around the territory.

"Whatever man," I laughed through the mind link before trotting off behind a tree so that I could shift myself. To be able to do the clean-up that was required I kind of needed my opposable thumbs back.

"How's Anna and JJ?" I asked Jax as I came up behind him with a bunch of logs and twigs that I'd collected from the woods in the surrounding areas.

"They're good, the rogues didn't even make it through our first line of defence so no stress there," he shrugged as we both deposited my collected wood into the centre of the semi clearing. Even if these wolves weren't part of our pack, it was important for us that they got a proper cremation, only then will their spirits ascend to the Moon Goddess. She can deal with them how she sees fit.

I nodded my head as I watched more warriors dump logs and bits of brush onto the ever-growing pile. We had gotten confirmation from our scouts that no more rogues had entered or exited our territory and with a sigh of relief from many around us, the mental alert we had all been sharing had gone from critical to just cautious.

"Where's Blaine by the way? I thought she'd be the first one here to question me about the safety of others and whether we were all okay," Jax laughed as he looked around the clearing.

I frowned before looking back up to where I had spotted Blaine disappearing off to. Jax was right, she knew the dangers of being out in the open, especially in the middle of an attack. After she dealt with that runaway she should have come straight back, believing in safety in numbers. The rogue she was chasing didn't look like he would have given her much trouble, so what was taking her so long?

Just as I was about to take a step in the direction where I saw her disappear to, I heard Blaine's voice whisper through our mate link and into my head. *"Xavier"*.

It wasn't much but it was enough to set me on edge as I froze on the spot. I heard Jax and a few others trying to gain my attention, asking if I was okay, but I couldn't answer. My sole focus was on the mate link as I tried to grasp it tighter. The link was weak, making me nervous beyond belief as I put everything into strengthening it.

"Blaine? Blaine, where are you?" I yelled, hoping my message was getting through all the static that was clouding the link.

I stood there for several seconds, frozen to my spot as I put all my energy into keeping this link alive. I was the only reason the link was still open, Blaine being too weak to hold it herself. *"Help,"* was the last thing I got from her before she slipped into unconsciousness, and it was like the snap of the link closing was a gun going off before you began a race.

I was off like a shot as I sprinted towards where I last saw Blaine, following the weak trail her scent had left. I could feel the presence of several pack members following closely behind me, but I paid them no attention, my vision focusing in like a laser at what was in front of me.

It was difficult to pick up her scent, the strong stench of blood in the air along with hundreds of wolves' scents muddling up with her own, and I thanked anyone that was listening that she had been in her wolf form when she took off. If she was in her human form, I doubt I would be able to pick it up.

I cringed as her voice filled my brain as she regained consciousness. She had only managed to scream my name before the link snapped back shut again, but it was enough to set my muscles on fire and my stomach to feel cold with dread. I had lost my sister and my parents to a rogue attack, there was no way I was going to lose Blaine to one too.

As I drew towards them, I shifted into my wolf, not caring for the scraps of fabric as they fluttered to the floor behind me. I just had to get to Blaine, as long as I got to her, everything else would work itself out, everything else would be okay.

I squinted into the distance and growled when I spotted a male figure leaning over Blaine as he held her throat in his hand. They were both naked, fresh from a shift, as I noticed claw marks running along Blaine's ribs and a considerable amount of blood leaking from a head injury on her left temple. No wonder she was struggling to stay conscious with a wound like that.

"Blaine!" I screamed through our link just before I tackled the stranger to the ground, effectively removing the stranger's hand from around my mate's throat.

He was larger than your typical rogue, showing a lot more muscle tone than I was used to seeing on a wolf without a pack, but I didn't let it faze me. Blaine's last lesson rang through my head, about how you never give them a second to watch you, and before I knew what I was doing, I attacked.

The two wolves who had followed me into the woods, Henry and a she wolf called Mel, attacked with me and it wasn't long before we had the rogue cornered in front of a tree. However, he didn't react how you'd assume a cornered rogue would. Instead of cowering in the corner and begging for mercy, this rogue stood tall and proud, as if we were the ones that were cornered, and he was the one that held all the cards. He didn't even bother to shift back into his wolf, and just that fact alone put us all on edge.

"Ah the Beta I presume?" The man questioned as he raised his eyebrows at me. "It is a pleasure to make the acquaintance of the *messenger's* right hand man," he smirked as he took the three of us in.

154

I growled at him as I felt my hackles rise, this man set me on edge, the confidence he portrayed unsettling me more than I cared to admit.

"Are you really going to put your lives at risk to try and save that girl over there, that... rogue?" He questioned as his smirk grew.

I growled at him, furious that he would even consider attacking my Blaine.

The stranger's smirk turned into shock as he stared at me, looking like he was trying to figure something out. His smirk suddenly returned full force as he looked over at the still unconscious Blaine before returning his gaze to me.

"You're her mate aren't you?" He asked, directing his comment at me. Whatever he found must've answered his question because it wasn't a second later that he let out a laugh like cough, almost as if he had just heard the punch line to the funniest joke he'd ever heard.

"Oh that is *rich*, the Rogue Killer is mated with a rogue?"

I growled at him again as I took a step in his direction, not liking that his attention wasn't completely on us. How dare he look at my mate.

"This is going to be *so* much fun," he muttered right as Blaine started to move, not too far behind us. It wasn't much, just a small twitch as she tried to push herself into a sitting position, but it was enough to distract the three of us long enough for the stranger to attack.

He shifted faster than I had ever seen anyone shift and went straight for Henry as he swiped him with his large paw. Henry went flying into a nearby tree, and I cringed as I heard the cracking of his ribs shatter at the contact.

The two of us quickly moved into action, attacking him on both sides to keep him busy whilst I changed the warning back up to critical through the pack link. It wouldn't take long for back up to arrive, I just had to keep him busy long enough for the cavalry to rally.

...

We'd tried our hardest, but with only two of us taking down that one rouge it wasn't easy. I had been completely distracted, listening out for any noises that could mean Blaine was in trouble instead of focusing on the fight in front of me. I was obsessing over the sound of her heartbeat, her soft shallow breaths, and the small groans in pain she let out every time she moved.

In the end the rouge had escaped, and I was still kicking myself over it. You should never let a rogue escape, it sends a bad message to both the rogues and the packs around you. But I had been too distracted, too caught up in my own head to pay attention to what was going around me. I had already apologised to Mel, knowing that she was kicking herself just as much as I was for what happened.

It was bad enough that he managed to give us the slip whilst being outnumbered, but he also knew about Anna. If that rogue decided to brag to anyone about who Anna was and where she could be found, we were in serious trouble.

I was now sitting in the hospital, in the private room Blaine had been assigned to. Thankfully she was strong, and her head and rib injuries had already started to heal. The doctor had induced her into a coma though, claiming it would help her brain heal faster after the trauma it had endured. It left me restless, not being able to talk to her and ask if she was okay, but if this was what she needed to heal then I was just going to have to accept it.

Henry was in critical condition, sustaining injuries like the ones he had was nerve wracking, even for a wolf. Not only had his ribs and thigh bone been shattered to pieces, but he also sustained internal injuries causing him to need multiple surgeries to try and reverse the damage of the internal bleeding.

I cringed as I heard Sarah crying in the hall down from where I sat, her friends offering her moral support as they waited for Henry to come out of his second surgery. If I had just anticipated the rogue's moves, done my job instead of focusing on my mate, then maybe Henry would be here right now and not in a room unconscious whilst the doctors tried to fix him.

I just hope he'll make it.

Chapter Twenty-One
Blaine's POV

The first thing I noticed was the noise, that irritating beeping sound beside my right ear, which confirmed to me where I was... in the hospital.

What happened?

The last thing I remembered was... the rogue attack? Maybe? I felt like something big had happened, something that I really should remember, but for the life of me I just couldn't put my finger on it.

"Blaine?" I heard a voice whisper not too far away from me. I frowned as I tried to open my eyes and see who it was, but groaned as the light entered the small slits in between my eyelids, burning my retinas. I cringed and went to lift my arm up and cover my eyes, hoping to shield them from the bright sunlight that was undoubtedly streaming in through the open blinds, but I only got my arm up a short distance before it was pulled back with a sharp tug.

I peeked through my eyelids and spotted my arm, restricted from movement by a tube feeding IV fluids into my body. It was attached to my left hand, with a bandage wrapped around it to help prevent the needle from being ripped out and I groaned at the sight. Great, looks like I'll be on more bed rest.

"Blaine, are you awake?" The voice asked again, and I looked to my right where I saw Anna sitting on my bed and holding my hand, the one without the needles, tubes and bandages attached.

I frowned at her for a second, my brain still trying to catch up with itself and figure out what she was saying, before giving her a short nod to confirm that I was.

"Oh thank you Goddess," she muttered under her breath as she looked up to the ceiling slightly. "We have all been so worried about you Blaine, no one knew when you were going to wake up, *if* you were going to wake up, after the amount of head trauma you sustained," she sighed as she reached up and wiped a single tear from her cheek.

"What happened?" I asked her, eager to fill in the blanks in my memory. Something just wasn't sitting right with me, and I just had to find out what it was.

"Umm... I'm not quite sure, Xavier hasn't spoken much since he found you and we can't seem to get anything out of him. He's pretty shook up," Anna explained as she looked down at my hand in hers, looking sad now for a whole different reason.

I looked around the room, expecting to see him passed out on the room's lumpy sofa or something, but when I came up empty, I frowned. He was never away from me last time I was in the hospital, and that was when I was conscious and doing fine, why wasn't he here now?

As if sensing my confusion at his absence, Anna sighed and squeezed my hand in reassurance. "More often than not he's here, sleeps on the sofa at night just like last time, he just needs to get away every now and then, when it gets too much for him. He's taking everything pretty hard and goes for a run or patrols the border when he can, it helps him to feel like he's helping," she shrugs.

I nodded and tried to speak but cringed as my voice came out all scratchy, god my throat felt like I smoked twenty packs a day.

"I'll go and get you some ice chips to soothe your throat," Anna smiled as she noticed me cringe at the weird noise I'd just made.

I smiled up to her in gratitude as she released my hand, silently thanking her for the thought.

"I'll be back in a second," she informed me, before leaving my room and walking down the corridor, leaving my door slightly ajar so that I could see out into the hallway.

I sat in silence whilst I waited for her to come back, not having a radio or TV to drown out the deafening silence, only broken by the continuous beeping from my heart monitor. I could hear quiet murmurs from other passers-by as they walked past my room, but barely paid attention to them, that was until I caught the faint voice of Anna talking to another lady just a few doors down from mine.

"It's going to be okay Sarah, Henry is a strong warrior and an even stronger wolf, if anyone can recover from this it will be him," Anna said as she reassured a fellow pack member.

The person she was talking to, Sarah, sniffed but otherwise didn't comment.

"We cannot lose hope. I haven't, so you shouldn't either," she continued softly.

"The Moon Goddess... has she...?" Sarah muttered weakly, her voice wavering as she struggled to finish her sentence. Anna must've understood her question though because she answered in a soft voice.

"She hasn't said anything to me, but please don't take that as a bad sign, in my opinion no news is good news," she reassured her. I couldn't see what was going on out there, but I could guess, knowing Anna she was probably comforting Sarah with a small hug. "Henry helped me out so much in my early stages here in this pack. First finding me and bringing Jax to me, and then escorting me when I went to confront the Leftens and get the photo of my parents back. I am praying for him every second that I have, I just hope that you don't lose hope whilst we wait for his body to recover."

I frowned at her odd words but otherwise didn't question it, maybe this was how Lunas were supposed to react around injured and grieving pack members? Saying that they could hear the Moon Goddess as if she was whispering in her ear. Whether it was to ease Sarah's concerns or console her in some way, it must've worked, because she just sniffed with a mumbled "thank you" before walking back into her room.

A second later my door was pushed open, and Anna made her way in with a plastic cup of ice chips in her hand.

"I've linked Xavier, he was on patrol, but he's found cover and heading over here now," Anna explained with a smile as she handed me the ice chips. Even though she was smiling, I could see her eyes glisten slightly with tears and I frowned at her, not liking seeing the girl that was always so happy and full of life, sad.

I scooped a few ice chips out of the cup and sucked on them before assessing my voice again, no way was I putting myself through that pain again if I could help it.

Once the chips had melted, I put the cup down on my bedside table and leant over to take her hand, gaining her attention. "What's the matter?" I asked, cringing at the sound of my voice but relieved that it wasn't as painful as before.

"Oh... umm it's just Henry," Anna mumbled as she wiped her hand under her eyes, making sure to catch any tears that may have fallen. "He helped me out so much when I first came to this pack and it just kills me to think of him fighting for his life in a bed a few rooms over from here and there isn't a single thing I can do to help," she sighed as she looked into the distance, as if she could see through the walls and was checking up on him.

"You weren't born here?" I questioned, I knew the answer to this, Xavier had already told me she was from a few towns over, I was just hoping to take her mind off Henry and onto something else.

Anna refocused on me again and sighed as she ran her hand over her forehead, looking more tired than I had ever seen her. "No, I was born into a pack about twenty or so miles from here," she explained as she settled into her seat. "I don't go around publicly announcing where I came from because it wasn't a great situation" she continued. "My parents were kidnapped when I was seven years old, and I was placed into what I thought was the foster system. Turns out the family I was placed with worked for the very Alpha who had kidnapped my parents in the first place, and it's safe to say I wasn't treated very well. Anyway, long story short I managed to escape and ended up running through the woods until I stumbled upon Jax's pack. Henry was one of the warriors on patrol that night and informed Jax about what was happening."

She didn't continue and I didn't push it. She had obviously gone through a lot of pain throughout her life, and I wasn't going to make her day worse by asking her loads of questions and having to relive old memories. I knew how painful that could be for someone and I wasn't about to put someone else through it, when Anna was ready to tell me her full story I would be here to listen.

"I'm sorry," I muttered, unable to get much volume in my voice but wanting to show her that I really was.

She shrugged as she fiddled with her hair, going through a sequence of plaiting, and unplaiting the same section of hair over and over again.

We stayed in silence after that, neither of us breaking the silence as we listened to the rhythmic beating of the heart monitor. It wasn't until we heard frantic footsteps running down the corridor a few minutes later that Anna lightly smiled.

"That would be Xavier," she announced and just like she said, seconds later, Xavier slammed the door open and strode over to me.

I smiled at his dishevelled look, not being able to hold back the smile as I took in his messy hair pointing in all directions and his t-shirt that was haphazardly thrown on, the label on full display on his side indicating it was on inside out.

"Blaine you're awake," he huffed, clearly out of breath from the running.

"It would appear so," I croaked as I looked down at myself in fake shock.

"I'm going to leave you guys to it," Anna announced from across the room and I smiled over at her in thanks before focusing back on Xavier.

He hadn't even acknowledged she was in the room as his eyes swept over my body, making sure that I was doing okay and that my injuries were healing as they should. Even if he couldn't see half of them due to the hospital pyjamas I was wearing and the blanket that had been draped over my legs. It didn't stop him from trying though.

"I'm so glad you're awake," he sighed as he walked over and sat in the seat Anna had just vacated. He looked tired, and I wondered how long I had been out for. He took my hand in his and kissed my bruised knuckles before bringing my hand up to cradle his face. Things must've been really bad if he was reacting like this.

"What happened?" I groaned, leaning over with my free hand to fetch the cup off my bed side table so that I could have a few more ice chips. It was tricky due to the leads and bandages, but I managed.

"You don't remember?" He questioned as he looked into my eyes with a frown.

I shrugged, but instantly regretted it as my side pulled, I obviously had stitches there then.

"Well I was kind of hoping you'd tell me, fill in the blanks a little. The guy seemed to know you somehow and we were hoping you'd know where to find him so that we could bring him to justice for what he did to you and Henry," he said as he looked into my eyes with a mix of sorrow and regret.

Anna had said that he'd been struggling with what had happened, and it was only now that I could fully see the extent of it. He had huge bags under his eyes,

The Beta and his Mate

indicating he hadn't slept in days, and there was a slight haunted look in his eyes that hadn't been there last time I'd looked into them. It was as if a little bit of his light had been stolen from him and he was lost in the dark, retracing his steps to try and find it again.

I sighed as I smiled over at him slightly, if justice was what he needed to be able to rest then I was more than happy to help, after all he had saved my life more than once now, the least I could do for him was help identify someone.

"Send over an image of what he looked like through the mate link, maybe I'll recognise him," I said as I squeezed his hand in mine.

He smiled gratefully before sending over a watery image of a larger man with rust brown coloured hair and a full beard covering the lower half of his face. At first, I couldn't quite pinpoint where I had seen him before, feeling that horrible feeling of recognition but not being able to put a name to the face. It wasn't until I got a good look at his icy blue, almost white eyes, that I remembered something.

I definitely hadn't seen him before, but he one hundred percent knew who I was, and more horrifyingly, he knew where my family were.

"I'll tell the family you say hi".

Chapter Twenty-Two
Blaine's POV

My heart rate increased as my palms started to sweat, panic filling my body with adrenaline causing my body to shake uncontrollably. The heart monitor next to me was screaming, telling the nurses outside that something was wrong, but I paid it no attention. That man knew my family, knew where they were, and I knew for a *fact* that he wasn't good news.

"Blaine? Blaine sweetheart can you hear me?" A female voice asked from somewhere to my left. I couldn't answer her though, I couldn't seem to focus my eyes or think of a coherent sentence, my vision blurring as I began to hyperventilate and become lightheaded.

I felt someone squeeze my hand and I instantly started to relax at the feeling of tingles that began running up and down my arm. Xavier was here, he was next to me and trying to comfort me. I didn't want to worry him anymore than I already had, not after everything he had been through, so I focused on his hand, just his hand, as it gripped onto mine as if his life depended on it.

My heart slowly started to calm down as I continued to breathe in shaky breaths, trying to get as much oxygen into my lungs as I possibly could.

"Blaine are you alright?" Xavier asked as he came and sat beside me on my bed, getting as close as he possibly could without accidently knocking me or dislodging the wires around me.

I nodded my head, but otherwise didn't say anything, not trusting my voice after the mild panic attack I'd just had.

"Blaine sweetheart," the female voice spoke up again and I looked over to see a middle aged woman leaning over the equipment on the left hand side of the bed. "Are you in any pain at all? Do you need me to increase your pain medication?" She asked as she continued to fiddle with the buttons on the machine whilst looking over at me with kind, motherlike eyes.

I cleared my throat before shaking my head, the last thing I wanted was more medication. I needed to have a clear head if I was going to be able to think over this recent development with my family.

She smiled kindly at me before nodding her head. "Okay dear, but if at any point you need me, just press the call button by your right arm and I'll be right in," she informed me before she gave a small smile to Xavier as she closed the room door behind her.

We sat in silence for a while as I calmed myself down and caught my breath. I could tell Xavier felt guilty about what just happened, but he couldn't be more wrong. Xavier had managed to help me get the first real clue I'd had on my family's whereabouts in over a year. Yes, it sucked to have a panic attack, but I was still beyond thankful regardless of my reaction.

"Xavier," I tried my voice as I looked over at him, his sad eyes looking into mine with regret.

"I'm so sorry Blaine, you're in no fit state to be doing anything right now and I was so focused on getting my revenge for you that I didn't even take into consideration your reaction."

I shook my head as I smiled at him, hoping it would calm his nerves in some way. "Xavier, I have no idea who that man was, but I do remember what he said to me right before I passed out. He knows my family, and most likely where they are. This is my first *real* lead in *so* long and I couldn't have remembered it without you giving me a little push in the right direction, so thank you," I explained as I squeezed his hand tightly.

"Your family?" Xavier questioned, suddenly straightening up at my comment.

"He said he'd say hi to them for me," I whispered as I looked down at our joined hands, feeling a wave of nausea hit me at the thought of them being anywhere near that man.

"Are you sure he wasn't just messing with you?" He asked, his eyebrows slightly raised and pinched together.

I thought about it for a second, before shaking my head and dismissing the idea. "No he knows… I can feel it in my gut that he knows where they are and my gut is *never* wrong," I muttered as I fiddled with Xavier's fingers.

Xav nodded as he looked deep in thought before standing up slowly and started to pace the small room. "Well, the trackers are still out looking for him, following the scent trail he'd left behind. With any luck they'll manage to find something that will hopefully lead us to him and your family," he explained as he continued to pace, still deep in thought. "If that doesn't work, we still

168

have a few more options to try. I've already sent out an alert to all the neighbouring packs in the area about this guy so hopefully word will spread about him and we can find him that way."

I sat in silence as I continued to watch him walk a hole through the floor. I needed to let him think, and to do that he needed silence.

"I mean... there is one more thing we could try, but I don't know if..." he muttered as he trailed off and looked at me, as if he was thinking hard about something. "Screw it, it's worth a shot," Xavier suddenly exclaimed as his eyes clouded over slightly, letting me know that he was using the mind link.

He was still for a good few minutes, communicating with whoever was on the other end of the pack link about the latest information gathered and what could be done to help. Xavier clearly had an idea, I just hoped it was enough to find my parents and siblings.

Finally, his eyes refocused and looked over at me, almost as if he was calculating his next move. I looked back at him in confusion, why did he look so worried and unsure all of a sudden? I was just about to ask when Anna knocked on the door before letting herself in, distracting us from the silent staring we'd been doing.

"Hey Anna," I greeted as I looked between her and Xavier, clearly she had something to do with this as they exchanged a worried, knowing look before both settling their eyes on me. "Is everything okay?" I asked, feeling uncomfortable with the way they were both looking at me.

"I heard about your family Blaine, I'm so sorry," Anna answered as she came and sat down next to me. "We are going to do *everything* in our power to try and get them back," she stated as she took my hand in hers, a fire burning in her eyes like I'd never seen before.

I smiled over at her before nodding my head in understanding. "Thank you Anna, that really does mean a lot to me considering I'm not even technically pack yet."

"You are just as much pack as everyone else, you've fought for us, guided us and protected us to the best of your ability, if that doesn't make you family then I don't know what does" she stated as she squeezed my hand tight.

I smiled at her statement, feeling more at home than I had in a long time.

"If only Xavier over there would get his ass into gear and mark you already, then we wouldn't even be needed to have this conversation," Anna whispered with a smirk. It was one of those fake whispers where you actually want the room to hear you, but you pretend you didn't.

"Hey!" Xavier exclaimed as he frowned at Anna, "we've kind of been busy over the past couple of weeks if you haven't noticed. Add to that Blaine always getting injured and ending up in hospital every five minutes then there's really been no time to even discuss it let alone complete the bond."

I smiled over at Xavier as he continued to look over at Anna, looking very unimpressed with her comment. "Besides if my memory's correct, I seem to remember you and Jax taking *forever* to mark each other," he smirks, looking chuffed with his comeback.

I smirked at the two but otherwise didn't comment, Anna had mentioned that she'd had a troubled past before coming here, so I imagined their wait probably had something to do with that.

170

"Now Blaine," Anna said as she suddenly turned serious and looked over at me. "Above everything else that a normal pack can do when they're trying to find someone, our pack has a little extra something to help us along the way," she explained. "Do you remember me explaining about my past and what happened to me before I arrived here?" She asked.

I nodded my head, suddenly feeling anxious. I had so many different emotions running through my head; fear for my family, confusion from all of Anna's and Xavier's secrecy, hope that I could finally hold my family in my arms again and then fear all over again *because* of the hope I was feeling. It was making me dizzy.

"Well, the reason why my parents were kidnapped was because of who my family are, or more accurately what we can do," she continued to explain.

I frowned at her, not understanding what she was trying to explain. Was she a special type of shifter or something?

"My family, or more accurately the women in my family, are closely linked to the Moon Goddess, unlike any other ordinary wolf," she clarifies as she starts to fiddle with the hem of her shirt. "I, like my mother was before it was passed down to me, am a messenger of the Goddess. I have a special bond with her, meaning I have abilities that would normally be impossible for the common wolf. Abilities like receiving messages from her, being her vessel for whenever she graces our earth and... spirit walking... amongst other things."

I frowned, unable to comprehend all the information she'd just unloaded on me. She couldn't mean what I think she meant, could she? But as I looked into her usual blue eyes and spotted the slightest hints of a translucent colour swirl through them, I sucked in a strangled breath in shock. "I can't believe you're... I didn't even know they even... how could you be..." I stuttered as I struggled to piece together my thoughts and come up with a single question.

"I know that this has probably come as a bit of a shock to you, and I am *so* sorry for keeping it from you for so long, but Jax and I decided when I first found out about my heritage that no one outside of our pack was allowed to know about me. Not only for the safety of myself and our future children, but also for the safety of our whole pack. The idea that my pack, my family, would be attacked every other week for the chance to get to me made me sick to my stomach," she explained, looking ever so slightly green at even the idea of someone getting hurt because of her. "It had happened once before with this delusional wolf named Matthew, and I had promised myself that I would *never* put anyone in that position ever again."

I continued to stare at her, my mouth no doubt hanging open, at the information she'd just laid on me. I still couldn't believe it; Anna was a Messenger? To the Moon Goddess?

"Blaine, because of Anna's ability to spirit walk, I'm hoping that maybe the Goddess will help guide us in some way to wherever your family is being held. Now we can't guarantee that it'll work or anything, but I thought... you know... it was worth a shot," Xavier explained as he walked over to my free side and took my bandaged hand in his. "I know what it's like to live without your family next to you... we both do," he muttered as he looked over at Anna, sadness shining in his eyes. "And I can promise you that we will both try *everything* in our power to get them back."

His voice held so much confidence, so much emotion, that I couldn't help but believe him. I knew Xavier and Anna, and I knew that both of them would try everything they could to help me get my family back. A few stray tears slipped down my cheeks, but I quickly brushed them away. I had never liked crying in public.

"I-I," I stuttered but failed to get any words out. I had waited over two years to see my family back together again, and in the short space of just a few hours I was closer to finding them than I had ever been before, all because of my mate and his amazing friends.

My amazing friends.

Chapter Twenty-Three
Xavier's POV

It's been four days since we'd told Blaine that Anna could possibly find her parents. We had all agreed that we weren't going to do anything until Blaine was all healed up and out of the hospital. Although reluctant at first, Blaine agreed to wait, knowing that there was no point in finding out where they were if she was still bed bound and unable to help or do anything about it. If anything, it would probably be counterproductive for her, she'd just be sitting in bed and worrying the whole time, feeling useless for not being able to do anything.

The day had finally come though, Blaine had been released from hospital this morning and, with strict instructions from the doctor on how and when to take her medication, we were off home.

We were now sitting in my living room, all staring at each other as we planned our next move. The one downside about Anna's ability to spirit walk was that she was as real there as she was here. In other words, if someone hurt her whilst she was in a spirit walk, they not only hurt her soul there but also her body here. It was dangerous, especially when we didn't know what she was getting into, but we had to have faith in the Moon Goddess, to keep her safe and protected. We had to believe that if things got too dangerous for Anna, the Goddess would pull her spirit out and put her back into her body.

"So how will it all work?" Blaine asked as she continued to snuggle up into my side. I smiled down at her as her fly aways tickled my nose, but I didn't move them, afraid that she would move if she thought they were annoying me. It was as if the more contact I had with her the more the ever-present void in my chest began to close, healed by her very presence.

I hadn't asked her about our bond yet, about whether she knew what type of bond we shared, but I knew I'd have to ask her soon. It would become obvious when we marked each other, and I thought it would be best coming from me rather than someone else.

"To you it will just look like I've fallen into a kind of deep sleep, my body will remain here, but my spirit will be taken elsewhere by the Goddess. It used to happen randomly, the Goddess would just take me wherever she thought I needed to go, but over time I've managed to control it a little. I can now call upon the gift whenever it's required, and I can control where I go... to a certain degree," Anna explained as she smiled over at Blaine.

If anyone knew how Blaine would be feeling in this second, it would be Anna. She too had to live through her parents being kidnapped and taken away from her.

"Okay... so what do we do whilst you're in your sleep?" Blaine asked as she played with my fingers as they rested in her lap.

"Honestly there isn't really much you can do, it's more of a waiting game for you lot until I get back," she shrugged as she kissed Jax on the side of his jaw.

175

Jax was never okay with her doing something dangerous, let alone something where he couldn't protect her, but he knew his mate, once she had her mind set on something she was damn well going to do it.

"Right shall we get this party started then?" Anna asked as she got up and shooed Jax off the sofa so that she could stretch out and get comfy.

"I'm going to be by your side the whole time okay little mate? And I want you to promise me that if things get too dangerous or you start to feel unsafe in any way you'll come straight back here." Jax asked as he knelt on the floor beside her head, stroking her hair affectionately as he continued to stare at her.

She smiled softly up at him as she nodded her head before taking a deep breath in and out to calm herself as she closed her eyes. She was out in seconds.

As she slipped into unconsciousness the moonstone in Anna's necklace started to glow a bright white/blue colour and Blaine gripped my hand in shock before looking up at me.

"Her necklace is a family heirloom, passed down through generations," I explained. "It helps her to link with the Goddess and control her powers and abilities. It was one of the reasons why her spirit walking was so sporadic when she first started, she didn't have the necklace to help ground her and guide her through the stresses the abilities put on her body," I explained. It was amazing, watching her grow her strength and practise her abilities through the years I'd known her, and with the help from her mum, she'd come on leaps and bounds in just a few short years.

She looked back at Anna in amazement, and I couldn't help but smile down at her before looking back over at Anna.

Looking at Jax as he stared down at his mate, like she was the only thing in the world that mattered, I realised just how far I had come in the last month. Before I'd met Blaine, watching them looking at each other like that, would have been like a dagger to my heart, slowly twisting as I felt the pain of being mate less grow until I could no longer take it. But now, as I looked down at my perfect mate as she rested in my arms, I realised just how lucky I was.

After my family died, I had vowed to never slack off on my Beta duties again. To never go off and have a good time and get drunk at a random party. Never wake up next to some unknown girl who I had used to try and numb the pain of having an incomplete blood bond, and never question the importance of the Beta role ever again. After all, that was what got my family killed in the first place, me and my stupid arrogant self.

"Is this all we do now? Sit around and wait for her to wake up?" Blaine whispered over to me, almost as if she was worried she'd wake Anna up if she spoke too loud.

I shrugged as I looked back at the couple on the opposite sofa before looking back down at Blaine, "pretty much yeah."

"Oh... well in that case I'm going to take a page out of Anna's book and go for a little nap. My sleep pattern is all over the place anyway so why bother trying to stay up when I'm dead on my feet," Blaine shrugged as she snuggled in and got comfy.

I smiled down at her as I watched her face relax and her breathing even out before looking back up at Jax who was still staring at his mate, looking for any sign that she was in trouble.

"You good if I have a quick nap too?" I asked him, feeling my eyes starting to drop. "I never sleep well on that hospital cot, and it's been ages since I've managed to get any decent rest."

"Sure man no worries, I'll wake you up if anything happens," Jax nodded as he lifted Anna's feet up and placed them back on his lap as he took a seat on the sofa.

I smiled over at him in gratitude before letting my eyes drop and before I knew it, I was out.

...

"Annabelle... Annabelle wake up... come on little mate...please... wake up!" I rose from my deep sleep to the sound of Jax's panicked voice and I sprang awake. Something had happened.

Slipping out from under Blaine I ran over to Jax's side as he knelt on the floor, softly shaking her shoulders to try and rouse her from her spirit sleep.

"What's happening?" I asked, frantically looking over her to see if I could see any injuries.

"I don't know," Jax muttered as he continued to try and wake her up. "One minute she was asleep and the next it was like she had been shocked by some electricity or something. Her whole body jerked before it went deadly still again," he explained as he sniffed the air. I did the same, looking for any changes in her body that might have caused her to have such a violent reaction.

We both froze at the same time, as we smelled the blood that was coming from her body.

"Anna!" I shouted the same time Jax shouted "Annabelle!" He frantically started looking over her body, looking for the source of where the blood was coming from, and when he found it, he froze, his whole hand covered in her blood.

"It's her head Xav, she's bleeding from her head," he whispered as he stared at his blood-stained hand.

"What's happening," I heard Blaine mumble from the opposite sofa, but I couldn't draw my eyes away long enough to answer her.

I moved so that I was on her other side and leant over the back of the sofa. "Blaine, I need you to come here and check Anna's head, she's bleeding and we can't check it without rolling her onto her side," I explained as I reached down to touch Anna' shoulder.

But as I made contact with her skin, Jax let out a low growl. I looked over to see that gold was swirling in his eyes and his teeth had extended slightly.

When your mate was injured, you went into overprotective mode, so it was completely natural for him to be territorial over Anna and want to protect her. But him standing guard over her wasn't going to help, and if we were going to check her injuries and see if she needed medical attention, we had to see how serious the cut was.

"Jax snap out of it," I growled as I let my own eyes swirl with gold. "You acting like an overprotective and jealous mate is not going to help her in any way, now help me lift Anna up slightly so that Blaine can have a look at her head."

It was a risk, yelling at your Alpha whilst his wolf was out, but it was one that seemed to pay off because in an instant Jax's eyes had gone back to their usual brown colour as he shook his wolf from his head. He nodded once, confirming to me he was all good, before reaching out and lifting her other side, both of us supporting her head and neck so that it didn't roll back.

Blaine quickly shifted her hair out of the way and with a small torch began to inspect the area where she was bleeding. "It doesn't appear to be a particularly big cut," she said as she continued to feel around Anna's skull. "My guess is that she was thrown against a wall and her head impacted with it," she explained as she continued to inspect it. "Honestly I don't think it's anything to worry about, I doubt she'd even get a concussion from it, but if you wanted to call the doctor out just to be on the safe side you can."

Jax nodded his head in understanding before lowering her back down, his eyes already unfocused with the telling signs of him using his mind link.

Just when we'd started to relax, I frowned when I saw a slight swelling appear on her cheek bone. "Umm Jax... I think you're going to want to see this," I muttered as I continued to stare at the beginnings of a bruise that was starting to form.

"God damn it Annabelle," Jax shouted as he punched the floor. "She promised me that she would exit the spirit walk if things got too dangerous," he growled as he got up from his spot on the floor and started pacing.

And then the worst part happened... four distinctive claw marks appearing on her stomach, the blood soaking through her t-shirt. Before any of us could say anything though Anna startled awake, taking in a huge gulp of air, as if she had been kept underwater for too long.

"Annabelle, are you okay?" Jax asked as he rushed to her side, his angry pacing long forgotten as he took her head in his lap.

She nodded, causing her to wince slightly as her head scraped against the fabric of the pillow she'd been lying on.

"Are you sure? I have the doctor on the way over now, to check you over and make sure nothings severely damaged," he explained as he stroked her hair back.

I looked over to see that Blaine had removed herself from our little group, as she wrapped her arms around her waist and looked over at Anna with regret. I smiled at her softly before walking over to her and taking her in my arms, comforting her the best that I could.

"It's not your fault Blaine," I whispered in her ear as I led her over to the other sofa, out of the way of Jax and Anna.

"How could it not be my fault," she mumbled, her voice muffled due to her face being buried in my neck. "*I* was the one who asked her to help me find my family, if I hadn't, she wouldn't be over there in pain right now."

I sighed as I rubbed her back comfortingly. "Trust me, no one makes Anna do *anything* she doesn't want to do. She wanted to help you, and she would have done this with or without your blessing," I tried to reassure her as I continued to rub soothing circled on her back.

"He's right Blaine, you didn't make me do anything," Anna muttered as she smiled over at us.

Blaine smiled back and nodded her head in thanks before settling back into my arms. I could tell she wanted to know what Anna had seen, but she also didn't want to press the issue, probably afraid that it would cause Anna too much strain after what she had been through.

I, on the other hand, knew she was fine and was just waiting for the go ahead from us to start talking. "So, what did you find?"

"Well... I didn't see your family, or maybe I did and I just didn't know it was them, but I *know* they were there. I just had this *feeling* that this was what we were looking for... you know?" She asked as she rested her hand over her eyes, blocking the light out with her fingers. She always got a headache after she forced a spirit walk.

"And what did you see?" Blaine tentatively asked, almost as if she didn't really want to know the answer, terrified of what her family was currently going through and where they were being kept.

Anna shifted out of Jax's lap and looked over at Blaine, sadness pinching the edges of her eyes. "Are you sure you want to know? What I saw wasn't... pleasant," Anna stuttered as she thought of a good enough descriptive word to use.

Blaine nodded her head, her shoulders set in determination.

Anna sighed as she ran her hand over her forehead before looking right into Blaine's eyes. "I found an illegal fighting ring and my guess is that your family is smack bang in the middle of it."

Chapter Twenty-Four
Xavier's POV

"I'm sorry, a what now?" Blaine exclaimed, disbelief lacing her tone.

Anna sighed as she ran her hand across her forehead, clearly struggling slightly. "I'll go get you something to help with your headache," Jax muttered close to Anna's ear before kissing her on the temple and rushing off to the kitchen, where he knew I kept some medical supplies under the kitchen sink.

Anna didn't restart up again until Jax had returned with a few pills and a glass of water to help her wash them down. What she had found out about Blaine's family, she obviously thought Jax needed to hear about it, otherwise she would have started without him.

I shifted uncomfortably in my seat. Just hearing the words *illegal fighting club* you just knew it wasn't going to be good.

"What did you see Anna?" Jax prompted as he took her hand in his, comforting her anyway he could. Anna was clearly shaken; you didn't have to be an observant person to work that one out.

"Well... it started off with this cave type thing at the bottom of a mountain range, I'm not quite sure where it was specifically," she muttered with a frown as she rubbed her forehead. "Then I saw a doorway, covered in weeds and vines of ivy, keeping it hidden from passers-by would be my guess, not that anyone could stumble upon it, seeing how out of the way it was.

"When I walked in the first thing I noticed was the smell, I always seem to notice the smell first, it was like a mixture between a seedy kind of bar and a cell block. The stench of beer, urine and blood was so thick in the air I almost threw up," she cringed suddenly, as if the memory of the smell alone was enough to make her gag again.

"I made my way through all these different deserted corridors; it was like nothing I had ever seen before. You could tell that they were all man-made tunnels and rooms, someone must've come across the cave a while back and decided to convert it into something bigger. There wasn't much lighting around so I couldn't make out a lot of features about the place, but I could tell I was walking through some form of holding cell. There were doors leading off the corridor every few steps, and after looking inside a few through what I'm assuming were their little feeding slots, I found wolf after wolf just lying there, motionless on the ground.

"Most of them had some form of injuries on them, only superficial ones, but enough to know that they were being harmed in some way. They also had collars on, of all different sizes and colours.

"The wolves paid me no attention, they just stared off into space with this ghostly haunted look in their eye, as if they were there in body but not mind, like their spirit had been broken somehow".

We all watched Anna as her eyes glazed over in pain and sadness. It was obvious what she'd just seen was something she wasn't going to forget any time soon.

"I eventually made it to the end of the corridor and found myself in a *huge* room, bigger than I thought a cave could possibly be, and that was when I figured out what was going on. In the middle of the room held a boxing ring of some sorts, it was bigger than your average ring and it had a chain link fence surrounding the edges and across the top, creating a cage. Blood stained the floors and claw marks had been scratched into the concrete floor, as if wolves had been dragged somewhere against their will or something.

"I was just about to leave the spirit walk, feeling beyond creeped out by what I'd seen, when I was hit on the head from behind and attacked. Thankfully the Goddess got me out of there before anything serious could happen," she sighed as she closed her eyes.

"Before anything serious? Anna you were knocked over the head, punched in the face and attacked by some wolf, I'd hardly say you got out before anything serious could happen to you," Jax exclaimed, obviously not overly impressed with the way Anna played down her injuries.

"Jax I'm fine, seriously it wasn't as big of a deal as you're making it out to be," Anna reassured him as she kissed him on the cheek.

"Then explain the claw marks," he growled as he shifted slightly, obviously feeling on edge at the mere mention of his mate's injuries.

"I was thrown into one of those cell rooms that held the captured wolves… with one already in there," she sighed, almost silently.

"You what!" Jax exclaimed at the same time I shouted "Anna!"

"I'm fine alright? I'm still whole and in one piece, see?" She quickly defended herself as she held her hands up.

Just then there was a knock on the door before doctor Tessler let herself in. "I heard my favourite patient is in need of some assistance," she smiled over at Anna as she made her way over to her, doctors' bag in hand.

"I'm only your favourite because I keep you so busy," she laughed, rolling her eyes.

"Now that's only half true," she smiled before stopping in front of Anna. "I hear you've had a little accident during your spirit walk?"

I snorted at her choice of words before standing up, taking Blaine with me. "That's right doc, she peed herself *again*," I laughed before swiftly making my way out of the living room and into the kitchen. Knowing Anna, she gave way worse than she got, and it always ended up being on the more physical side.

I walked into the kitchen with Blaine following close behind me, but if it wasn't for her hand currently clutched into mine, I would have thought she'd stayed behind with the others, she was so quiet. I turned around so that I was facing her, intent on asking her what was wrong, but when I got a look at her face I froze. She was crying.

With everything I had seen Blaine go through, from the physical injuries to the hateful words I had told her right at the start of our meeting, I had never seen her cry. She was like a stone, always keeping her feelings close to her chest and never letting them out in the open. She never talked about how she was doing, and she never openly showed me how she was feeling. Like a wall had been built around her emotions a long time ago and she refused to let it crumble.

Looking at her now had my heart almost breaking in two. She had big droplets of tears streaking down her freckled cheeks, her big green eyes glistening as they caught the kitchen light. Her nose was pink from her rubbing it a couple of times and her hair was all over the place from her running her hand through it constantly in distress.

I looked her over before taking her into my arms, already understanding what had gotten her so upset. Throughout the whole conversation of Anna explaining her findings to us, Blaine hadn't said anything, not one word, she just sat there in my arms as she digested everything that was being said.

"It's going to be okay Blaine, we're going to get them back," I reassured her as I continued to hold her tight in my arms, stroking my hand up and down her back occasionally in the hopes that it would soothe her in some way.

"How can you know that?" She mumbled into my neck, not bringing her face out from her little hiding spot.

"Because I know my pack and I know you," I muttered as I continued the soothing strokes. "We will stop at nothing to get your family back Blaine, that I can promise you."

She stayed silent, not having anything to say, as I held her securely in my arms.

After a while her tears died down and dried up, and the only evidence of them even existing was the wet patch that she had left on the collar of my shirt.

"What if they're in pain Xav," she finally spoke, her voice sounding thick from the recent tears that had just been shed.

My heart rate kicked up slightly at the use of her nickname, but I forced it to remain as neutral as possible. The last thing she needed to deal with right now was an excited mate.

I sighed before kissing the top of her forehead delicately. "If we find them in pain then we'll just have to do to the rogues what they did to your family. An eye for an eye."

I continued to hold her close as I breathed in her scent, using it to calm me down and not let my wolf take over. I always got particularly worked up over thinking about someone close to me in pain. After… What happened... I had promised myself that I would never let anything happen to my friends and family again, and seeing as Blaine was my mate, her family were now my family.

"You're my family now Blaine, and I will do everything in my power to protect you and make you happy for the rest of our lives," I vowed, kissing her firmly on her forehead once again.

Blaine retracted herself slightly from my arms so that she could look up at me. Even with her slightly puffy eyes and bright red nose, she was the most beautiful woman alive. I mean I may be a little biassed due to the mate bond and everything, but she damn sure was the most beautiful woman out there. Fact.

"Xavier I-," she stuttered as she looked up into my eyes. "I umm..." she tried again before sighing and looking down at our feet, her head resting on my chest. She sighed as her shoulders slumped in defeat as she looked back up at me, a soft smile gracing her full lips. "Thank you," she muttered before resting her head back into the crook of my neck.

I stood there for a second, frozen, as I thought about what she had just said, or more accurately, what she *hadn't* said. Was she really trying to say what I think she was?

I looked down at her, trying to get a look at her face and see if I could read her expression, but all I was met with was a mass of curly red hair as it twisted in different random directions. I smiled for a second before squeezing my arms tightly around her. I knew what she was wanting to say, I wanted to say it too, but with everything that was going on, and because of my cowardice, I decided to hold my tongue and not say the three words I so desperately wanted to.

Instead, I just whispered into her ear. "It's going to be okay Blaine; it's all going to be okay."

Chapter Twenty-Five
Blaine's POV

I lay awake that night, completely unable to sleep. Ever since Anna told me what she'd seen, I'd had these images of my whole family, being stuck in that hell hole going through god knows what, in my head. It was times like this when an overactive imagination can really be a downside. No matter what I did to try and distract my brain, it always somehow led me back to my family and what they were currently going through.

Everything I thought about just seemed to make me madder and more terrified. If I thought about food, it just seemed to make me think of my brother and how much he enjoyed eating, no matter how much I teased him about becoming fat one day.

If I thought about fighting or running or anything remotely physical, it just made me think about my dad. He was the one that taught me everything I knew about how to survive as a rogue out in the forests.

If I thought about Anna or Hannah, it just reminded me of my little sister. She was so similar to them it was almost comical. I never thought she really belonged in the rogue lifestyle, and my beliefs had only solidified since I've gotten to know my two girlfriends here. They were thriving in this kind of pack environment, and I couldn't help but wonder how different Julie's life would have been if we hadn't been born as a rogue.

The person that really broke me to think about though was my mum. She was such a kind-hearted and free-spirited person; I couldn't help but shudder when I thought about her being involved in something as horrible and gruesome as a fighting ring. She could never harm anyone, even when we were fending for ourselves, so the idea of her having to fight some strange wolf just for the enjoyment of the onlookers made me physically sick.

I sighed as I sat up in bed, the duvet falling from my shoulders as I made myself comfortable against the headboard. I knew there was only one thing, or rather one person, that could help ease my mind enough to fall asleep right now, but I just couldn't bring myself to go to him. We had come so far in our relationship since our first meeting, and I was worried that if I did go to him, to wake him up and ask for some company, it would backfire on me.

It was weird, at this moment I had more people looking out for me and genuinely wanting to be in my company then I ever had before, but at the same time I had never felt more alone. The pain I felt from the absence of my family was like a gaping hole in my chest, a hole I knew could never be filled or healed, until I found them and had them back in my life and in my arms.

I groaned again in frustration before thinking *to hell with it.* If I couldn't go to Xavier in my hour of need without him having a bitch fit, then maybe it was a good thing that we hadn't let things escalate. Mates were designed to be there for you, whenever they needed you, and if Xavier didn't want to be with me and deal with what was going on then maybe he didn't deserve to be my mate.

I flung the covers off my legs before walking over to my slightly ajar door and across the hallway until I was standing right outside his bedroom. I stood there for a second as I thought about what to do next. I mean do I knock, or do I just walk straight in? It was extremely likely that he was asleep right now, so he probably wouldn't hear me if I gently knocked, but the idea of walking in and standing over him whilst he slept seemed kind of weird. What if he woke up before I got a chance to wake him and he just saw me standing over him, watching him whilst he slept. No thank you.

I eventually went with knocking on the door whilst also letting myself in, hopefully I could wake him up before getting too close to him and seeming like some sort of creep.

"Xavier," I whispered as I walked into his room. I don't know why I whispered, my goal was to wake him up, so why did I say it in such a quiet voice? Even I wouldn't be able to hear that, and I was a light sleeper, well I had been before coming here anyway. There was something about this place, this house, that made me sleep like the dead.

"Xavier," I whispered again, a little louder this time as I stayed near the door. He groaned as he heard my voice before shifting in his sleep and passing out again.

Really? I sighed before walking a little further into his room, whispering his name repeatedly as I went.

Finally he stirred again, rolling over so that he was on his back. He didn't open his eyes, meaning he was probably still half asleep, but at least he was moving now. I stared at him for a second, a small giggle escaping my lips, but when Xavier finally muttered something, I stopped dead in my tracks.

"What do you want Lou," he grumbled. Even with his voice still thick with sleep, there was no denying what he had just said. He'd called me by a different name.

"Really?" I yelled as I walked over to him, there was no way that I was going to let him get away with that. "After everything we've gone through and everything I'm *currently* going through, you go and call me by a different *name*?" I screamed at him, no longer trying to gently wake him up.

"Blaine?" He mumbled as he rubbed his eyes, confused about what was going on.

"Oh, so now you get my name right?" I rolled my eyes as I stood over him, with my arms crossed and my hip popped, there was no denying that I was pissed off.

"What the hell are you talking about?" His own duvet fell from his shoulders, leaving his chest bare for me to see. I stared for a second, admiring the way his chest tensed whilst he stretched, before shaking my head and looking back up into his eyes.

I know he'd seen me admire him, but thankfully decided not to mention it as he got up and walked over to me. I tensed as his steps brought him closer, but I otherwise didn't move. No way was I going to be the girl that cried and ran away as soon as they found out they were being cheated on. If Xavier was seeing someone as well as me, he deserved to feel the full force of my fist.

"What's the matter Blaine, you look like someone just spat in your cheerios," he chuckled as he gently placed his hands on my shoulders. He tried to pull me in for a hug, but I remained stationary, not allowing him to draw me close enough to wrap his arms around me.

"I honestly didn't think you had it in you," was all I replied with as I stared into his eyes. They showed nothing but confusion and a little hurt that I hadn't allowed him to hug me, but otherwise nothing. No guilt and no remorse.

"Didn't have it in me to do *what*?" He questioned, sounding exasperated as he tried to clear the sleep from his eyes.

"To cheat," I clarified as I continued to stare him down. I mean why else would he mutter another girl's name when I had walked into his room and woken him up.

"Cheat?!" He exclaimed as I watched his eyes bug out of his head, "Why on God's green earth would you ever think I could ever do something like cheat on you?" He questioned as his grip on my shoulders tightened, as if he was scared that I would disappear if he let go.

"You called me by another girl's name when I came into your room and woke you up, that's like red flag number one! When a guy calls you a different name you run for the hills, every girl knows that!" I yelled.

He looked at me confused for a second before realisation seemed to dawn on him and he sagged slightly. I guess he knew he'd been caught in the act. "I-I said Louise, didn't I," he muttered, seeming almost pained when he stuttered out the other girl's name.

"You called me Lou, yeah," I confirmed as I re-crossed my arms, making sure they were secured so that I couldn't reach out and comfort him after seeing the look of pain in his eyes.

"Blaine, I'm not cheating on you," he sighed as he turned around and took a seat on the edge of his bed, quickly resting his elbows on his knees and his head in his hands. "Louise is... she's my sister... *was* my sister" he muttered, not looking up at me.

I stood in silence for a second in the middle of his room, unable to move. Had I really just gone off on my mate and accused him of cheating on me all because he'd called me his dead sister's name whilst still half asleep? I didn't think it was possible to feel worse than I had a while ago, when I was staring at my bedroom ceiling alone, but I can confirm that I definitely could. I felt like the biggest bitch on the planet.

"Xavier I'm-,"

"No no it's fine," he cut off my apology as he waved his hand dismissively in the air. "I would have probably thought the same thing if you'd called me a different name," he chuckled, still not bringing his head up from his hands.

I stood there for a second, unsure on what I should do, but after studying his broken stature, sitting slumped forward on the edge of his bed, my heart broke. He needed me, my mate needed me. I walked over so that I was sitting next to him on the bed before taking his hands in mine and pulling his head so that it rested on my shoulder.

I knew the basics about what had happened to his family, a rogue attack, but he had never gone into much detail about it.

"I'm sorry, talking about your family must have made me think of mine without even realising it," he muttered as he wrapped his arms around me, shifting us so that I was now resting in his arms. "I used to do stuff

195

like this all the time, confusing people with certain family members, but I haven't done it in a long time."

"It's okay," I shrugged as I settled into his arms. "I *am* sorry though," I muttered. "I feel like a class A bitch right now for accusing you of doing something like that."

"It's honestly fine," he smiled slightly as he kissed my forehead and squeezed my shoulders. "I'm just glad you're here," he mumbled as he held on tight.

It was hard for a mated pair to cheat on the other, both physically and mentally, but it was even harder for a pair like us. A couple that shared a blood bond, even one that wasn't fully formed yet like ours, meant you physically could not live without the other. It was as if the Moon Goddess knew that we would struggle with our pairing and so formed a blood bond between us so that we could never live, breathe, *survive,* without the other.

A blood bond was similar to a normal mating bond, only a lot stronger, and once it was formed it could never be undone or broken. I had cursed it in my earlier years, hating how an unformed blood bond had made me feel, so hollow and empty at times. Now I'd met Xavier I cherished it. With Xavier by my side, I felt whole, and nothing was going to stop me from being with him, he was my drug and right now I was as high as a kite.

Chapter Twenty-Six
Blaine's POV

We lay in Xavier's bed in silence, neither of us wanting to break the little bubble that had formed around us. I still felt awful about how I had reacted to him calling me by his sister's name, but we had cleared the air and things no longer felt uncomfortable or awkward.

I was currently lying on Xavier's chest with his arms wrapped securely around me. It was as if he didn't want to let me go in fear that I would disappear, just like his family. Just like my family. We were both so broken in our own way, yet with each other at our sides we were slowly but surely starting to heal.

"Xavier?" I whispered into the darkness of the room, looking up at him even though I couldn't see him.

"If you apologise to me one more time, I'm seriously going to tickle you to death," he chuckled as he shifted his arm to my rib cage. I knew he wouldn't because I was still slightly tender there, but it didn't stop me from twitching ever so slightly at the threat.

"No," I laughed as I settled back down on his chest. "I wanted to ask you about something, about something to do with our mate bond," I muttered quietly. It was a conversation that had popped up more and more in my head over the last few days and I knew that eventually it would have to be addressed. I could not ignore it any longer.

"What about it?" Xavier asked. He tried to sound casual, but I could hear the slight edge that was making its way into his voice.

"I was just wondering... I mean I just wanted to make sure that you knew about...," I stuttered, but thankfully Xavier helped me out.

"Yeah I know," he interrupted me. "I've known since the day that I shifted," he explained. "My mum had a load of these really old history books and I always found myself reading them when I was younger. For some reason I found them so fascinating, all about the wolf's history and what we could do," he shrugged. "I came across a particular entry when I was reading up on mate bonds, it pretty much explained everything for me."

I nodded as I listened to him. I felt a little envious of his knowledge of our bond so early on. Being a rogue meant I didn't have access to all the fancy old pack books dating back to god knows when, I had to find out through word of mouth about what a blood bond was and what it meant for me and my destined mate. "I found out about a year or two after I shifted. I couldn't understand why I was craving contact so much with another wolf. I mean my older brother never felt like that when he had shifted, so I just assumed I was being a wimp about not having my mate by my side," I explained with a sigh.

"Just because I knew why I was feeling the way I did, didn't mean it was any less painful for me," he shrugged. "I had to watch so many people find their mates before me, it made me so angry, at the world and at the Goddess, that I hadn't found mine yet."

"Bet you had the shock of your life when I suddenly turned up," I chuckled.

He laughed along with me as I felt him nod his head. "Yeah, you were a surprise, to be honest I thought you were some cruel joke the Goddess played on me. After hunting down and killing so many rogues for what happened to my family, I was suddenly stuck with one."

"Stuck with me hu?" I teased him as I poked his side slightly.

"You know what I mean, seeing as we couldn't reject each other because of the type of bond we shared, I had two options. I either had to get over myself and my hatred for rogues or live the rest of my life mate less and slowly go stir crazy," he shrugged. "I'm glad I chose the first option," he whispered as he looked down at me.

I smiled slightly into the darkness at his confession. "I'm glad I got over myself too," I nodded. "I had sworn from a very young age, all three of us siblings had, that we would never get involved with a pack. After hearing about my parent's past and having to live with the consequences, I had vowed never to put myself through that. If our mate was pack, we said we could offer them one of two options, we'd either leave them forever or welcome our mate into the life of a rogue to be with us," I explained.

"After meeting you and figuring out that you were a Beta, I knew you'd never leave your pack, not for anything," I explained. "That's why I ran that day, when we first met."

He stayed silent for a moment, before quietly muttering "I'm glad we caught up to you and Anna made you stay."

"I'm glad she did too," I smiled. "At least we now know why we were given a blood bond, we literally had everything stacked against us," I laughed. "There is no doubt that we would have rejected each other given half the chance."

He laughed along with me but otherwise didn't comment, instead just wrapped both his arms around my waist and held me tight. I could hear his heart beating wildly in his chest and I smiled slightly at the effect I was having on him, the same effect he always had on me.

"Blaine? There's something else I wanted to talk to you about before we head off and find your family," Xavier mumbled hesitantly.

I tried to look up at him but his hold on me was firm and I only managed to move my head a few inches before I gave up. "What's that?" I asked. If he's planning on telling me to stay behind whilst he goes and finds them, he's out of his mind.

"Well... seeing as we're going into unknown territory and performing a rescue mission that is quite possibly life threatening... I was wondering if... umm... you would... I wanted to...,"

"Spit it out Xavier," I laughed as I listened to his stuttering.

"I think we should mark each other," he rushed out as he looked down at me. "I've been wanting to bring it up for a few days now, but after hearing what Anna had to say, it only solidified my thoughts. We don't have to if you think it's too soon, but just so you know, I'm suggesting it because I want to and not because I feel like we have to. Even if everything was fine and dandy in our lives, I'd still ask you because I think we're good together and I don't want anything to get in the way of that."

I stayed silent for a second, letting him finish his rambling speech, in complete shock. He wanted to mark me? I know it shouldn't come as a surprise, we were mates, and it was going to happen eventually, but still, hearing the word coming out of his mouth still stunned me into silence.

"So...? What do you think?" He asked, nervous as my silence continued to stretch into the darkness of his room.

"I think... yes," I whispered as I looked up at him, finally able to as he'd released his vice like grip on me.

"Wait... what?" He stuttered, almost not believing I'd agreed.

"Yes," I repeated as I nodded my head slowly. "Why... did you think I'd say no?" I chuckled.

"Honestly? A small part of me did yeah," he laughed. "With the timing and everything I thought you'd say it was too soon, or that you wanted to wait until we got your family back," he laughed.

I quietly laughed along with him before getting up slightly so that I was resting on my elbow. "I've been thinking about it too," I admitted as I smiled down at him.

"Yeah?" He asked, sounding slightly excited at the idea of me thinking about marking him.

"Yeah," I nodded. This was actually happening; I was going to mark him and get marked in return. I had been speculating about this day for years now, about whether it was even in the cards for me, and now here we were. I was sort of nervous, which was stupid because this was Xavier we were talking about, but I couldn't help it as i felt my heartrate increase and my palms start to sweat.

"Blaine?" Xavier whispered, closer to me then I had originally thought. "I-I love you," he whispered into the darkness, and that was it for me. Before I knew it, I was kissing him and he was kissing me.

It started off harsh, like we were both starved for each other, and we couldn't get enough, but when Xavier's tongue touched mine, I melted. I sunk into the soft pillows beneath me as Xavier hovered over me, making sure all of his weight was on his elbows so that he wouldn't crush me.

His lips felt like velvet against mine, and when he moved from my lips to my chin I almost groaned in frustration, not liking the fact that I couldn't kiss him. My frustration was short lived though, because I soon felt his lips trail down the side of my neck, leaving light kisses in their wake as he sucked and nibbled along my overly sensitive skin.

I wrapped my arms around his neck and flung my leg over his hip, desperate to have him as close to me as physically possible, and when I felt the first scratch of his extended canine teeth against my skin I groaned in pleasure. I was sure my eyes were swirling bright gold as my wolf emerged to the surface, I didn't push her down though, this experience was as much for her as it was for me.

"Are you ready baby?" Xavier growled against my skin, and I couldn't help the tingles that ran up and down my spine as my skin hummed with his presence.

I didn't think I could form a coherent word, so instead of trying to talk I just nodded my head with a groan as I ran my fingers through his hair, hoping my actions were confirmation enough for him. Thankfully he got the hint because before I knew it I felt his four sharp canine teeth pierce through my skin on the right side of my neck. It only hurt for a second, before the sheer bliss of the forming bond weaved its way through my mind.

I had never felt anything like it. It was magical. Bliss. Heaven.

He held onto me for a few seconds, before slowly retracting his teeth and licking the wounds to make sure they were clean and would start to clot.

"You okay?" He asked husky, a slight lisp to his words because of his still extended teeth as they stuck out past his lips.

I nodded my head with a small "uh hu," I was more than okay.

"Your turn," he grinned as he easily flipped us over so that I was now on top, obviously eager to feel my mark on him. The bond wouldn't fully form until both of us had marked each other, and so before I wasted another second I leant down and positioned myself right in the crook of his neck, where his shoulder met his neck.

"Xavier?" I growled as I inhaled his scent. He didn't respond, feeling exactly how I felt when he was that close to me, too caught up in the moment to be able to say a coherent word. "I love you too," I whispered against his skin right before I bit down hard into his skin.

I'd felt nothing like it, the feeling of pure belonging, as I fully sank my teeth into his skin, my canines buzzing with the feel of our blood bond fully forming. I stayed there for a second, wanting to make sure the bond had enough time to fully form, before slowly retracting my teeth.

I collapsed onto his chest after I was sure his mark was clean and sighed at how amazing I felt. My parents had spoken to me about marking briefly in the past, to prepare me for when I would eventually meet my mate, but I don't think anything could prepare me for what I felt right now. I felt complete, whole, *invincible*, like nothing could touch me as I felt Xavier and his wolf worm their way into my brain just like I was doing to him. I had spent my whole life cursing the blood bond, but now I couldn't be more thankful that we shared it. I couldn't imagine feeling anything less than what I felt for Xavier at this moment.

I almost felt dizzy as we both lay there in silence, and I knew that as I drifted off to sleep, I had the biggest smile on my face.

Chapter Twenty-Seven
Xavier's POV

When I woke up the next morning Blaine was nowhere in sight. I panicked for a second, thinking that maybe we had gone too far last night and that she had left me, but when I heard pots and pans clattering downstairs I relaxed. She was just downstairs, cooking herself some food.

I lay in bed for a moment longer, just enjoying the feeling of finally being whole as my brain explored the formed mating bond. I'd felt like something was missing from my soul since I was sixteen years old, but right now in this moment, I felt complete.

I smiled as I reached up and felt the four scabbed over puncture wounds that now sat proudly on my skin. That girl sure did have a bite on her. It was a known fact that the more powerful the wolf was the more obvious the bite would be, and I knew that with the size of her canines there was no doubt that my mark would be impossible to miss.

The sizing of the bite was more of a genetic thing than a Moon Goddess thing. The bite showed other rival wolves how powerful their mates were, the bigger the mark the more stupid it would be to cross the line with their mate.

After going to the bathroom and staring at myself for a good five minutes in the mirror with a huge goofy grin on my face, I decided to finally go downstairs and give my mate a hand with breakfast. I still couldn't wrap my head around it, she was *my* mate, *mine* and no one else's. *Forever.*

When I walked into the kitchen, I couldn't help but laugh. Blaine was still in her pyjamas from last night and was dancing around the room to some song that was playing on the radio. She hadn't seen me yet as her back was to me, so I leant on the door frame and watched as she swayed her hips to the music from side to side. God she was gorgeous. She had her crazy hair in a knot on top of her head, but it still didn't stop the odd loose lock from escaping and bouncing around her face every time she moved.

"I didn't know you were a dancer," I chucked, finally announcing my presence.

A scream escaped her lips as she stopped stirring whatever was in the frying pan she had in front of her, her hand resting on her chest as she stared over at me with accusing eyes. "Jesus Xavier, what are you a ninja?"

I laughed harder at her shocked expression before making my way over to her and pulling her in for a hug. "Nope, not a ninja, just really sneaky," I replied as I kissed her cheek, silently feeling chuffed at the scars and bruises dotting up and down her neck and shoulders. I got her good last night. "What's for breakfast?"

"Umm... well I'm having scrambled eggs on toast, don't know what you're having though," she laughed, flashing me a cheeky grin.

I acted hurt as I clutched my chest as if I was in pain, "my own mate didn't cook extra for me?"

She played along for a second, acting as if she didn't care, but after a few seconds she rolled her eyes and turned back to her still cooking eggs. "Relax, I cooked enough for you too," she smiled as she turned the gas off. "Don't go getting used to it though, I'm not the type of mate that'll cook all your meals and wait on you hand and foot," she commented as she pointed the wooden spoon she was using out at me before turning back around.

I smiled at the back of her head before pulling her into a hug, her back to my front. "I wouldn't have it any other way," I whispered as I kissed down her neck, sucking slightly on her mark as I went. This was what marking did to wolves, it made them euphoric. After the bond is complete, the brain releases a massive dose of chemicals and endorphins which makes you the happiest you've ever felt in your entire life. It's addictive, and makes you want to experience that rush again and again.

"Blaine? Xavier?" A voice suddenly called from the front door, and we instantly sprung apart, as if we were teenage kids and didn't want to be caught doing something we shouldn't.

"Kitchen," I yelled back as Blaine went over to the counter and started buttering toast. I went over to the eggs and stirred them, making sure they weren't burning, before I remembered that Blaine had turned the gas off already and my actions were completely unnecessary.

"Why does it smell so... ho-ly crap," Anna laughed in the doorway of my kitchen. She took in both Blaine and I for a second before squealing and running over to Blaine and crushing her into a huge hug. "Congratulations!" She yelled into her ear before running over to me and pulling me into my own bone crushing hug.

"Annabelle, why are you screaming?" Jax yelled from the doorway, baby JJ in his arms. No explanation was needed though because as soon as he got a look at us, well more specifically our necks, he knew.

"Congrats man," Jax nodded my way before looking over to Blaine with a smile. "Welcome to the family," he grinned as he walked over to Blaine and gave her a small, one-armed hug.

The emotions that rushed through me nearly knocked me off my feet. Not only was I feeling my emotions, the love and gratitude for two of the most important people in my life, but I was also feeling Blaine's emotions as well.

I knew Blaine had always felt a little out of place here, in my pack and my home. She had grown up as a rogue and had never had to rely on anyone or be looked after by anyone other than her family before. It was in this moment however that she felt it, loved and accepted by the people around her.

"Thank you," she whispered, feeling overwhelmed by everything, before she turned around and finished off buttering the toast. I smiled at the back of her head before walking over to her and taking her once again in my arms, not wanting to pull her away from her task and distract her but still wanting to be near her and for her to know that I was there for her.

"I love you," I whispered in her ear, so soft only she could hear me.

She relaxed into my arms and stopped what she was doing as she looked up into my eyes, her eyes were glossed over slightly as she struggled to hold back her tears. "I love you too," she whispered back and closed her eyes as my lips made contact with her forehead.

I savoured the feeling of her for a second longer before moving away and resting my hip on the nearby counter, "so why are you guys here?" I asked the two of them as they sat on the floor with a crawling JJ.

"We just came by to let you know that I've called a pack meeting about our plans to rescue Blaine's family and any other wolf we find trapped in there," Jax explained as he looked up at me, JJ smacking him in the cheek with his tiny fist.

I nodded before walking over to the now slightly chilled eggs and started plating them up as Blaine finished buttering the last slice of toast. "What time?"

"Twelve sharp," he replied as he smiled over at his mate and son who were now playing together with a little fabric book.

I nodded my understanding before taking both plates of food and sat them down on the dining room table. "Okay thanks for letting me know, do we know what the plan is yet?" I asked as I started digging into my breakfast, making sure that Blaine had everything she needed before she too started picking at her eggs.

I could tell that her earlier feelings of happiness had now shifted. Just the mere mention of her family and the battle that we'd most likely have to go through made her sombre as she scooped small mouthfuls of food into her mouth.

"Well from what Annabelle had described, it doesn't sound like the place is that well guarded. I'm thinking maybe only bringing a few warriors with us and performing a stealth mission, the less that go the less chance we have at being detected," he shrugged as he sat next to me.

I thought the plan over for a second before nodding my head, out of the limited options we had, that would be the best option. In our absence we still needed to make sure the pack grounds were safe and guarded, and the only way to do that was to leave some warrior's behind.

"I have already contacted the elders and filled them in on what's going on, they have arranged safe passage for us to wherever we need to go," Jax continued to explain. The elders were pretty much useless nowadays, they were there more for the tradition than anything else, but at least they came in handy occasionally. With them giving us safe passage, it means that we can cross any land, whether it's pack land or not, and not have to worry about some Alpha becoming territorial and denying us entry.

"I'm thinking maybe fifteen of us," he continued. "A few trackers, a few warriors and us two-".

"And me," Anna piped up from the kitchen floor where she'd stayed to continue playing with JJ.

"Annabelle we've been through this; you can't come with us," Jax sighed as he ran his hand through his hair. They had obviously already had an extensive conversation before they came over about Anna coming with us, one that still hadn't been resolved.

"Exactly, we *have* already been through this. You don't know every single detail that I saw, you don't know what you're going to be up against, and you don't know if you're going to need my help somewhere down the line," she explained as she walked over to us.

"Little mate-,"

"Don't you Little mate me... I refuse to be one of those Lunas that sit on the side-lines whilst everyone else does everything they can to help. I won't do it Jax," Anna basically growled as she advanced on Jax, baby JJ secure in her arms.

"I'm coming too," Blaine nodded as she put her knife and fork together on her plate, having finished her breakfast. I had barely even touched mine yet.

"Blaine," I frowned as I looked over at her, not liking the idea of her getting in harm's way. I knew she could handle herself; she had demonstrated that over and over again, but the girl didn't have the best track record when it came to getting injured.

"Nope, I'm with Anna on this, we're coming with you," she stated. I could see the determination in her eyes, and I knew that I could argue all I wanted with her about this, but I would never win. Besides, it was her family, if anything she had more of a right to come than anyone.

"Fine," I sighed as I took her hand in mine. "But you just have to promise me you'll be careful, no running off and getting hurt like you tend to do," I smiled.

She nodded her head in confirmation before getting up with her plate in her hand. "Promise. Now I'm going to go for a quick shower before the meeting, see if the water will help with this mane of bed hair," she smiled before walking off.

I couldn't help but watch her as she walked out of the room so that she could head upstairs and take a shower. She was so magnetic my eyes were just drawn to her.

"You'll catch flies," Anna laughed as she took a seat in front of me.

211

"Oh shut up," I rolled my eyes before looking back at Jax. "So, after the meeting when do we roll out?"

"As soon as possible, we're going to hit them when it's dark, hopefully that's when the least amount of people will be around."

I nodded as I tucked into the rest of my breakfast. I guess all that was left to do now was hope and pray that everything runs smoothly.

Chapter Twenty-Eight
Xavier's POV

It was about four o'clock by the time the small group of us were ready to leave. Anna took the longest to get ready, between dropping JJ off at her parents and stopping off at the hospital to check on Henry. It was threatening to get dark before we had even left the pack lands.

Blaine had been jittery throughout the day, not being able to sit still and shaking her legs whenever she sat down for too long. I could understand how she was feeling, if I had a chance to see my parents and sister again but was waiting on others to get ready, I'd be feeling anxious too.

We were finally off though, with a small group of eighteen including a few trackers and warriors, Will, Jax's younger brother being one of them. We were all following Anna's lead, who seemed to know where she was going better than any of our trackers could. When I asked her how she knew where she was going, she just replied with "I just do" as her necklace glowed softly in the shadows of the tree under her t-shirt. It was a good job she'd insisted on coming with us, without her we probably would've gotten lost long ago and forgotten where we were even heading too.

Apparently, she had some form of internal compass, with the Moon Goddess' help showing her the way to where the caves were, as her wolf helped show her the way. I asked if it was anything like google maps, where you can drop a pin in the map and save the location for future reference to come back to, but she just rolled her eyes at me and laughed before walking off to catch up with Jax.

"Is it weird that I'm nervous?" Blaine suddenly asked next to me as we hiked through the woods. We had decided to travel in our human forms, making it easier to both cover our scent and walk through human populated towns if we needed to. The last thing humans needed to see was a pack of wolves running through their town centre as they yelled for animal control. This also meant that we could travel by car for most of the journey, saving us both precious time and energy.

"It's not weird at all," I reassured her as I took her hand in mine. "You haven't seen them in a long time, I'm sure your nervous and adrenaline are shooting all over the place right now." Now our bond was sealed and had settled down, I could feel her emotions trickle into the back of my mind, making me aware of just how anxious she was about meeting back up with her family.

She remained silent after that, but the grip she had on my hand became ever so slightly tighter the further we travelled from our pack lands and into the darkness of the woodlands. I wish there was something I could do to make her feel better, something I could say that would calm her down enough so that she wouldn't feel so anxious, but I knew there wasn't anything that could be said in a situation like this. The only thing that would make her feel better right now would be to see her family back on our pack lands, safe and sound and out of harm's way.

I wondered if I would get along with her family. My prejudice against rogues has significantly decreased since meeting my mate, but a small part of me wonders what I'll feel when I finally do come face to face with them.

A long time ago a doctor had told me that I could have been suffering from post-traumatic stress disorder. Whenever I saw a rogue, especially after the attack had just happened, I would see red and before I knew it, they were dead at my feet. I didn't believe her of course, I just blamed it on my wolf wanting revenge for what happened to them, but the more I thought about it the more it kind of made sense. The only thing that ever snapped me out of that thought process was my mate. My Blaine. My saviour.

Then there was the issue of whether her family would even like or accept me. Her family had obviously gone through something horrible for them to willingly leave their pack and raise children out in no-man's land. I knew why her parents had done it, and why they had such little faith in packs, but would it change their opinion of packs when they realised that their daughter was now happily a part of one? Or would they decide to continue their life of being a rogue and leave. Would that mean Blaine would leave me to be with them?

My palms started to sweat at the mere thought of Blaine leaving me, but thanks to the newly formed mate bond Blaine could feel my anxiety creeping in and reached up to give me a kiss on the cheek. It was a small act, but it was enough to calm both me and my wolf so that we could focus on the task at hand. Speaking of...

"It's over there," Anna suddenly piped up from the front of our small group of people, pointing to a small mountain range that was out in front of us, about two miles away.

"Okay, stay close, stay hidden and stay silent. Any forms of communication from now on must be through mind link only, understood?" Jax asked as we all flicked our eyes between him and our destination.

We all nodded in response before turning around and headed towards the mountain range, looking around and staying on guard to make sure there were no scouts or wolves on patrol.

By the time we made it to the mouth of the cave we were all a hot and sweaty mess, the hike hadn't been an easy one, and within a mile we all had to take a break so that we weren't completely exhausted by the time we reached the caves. There definitely had to be an easier way in, but seeing as we were trying to sneak in, the last thing we needed was to walk straight through the front door, especially when we knew at least one of the guys working here had seen our faces. We'd be recognised in a second.

"Alright this is a straightforward in and out rescue mission," Jax said over the mind link as we all tried to collect ourselves before walking into the man made cave. *"Because the pack link hasn't solidified with Blaine yet, she'll run everything through you Xav and we'll do the same, that way we can know which wolves are your family and which aren't."*

"But Jax what about the other wolves in there, we can't just leave them in the state that they're in," Anna piped up. I had to agree with her on this, if what she had described was true, then no wolf should be subject to that

216

kind of treatment. To be locked in a cell and forced to fight other wolves, all for the enjoyment of onlookers who no doubt got drunk and bet obscene amounts of money on them, it was sick.

"I know little mate, but our main priority is to get everyone back safely, including Blaine's family. I will not risk the safety of my pack for an unknown wolf. If it comes to it, I will inform all the packs on what we've seen here and they can choose whether they want to rescue them or not."

I didn't agree with it, but I understood it. Our main priority above all else was to not lose anyone, and if that meant leaving a few wolves behind until we could regroup and get back up, then so be it.

"Alright, we'll go in a few at a time so as not to raise suspicion, if we all walk in there now guns blazing we'll draw too much attention and the rescue mission will be over before it's even begun. Xavier, you and Blaine go first, and don't forget to stick together, you're our only connection to Blaine and if you two get separated we're sunk."

I nodded over at Jax to let him know I'd understood before I reached up and pulled my hood up and over my head. *"I'll let you know what we find, see you in a few,"* I linked to Jax before turning around, taking Blaine's hand in mine and proceeded to walk through the wall of ivy.

As we walked through the dark stone corridor there wasn't anything that specifically stood out, the walls were empty and there wasn't a soul in sight. Apparently, this was where Anna had found all the imprisoned wolves, but right now I couldn't see anyone, all the cells were empty and there wasn't a single noise coming from anywhere. It was like the place was deserted.

I frowned over at Blaine, but she was looking straight ahead, at something I couldn't see or smell.

"What's the matter?" I asked her through the link, alert as I tried to find out what she was seeing.

"They're this way, I can smell them" she said as she started to slowly walk along the corridor.

We walked for a few minutes, but as we went further and further into the cave, my wolf was becoming more and more on edge. Something wasn't right.

"Oi you two," we froze as we heard a gruff voice call out to us, "you ain't allowed back 'ere, if you're 'ere to watch them matches you've gone the wrong way," he said as he came into view.

Thank god we had put our hoods up, otherwise he would definitely be able to tell that we weren't supposed to be here, we were too clean to be seen as a rogue.

"Yeah, sorry about that man, we got lost," I spoke up, making sure to cover Blaine slightly with my body so she doesn't have any of this guy's attention.

He wrinkled his forehead slightly in suspicion as he looked us both over but seeing as we'd just done a huge hike and we were kitted out with clothes covered in mud and sweat, he must've thought we belonged because he grunted slightly before turning back around and walked through the hallway. His presence made the hair on the back of my neck stand up, but I held in my urge to punch his lights out long enough for him to lead us to a closed door.

"Betting is over next to the bar," the guy informed us before leaning forward and opening the door. What sat on the other side was something I knew I would never be able to unsee. This was obviously the place Anna had seen when she'd had her dream walk, the only difference was that when she'd been here it was an empty room. Now though, it was packed.

Well, there goes our plan of sneaking in and out undetected.

Chapter Twenty-Nine
Blaine's POV

When the bald headed, burly looking man opened the door, and I got a look at what was on the other side, I instantly froze.

The place was packed, filled with werewolves, witches and even humans as they all pushed past each other to get to where they wanted to go. I don't think I've ever seen so many people packed into one place before. Everyone was crammed into the space near the middle, surrounding a chain link cage, and yelling at the action that was going on inside. I couldn't see what was happening, but based on the noises, I could hazard a guess as to what they were yelling at and betting on.

Xavier gripped my hand tightly and slowly led me into the room, his eyes taking everything in as he surveyed the area around us. I was glad that I had him by my side, there was no way that I could have done this and been here without him.

"Do you sense them anywhere?" Xav whispered to me, close to my ear so that it could be heard over the roar of the crowd.

I stopped walking and breathed in my surroundings but frowned when I came up empty. "No, there's way too many people in here for me to identify anyone," I sighed, disappointed that their scent had vanished.

"It's alright we'll find them, we just have to keep looking," he whispered in my ear before placing a small kiss just below my ear, helping to calm my nerves.

I squeezed my hand that was wrapped around his before we both started heading off towards the bar. "Let's go and check out the betting area, maybe they'll have names up of who's fighting who and when," Xavier said as he let go of my hand and wrapped his arm around my shoulder, pulling me close to his side, shielding me from the over enthusiastic crowd.

The place was packed with bodies, all jostling around as they tried to fight their way to the front, wanting to get a better view of the current fight that was taking place a short twenty feet in front of us. I pulled my hood further over my head, hoping that it would shadow my face and cover my very distinctive looking hair. I loved my bright red, almost ginger mane, but right now I wished that it was a typical brown colour so that I could easily blend in with the surrounding crowd.

We eventually made it over to the betting area with only a small amount of beer being spilled over us from the excited onlookers, too engrossed in the fight to notice that their wild gestures were causing them to spill their drink that they had undoubtedly spent ages queuing for and spent a fortune on.

Just as we were getting close enough to see the blackboard, explaining who was fighting next, there was a massive uproar from the crowd, causing us to be pushed around left and right. I tried to figure out what was going on, but before I could I felt Xavier's hand slip from around my shoulder.

"Xavier?!" I screamed through the mate link, knowing that he wouldn't have a hope of hearing me over this crowd if I yelled out loud.

"Blaine where are you?" he yelled back, his panic seeping into the back of my mind through the bond.

"I-I don't know," I muttered as I looked around to try and take in my surroundings, hoping that I could find a landmark that would tell me where I was in this sea of people. All I saw were bodies as they all pressed up against me and each other, pushing me this way and that until I felt dizzy.

It was like that game we used to play as kids, you were blindfolded and spun around by someone, and you had to try and find your way back to your group of friends. Except this time I wasn't blindfolded, and the consequence of not finding my friends was far greater than just losing the game or tripping up on something and scraping my knee.

I suddenly found myself at the front of the crowd, being pushed against a metal pole as I looked up at the slightly raised cage, and what I saw made my blood run cold and a sheen of sweat appeared on my hairline.

It wasn't the fact that I was looking at two wolves, one with his jaw clamped around the other's throat as he seemingly waited for the command to clamp down. It wasn't that I was on my own, away from Xavier, and surrounded by a bunch of hot-headed rogues, all waiting for the final blow. It was the fact that the wolf who held his opponent in his mouth, waiting for his order to clamp down and spill blood, was my brother.

I stared up at him in shock as I looked him over. He had changed so much since I had last seen him all those years ago, gone was the caring older brother who had once taught me how to hunt and ride a bike. Gone was the brother who'd held me tight as a child, waiting for the all clear sign from our parents that it was safe for us to come back out of our hiding spot. In his place was a menacing wolf, who showed no remorse as he snapped his jaws closed around the losing wolf's neck and stepped away from the lifeless body.

The crowd cheered as they watched the life drain out of the losing wolf's eyes, but all I could hear was a constant ringing in my eyes as my eyes stayed fixed onto my brother's frame. What had they done to him?

I could feel Xavier poking at the mate link, trying to get a hold of me, but I blocked him out. I didn't want him to see my brother like this, he was only just starting to accept the fact that all rogues weren't evil. If he saw him like this, I shudder to think how he'd react.

Without looking around or even looking down at the wolf he'd stolen his life from, Daniel stalked out of the ring, through a caged corridor that had opened, like when humans moved large animals around at the zoo. The trap door quickly snapped shut behind him, leaving the dead and already forgotten about wolf lying lifeless on the blooded, concrete floor.

I quickly pushed my brain clear of all sympathy I felt for the poor wolf as I turned around and fought my way through the crowd. I had a job to do and there was no way I could get it done if I was consumed with regret and grief for another wolf.

"Xavier, follow that wolf that went through the metal tunnel, I'll meet you there at the other end."

"Blaine be careful, we don't know what these guys are capable of," Xavier cautioned. *"I've linked the rest of the pack waiting outside, they're going to blend into the*

crowd and wait for our signal. Once we find your family we're out of here."

I followed Daniel at a safe distance, making sure that I wasn't drawing attention to myself, and waited by the wall where the corridor disappeared through the stone wall for Xavier to catch up. I was ninety percent sure that all the wolves, my family included, were being held just beyond this stone wall, waiting for their turn to be called into the ring.

Eventually, Xavier made it to my side, and instantly pulled me into an almost bone crushing hug. "Blaine are you alright? Are you hurt? Don't disappear and cut me off like that, I almost had a heart attack when I couldn't get a hold of you through the link."

I smiled at his worried tone as I buried my head into his neck. "I'm fine Xav, but I think I found where my family are being held," I explained as I gestured to the now closed trap door leading outside the room.

"Nice work," he smiled as he looked over the wall, trying to find a door that we could use to get through to the other side. "I'll link the guys and let them know, maybe there's a way to access it from the outside or something. That way we can just slip in and out without having to go through the crowd."

I nodded as I followed his lead and started scanning the surrounding walls, desperate to get through to them. I hadn't seen them in over two years and to know that they are right behind this wall, right on the other side of a bit of stone, it was killing me.

"Anything?" I asked, hoping that he had seen something that I hadn't.

"No," Xavier sighed as he ran his hand over the back of his neck. "The pack hasn't found anything either."

I could feel my heart cracking at the possibility of not being able to get to my family. The expression *'so close and yet so far'* has never felt more accurate than it did in this moment. "Xav," I whispered as I looked down at my dirt covered boots. "What if we can't get to them?" I mumbled, losing hope with every second that ticked by.

Xavier gripped my shoulder tightly with one hand as he tilted my chin up with the other, making me look up at him. I saw love and determination bubble away in his eyes, and I could tell in that moment that he was never going to give up on finding them. This meant just as much to him as it did to me. "We will get them back Blaine," he told me. "I promise you I will do *everything* in my power to get your family back home and safe where they belong."

I smiled up at him with what I hoped was love and gratitude, this man was giving me so much more than I could ever think possible. Before I met him, I was a lone rogue, believing I was destined to be alone and fend for myself for the rest of my life. And now, not only was I getting my family back, but I also had the most amazing mate I could ever wish for, a mate who loved me and supported me unconditionally.

I pulled him in for a kiss, keeping it short so that we wouldn't draw attention to ourselves. A fight wasn't currently on, meaning that the audience's attention wasn't distracted by anything as their eyes wandered around the room.

"Guys keep it in your pants will you," I suddenly heard Anna laugh from beside me, making me quickly pull away from Xavier a little sheepishly.

"What are you guys doing here? I thought you were supposed to be blending in with the crowd and keeping a low profile?" I asked as I battled with the slight blush that was forming on my cheeks at being caught.

"We were, but then I had a feeling that you needed our help. Well my help, but Jax tagged along," Anna smiled up at her mate before looking back at us with her hands on her hips. "So what's up?"

"We think Blaine's family are on the other side of this wall, but we can't find a way in," Xavier explained as he gestured to the wall we were leaning up against with his thumb.

"Alright, well why don't you boys go and search the wall on this side of this...long metal cage thing... and me and Blaine will search the other side, that way we'll get it done twice as fast and meet in the middle."

"I don't know..." Xavier mumbled as he reached out and took my hand in his, "Blaine isn't linked to the pack yet, what happens if she needs me for something?"

"That's what I'm there for," Anna responded in a *duh* tone.

I kind of agreed with Xavier, but I wasn't going to go against Anna's wishes. She was my Luna and if I was being completely honest, she kind of scared me a little bit, plus she was connected to the Goddess. If she thought these were the groups we needed to split off in, then I was going to go for it.

"I don't know Anna..." Xavier continued to question.

"The girl's will be fine," Jax piped up as he slapped his hand on Xavier's shoulder. "Besides we'll blend in more if we split up, just looking around now I can tell this isn't really a place where you meet up with your mates and their friends for a catch up. If we stick together, we could look more suspicious."

It took a tiny bit more convincing, but finally Xavier agreed with splitting up. With a quick kiss goodbye and a promise that I will stay in constant contact with him, the boys were off and we were going our separate ways.

"So I have to be completely honest," Anna said as soon as the boys were out of ear shot. "I made sure Jax was on board with the whole splitting up plan before I brought it up. I wanted to check in on you quickly without Xavier around, just to make sure that you are doing okay. Reuniting with your family after being apart for so long is difficult enough, let alone when they've been through something as traumatic as this."

I smiled over at her as I squeezed her hand tightly in mine, thankful that I had an amazing friend like Anna in my life. "I'm doing okay," I replied as I sidestepped a man's arm as it swung out and nearly accidently hit me in the face. These people were starting to get rowdy now that there wasn't a fight to draw their attention.

My stomach flipped slightly at the mere thought of my brother in that fight earlier, but I pushed the mental image down. I couldn't let myself get distracted, especially in a place like this.

"Good, oh and I know how to get into the other room with your family," she smiled over at me as we suddenly stopped.

I froze in front of her with a slightly shocked expression, how the hell could she know that?

"The Goddess showed me the way to the hidden doorway," she whispered as she gestured to a dark dip on the cave wall behind my left shoulder. If I hadn't known something was there it would have blended right in, but now Anna had pointed it out to me it was as clear as anything, a small fake door posing against the stone surface of the wall.

Gotcha.

Chapter Thirty
Blaine's POV

"It sure is creepy down here," Anna whispered as we crept along the hidden tunnel, making sure we stuck to the shadows so that we had less chance of being seen. Her voice bounced off the stone walls and I had to quietly "*shhh*" her so that her voice wouldn't echo back up the tunnel and towards some guards.

That would be just our luck.

"Sorry," she whispered, a lot quieter this time so as not to cause her voice to travel.

We continued the walk down the dark tunnel in silence, the only light coming from the odd electric lamp that had been drilled into the stone walls. Unlike the rest of the cave, this corridor was a lot more rough around the edges. The stone had sharp edges where it had most likely been chiselled at to help make the opening wider, and the floors were covered in dirt and rocks. Obviously this path was not designed to have many visitors.

Where is this thing taking us anyway? I felt like we had been walking for ages and we still hadn't found anything.

"Are you sure this is the right way?" I whispered over my shoulder to her, making sure I kept my voice as low as possible.

"I'm sure. It's not too far now I promise," Anna whispered back to me as we continued to creep through the hallway.

True to her word, a short distance later, a scent hit me that made bubbles of nerves appear in my stomach, my brother was here.

"Anna on your left," I whispered as we came to a fork in the road.

"You sure?" She questioned as she surveyed our two options, weighing them up to see which one would be the best way to go.

"One hundred percent," I nodded, having complete faith in my nose and what it was telling me. The nerves that were still brewing in my stomach hadn't disappeared, if anything they had only intensified. I had a million and one questions swirling around in my brain which only seemed to spin faster the deeper we got into the cave.

What if they didn't recognise me? What if they had turned feral after being trapped in their wolf form for so long in those little cages, forced to fight for their life's day in and day out. What if... what if they'd died in one of those fights before I got a chance to get them out?

"Blaine are you alright? I can feel your emotions seeping through the bond they're so strong," Xavier questioned.

I took a deep breath trying to calm myself down, before replying. *"Yes we're both fine, Anna found a hidden door in the side of the cave and we're heading down it now to try and find my family. I think this is where they keep them all when the fights are going on, there are a lot of wolf smells down here."*

"You're where?! *Why the hell didn't you tell me you'd found something? Tell me where it is, and I'll come to you,"* he demanded through the link.

I wasn't sure whether having Xavier here with me would be the best idea. I had no way of knowing how my family would react around me, let alone Anna, and then an unknown male smelling like pack, it was probably safest to leave him out there just in case something was to kick off down here. Besides, my dad and brother were fairly hot headed at the best of times, I don't think they'd react particularly well to my mate storming in and trying to keep me from them, that's if they're still the same as when I last saw them.

"Xavier just stay there, I promise we are both fine and we'll be careful. If anything does happen, I'll let you know straight away."

"But Blaine-,"

But I didn't let him finish as I interrupted him. *"Do you trust me?"*

"Of course I do-,"

"Then trust me on this, Xav... please. I've been looking for my family for so long now, the least you can do is let me find them." I didn't feel particularly great about guilt tripping him into letting me find my family on my own, but I meant every word I'd said. I had been searching for my family for over two years, and if I'd allowed him to come with me he'd just bulldoze the whole thing and have me hiding behind his back the entire time whilst he did all the work.

The link was silent for a second, making me question whether I had pushed him too far, but thankfully Xavier finally replied through the link. *"Fine, but I want constant updates from you about what's going on and where you are... okay?"*

"Deal," I nodded, knowing it was the best deal I'd get out of him.

I looked over at Anna after I had shut off the link and noticed that she too had glazed over eyes, and I could tell just from her expression that she wasn't too happy. Looks like Xavier had let it slip that we weren't exactly where we said we'd be.

"Everything alright?" I asked when I noticed she'd closed the link off.

"Yeah fine, I hadn't exactly been completely honest with Jax about where we'd be going and now he's super pissed," she sighed with an eye roll. "It took me long enough to convince him to let us go on our own in the first place, now he's not going to let me out of his sight," she groaned. "It's fine though," she shrugged as she turned and continued walking down the hallway, "I'll just offer to change JJ for the next two weeks and Jax will be back to normal," she smiled. "You'd be surprised what changing babies' nappies could get you out of," she laughed as she recalled some distant memory.

I hoped me and Xav would be as happy as Anna and Jax clearly are one day.

We continued to walk for another few hundred yards, before coming face to face with an old wooden door. It was the type of door you'd find in old mediaeval movies, with the cast iron cut out so that someone could peek out and ask for the password to get in. Safe to say we didn't have it if someone asked us.

Thankfully no one was on the other side of the door, from what we could hear and smell anyway, and with one solid push from the both of us, the door creaked open to reveal a small, dimly lit room.

"What is this place?" I muttered, my eyes not having adjusted to the lack of light in the room.

At the sound of my voice a sudden rumble rang through the room, a rumble that was unmistakable to any wolf who came close. Growls. Warning growls.

Anna pulled a small battery powered torch from her pocket and switched it on before sweeping it around the room. What we both found made us gasp in shock and horror as we took in the scene in front of us.

In front of us there must have been at least forty to fifty cages, all lined up in rows, and each contained a wolf who was crammed into the space, hackles raised and teeth on show as they stared at us through the bars.

"Holy crap," Anna whispered as she swung the small torch from side to side, the beam far too small to light up a large enough area for us to take everything in. "How could this..." she stuttered, unable to finish her sentence, too shocked to be able to form any words that could describe what we were seeing.

I stood there in silence as I took everything in with tears in my eyes. This was where my family had been this whole time? Whilst I had been prancing around with my new mate and complaining about my so-called issues, my family had been suffering through this?

I sniffed but still made no effort to move, I had honestly been rendered speechless.

The cages were so small the wolves couldn't even stand up properly or walk around in them, being forced to lie on the iron flooring of their cage as they sat there and waited for their turn in the ring. The room stank of blood and urine and there was no doubt in my mind that these poor people were being forced to sit in their own waste. They were being treated like dogs, like vermin, and my blood boiled. No one did this to our kind and got away with it.

A flash of ginger and gold suddenly caught my attention and my eyes snapped over just as Anna's torch had moved on. I'd know that coat anywhere, that was the colour of my sister.

Instant relief washed through me as I realised that both of my siblings were still alive, but I knew the fear that was flowing through me wouldn't completely disappear until I had my whole family out of here and back at the pack lands. Safe.

"Anna over there," I whispered as I pointed towards the general direction of where I believed she was being held.

As we walked over to her the grumbles and growls from the surrounding wolves intensified, but thankfully they didn't increase in volume. It was as if they were scared to make too much noise, their voices never reaching a level that would be deemed appropriate for the situation they were in. If a wolf was feeling scared or threatened, they'd make as much noise as possible to seem like a bigger threat to the newcomer, it was only in our nature to do so, so why were these lot being so quiet?

"Which one Blaine?" Anna whispered from in front of me.

I refocused on where I was going and pointed out to where I thought I'd seen my sister. "Right at the back, in between these two cages there," I whispered as I pointed to the far end of the room.

I almost cried in relief when I smelt her. My baby sister was pressed up against the back wall of her cage, baring her teeth at me to try and scare me away. It was clear that she didn't recognise me, and my heart broke as I took in her rigid and threatening posture.

Like my mum, Julie had always been a quiet and gentle soul. We had always joked that she couldn't even seem to harm a fly, let alone come on a hunt with us to try and catch some dinner. Knowing her, she probably would have given our position away purposefully just so she wouldn't have to see the animal die.

The *one time* she'd agreed to go on a hunting trip was with my brother, just over two years ago. She told us that she needed to start doing more to help out and thought if she managed to catch something to eat she'd get over her fear of killing an animal. I never got to ask her if her theory worked.

Yes, I had joined in on the joking, but I had always secretly admired the innocence that always seemed to surround her. How pure she was, even when living in the situation we were in.

Looking into her eyes now though, I could tell that her innocence had gone, all that was left was anger.

"J-Julie?" I whispered as I crouched down towards her. "Julie it's me, Blaine."

The only response I got was a threatening growl as she snapped her teeth at me slightly and backed as far as she could away from me. God knows what she'd gone through to turn her into this.

"Julie please... don't you remember me?" I whispered as a tear escaped my lids. Seeing my little sister reacting this violently towards me was like a stab to the chest. The light in her eyes had completely vanished, and all that was left was sheer hatred and fear.

I felt Anna's presence behind me, lending me some moral support, but I didn't look back at her, I just kept my eyes solely focused on Julie.

I lifted my hand from where it had been resting in my lap and reached out towards her, hoping that my scent would trigger something in her mind and she would somehow remember me, but it only seemed to make matters worse. As soon as my hand touched the cold metal of her cage my sister let out an almighty growl before whining and collapsing to the floor in pain.

"What the...?" I whisper shouted as I felt a spark run through my fingertips.

"Blaine it's her collar," Anna whispered as she pointed to a thick strip of metal that was looped around my sister's neck. "I've seen these types of collars before, but only ever on domestic pets. They're used by humans when they can't get their dog to stop barking. It issues an electric shock every time it senses vibrations from the wearer's voice box, they must've adapted it somehow to make the shock stronger."

I shivered as I thought about the type of torture they'd been put through, no wonder all the wolves around us were staying quiet, they knew that if they made a noise they'd be shocked just like Julie was.

"Oh Julie, what have they done to you?" I whispered as I watched her lay there on the metal floor, convulsing slightly from the electrical currents still running through her body. "But don't worry, I'm going to get us all out of here," I muttered as I looked up at Anna.

Chapter Thirty-One
Xavier's POV

We hadn't found anything of relevance since the girls had left.

When I first found out that Blaine had gone off and was searching the hallways and caves without at least telling me first, I had been fuming. Jax had to tell me to calm down as my body language and attitude had started to draw some unwanted attention from the onlookers around us.

I couldn't believe that Jax had been okay with Anna heading off on her own to begin with. He had thankfully managed to talk me down and we were now walking around the edges of the large cave type room trying not to look suspicious and out of place.

I knew that the others from our pack who'd joined us were also within the room, but it was so jam packed full of people I was having a hard time finding a familiar face.

"Stop fidgeting man, you're going to give us away," Jax muttered next to me as he took a swig from the beer he had bought from the bar. He said it was to try and help us blend in, but I think it was more to try and ease his nerves about him and Anna being apart. He knew the Goddess would take care of her, hence why he wasn't storming off and looking for her as we speak, but it didn't make the separation any easier.

"I can't help it," I defended myself as I again swept the room for any sign of someone or something out of the ordinary. "Not knowing where she is or whether she's in danger is really setting me on edge," I grumbled as I ran a hand through my hair and along the back of my neck.

"I get it, but just try to take it easy. You have the mate bond now, not only that you have a *blood bond*, use it to your advantage," he said as he slapped his hand on the back of my shoulder.

"That's great advice and all, but if you haven't noticed we haven't exactly been mated all that long, I'm not even one hundred percent sure how it works yet," I sighed. Jax was right in the sense that we did share a strong bond with each other, one the Goddess thought was needed for us to get through being with each other, but without practising and truly understanding one another, there was no way of telling how this thing worked. It's not like a one size fits all type thing, every mated pair was different, and every bond linking that pair was different.

"Just try alright?" Jax sighed as took another drink and sidestepped a huge bald guy wanting to get past us. "You've probably read every book known to us about the blood bond, surely that must count for something? Just try something easy like focusing on her emotions, I know that helps me stay calm when Anna's away from me. Like right now for example, I can tell that she's a little confused as well as on edge and upset, but it also tells me that she's not in any sort of danger, if she were she'd be feeling scared."

"You're keeping tabs on her?" I chuckled as I raised my eyebrows at him. "Does she know this, or does she think you're just being a super supportive and trustworthy mate?" I chuckled.

"I trust her!" He defended but otherwise didn't say anything. In other words, no she doesn't know and if she did find out he's in the dog house, excuse the pun.

I snorted but quickly shut up as I saw out of the corner of my eye a group of less than friendly looking guys looking in our direction. "Jax three o'clock," I muttered as I turned around with my back to them so Jax could get a look at them without it being too obvious. "Think it's anything we need to worry about?" I asked, but before Jax could respond a flash of fear shot through my system making my body freeze up and my pupils dilate.

It wasn't the fact that the fear itself put me on edge and almost paralyzed me, it was the fact that the unmistakable chill of fear wasn't my own, it was Blaine's.

I took one look at Jax and without even voicing my concerns I know that he was feeling the exact same thing. This could only mean one thing; the girls were in danger.

Without another second wasted Jax dropped his beer, letting it smash to the ground, and turned around to make his way back to the point where we split off, hoping that we could find their scent and follow it to where they were.

But before we could even take two steps, the crowd seemed to part around us and we were swarmed by guys, all tattooed up and grinning at us. They were all strangers to me, all but one.

My eyes locked onto him as soon as I spied him in the gang of people, the rouge who had hurt my Blaine during the attack.

"Long time no see Rogue Killer," he grinned as he flashed his slightly extended teeth at me.

I growled at him as my wolf started to show through, my eyes no doubt burning gold with rage at finally being face to face with the wolf who'd hurt and nearly killed my mate. "Not soon enough," I growled as I stared him down.

We had quickly attracted quite the crowd, the ring of people around us growing by the second as they gathered to see a possible fight, one that hadn't been pre-arranged and trapped inside the chain link cage.

"And not only do we have the Rogue Killer with us ladies and gentlemen, but we also have the Alpha himself gracing us with his presence... welcome to my humble abode," he grinned as he shifted his gaze over to Jax who was standing tense beside me.

"If only you would have brought your beautiful mates along with you so that they could witness the show," he sighed as he looked around the crowd with an evil grin plastered on his face, his teeth still out for all to see. "But wait... what is that I hear?" He asked as he made a gesture of putting his hand to his ear and listened to something happening in the background.

At first, I heard nothing, just the breaths and sniggers of the people who surrounded me, but it wasn't long before I heard something that made dread seep into my veins and this time, the fear was completely my own.

"Get your hands off of me you slimey excuse of a man," Blaine growled as I heard scuffling not too far from us. They'd been found.

240

I growled as I realised an unknown wolf had his hands on my mate and was probably hurting her. No one hurts my mate and gets away with it.

Blaine and Anna suddenly broke through the ring of onlookers and were forced into the little clearing that Jax and I were standing in, both of them with their own escort tightly holding their biceps in firm grips.

"Let go of her," Jax growled as he started to advance on the man holding his mate. He was quickly held back as a few of the surrounding guards interfered and held his arms back, effectively stopping him from getting anywhere near the girls.

"Not so fast little Alpha," the head guy laughed. "The people here came for a show, and I think it's only fair that we give them one," he continued to laugh as he looked around the room with his hands in the air, loving the cheers from his onlookers as they agreed with him.

"Now, I was going to have the big bad Alpha face off with a few of my best fighters, after all we've never seen an Alpha fight in hand-to-hand combat this close before," he shrugged. "But I think I've thought of something *ten times* better," he laughed, his voice increasing in volume so that the whole room could hear.

"You see everyone," he continued as he walked around us, circling us as if we were his prey and he was just toying with us, waiting for the moment to strike. "The Rogue Killer is mated to the fiery little redhead over there... who is a rogue herself," he exclaimed, his onlookers laughing along with him as he continued his speech. "Quite recently to by the looks of those bite marks on the side of your neck," he guessed as he pointed to the side of my neck where Blaine's mark stood proud on my skin.

"Now the real kicker in all of this folks, is that not only is his mate Blaine over here," he explained as he gestured to my mate who was currently looking over at the man with daggers in his eyes. "I've been looking for her for the better part of two years. You see not only do I have her brother as one of my prize fighters; I also have her sister, her mother *and* her father too," he laughed. "And what can I say," he shrugs as he looks between us with a glint in his eye. "I'm a collector."

The crowd laughed along with him at his last comment, but Blaine growled, her eyes turning bright gold and her teeth extending to their fullest at the mention of her family being nothing more than a collector's item.

"You're a sick son of a bitch, you know that?" I growled at him, my speech having a slight lisp to it due to my extended canines.

"I prefer to look at it as pure genius," he shrugged.

There was one thing I'd learnt about this guy; he loved a show, and he loved the attention to be all on him. In his eyes he was the Alpha of this place, the one barking out all the orders and reaping all the rewards, and that had been made glaringly obvious by this little show he was putting on now.

"So what's your big plan then? Kill my family in front of me or something just so you can entertain all your buddies?" Blaine hissed as she again struggled to get out of the hold the guy had on her.

"You know that *had* crossed my mind," he nodded, as if he was deliberating the option. "But then I thought, why waste a perfect opportunity with just simply killing someone? Why not do it our style, and have them fight in the cage," he grinned over at her whilst the crowd shouted and cheered him on.

That was the last straw for me. The idea that he was going to steal my mate from me and put her in a cage to fight off her own family made me sick to my stomach, not to mention the fact that it would probably kill her to even lay a hand on one of her family members.

"Take me, let the rest of my pack go and I will give you a show like you've never seen," I said as I turned away from Blaine and looked at the guy square in the face. I could hear Blaine scream at me not to, begging me to stop talking and to just let her handle her own family issues, but I ignored her. This was something I had to do.

"Think about it," I continued. "The Rogue Killer fighting a rogue for all to see," I shouted, raising my arms up and gesturing to the crowds around me. "Now wouldn't *that* be a show for your adoring fans to see."

"Xavier no!" Blaine screamed.

I turned to her with a sad smile as I looked her deep in her eyes, hoping she would understand just how much I loved her. "I've already watched my mum and my sister die; I can't stand aside and watch you die too," I sighed before looking back over at the guy calling all the shots. I knew that it was pointless trying to fight our way out of here, we were surrounded, and any attempt at escaping would mean certain death for all of us.

"So, what do you say big man, am I worthy enough to be entertainment for you and your little group?"

The room was silent as we waited for him to decide, the tension thick as I waited for the decision that would surely end my life. I knew I couldn't kill a member of Blaine's family; they were a part of her, and I knew that if I harmed them Blaine would never forgive me.

243

"Fine," the guy finally shrugged as he pointed over to the cage. "Let's see what you're made of," he growled with a cruel grin on his face.

Blaine and Anna screamed as the guy finally agreed to my proposal, but I couldn't look over at them as I walked past them and towards the cage that was sure to be my death sentence.

Chapter Thirty-Two
Blaine's POV

I always find there's a moment of peace before any fight between two people. I know that sounds odd and a little contradicting, but it's true. It's the moment where the two people involved stand opposite each other, sizing the other one up, to see if they could find any weak spots or vulnerabilities.

I had always found this moment particularly fascinating, watching the two opponents sizing the other up and wondering what was going through their mind. Whether they saw the slight limp I'd seen or wondering if they'd noticed something that I'd missed.

But that was not something I was feeling right now, I felt the furthest away from calm I'd ever felt. The only emotion that was coursing through my veins was fear as I watched my mate willingly walk into the cage to fight someone to the death so that we could all go free.

My voice had gone scratchy from yelling so much, and the hands clasped tightly around my biceps, holding me back, were no doubt going to leave finger shaped bruises once he released his hold on me. *If* he released his hold on me. Every attempt I'd made to escape his grasp had only wound up with me worse off, every time I tried to fight back, I'd just have five guys tower over me and

245

remind me why it was in my best interest to remain where I was.

So I stood on the side-lines, helplessly, as I watched the love of my life get trapped inside the steel confines of the cage, where a mere half an hour ago my brother had stood and killed a wolf in cold blood for sport.

"Oh boy, do we have a treat for you lot tonight!" The announcer suddenly shouted into a microphone, making his voice echo off the stone walls as it came through the speakers. "Tonight, we have the one... the only... Rogue Killer!" He screamed into the microphone, leading everyone else to join in with his enthusiastic hollering.

My eyes stayed fixed on Xavier's as I watched him walk up to the chain link fence and place his hand against the cold metal. His eyes never wavered from mine as I watched a sad smile grace his lips.

"I'm so glad I got to meet you," he told me through the link.

The shouts and cheers from the crowd died away and suddenly all I could hear was the buzz of energy as I focused solely on the link.

"There hasn't been a day gone by where I regret finding you and getting to love you," he continued.

"I love you so much Xavier," I replied as a lone tear escaped my eyelashes. *"Thank you for teaching me how to love, and for making me feel whole again after feeling broken for so long. You taught me what it was like to live, and for that I could never repay you. You mean the world to me, and* when *we get out of here, I can't wait to spend the rest of my life showing you just how much you mean to me."*

246

I was glad that we were talking through the link, because I knew that if I was saying all this out loud, there was no way that my voice wouldn't have shaken with all the emotion I was feeling.

"You are the best thing that's ever happened to me, " he smiled sadly. *'Just promise me that no matter what happens, you'll get out of here okay? Even if it means leaving me behind, "* Xavier replied in a sad tone before turning away from me to face the entrance where his opponent would be appearing.

I tried to link him back, scrambling for any form of connection I could find so that I could beg him to make sure he came back to me. I needed to tell him that I could never leave him here, that I would rather die than leave this place without him by my side, but before I could he'd cut me off, severing all ties with the mate link.

"XAVIER!" I tried to get his attention, but with the noise of the crowd my voice was quickly drowned out.

"Okay ladies and gentlemen, it's time we meet our challenger," the announcer shouted through the mic just as the door connected to the cave wall opened and a dark brown wolf emerged.

My breath got stuck in my throat and my vision became dizzy as my eyes landed on someone I hadn't seen in years, someone who had taught me everything I knew and had always sworn to protect me for as long as he lived. My father.

My dad hadn't been much of a fighter when he ran away with my mother. He'd gone through the basic training that every wolf had to go through at a young age, but apart from that he mainly just stuck to his day job and kept his head down. It was only when they'd run away together and became rogues that he started paying attention.

He started by learning hand to hand combat in his human form against other humans, learning the basic skills that everyone would need to know in case they were approached and attacked. Once he was satisfied that he'd learnt everything that the humans could teach him he started to teach himself how to fight in wolf form. With his knowledge of fighting in human form he'd picked it up quickly, and before Daniel was even born he'd become quite well known in the rogue world for holding his own in a fight.

That's where I had learnt all my moves from, all my tips and tricks when it came to fighting off rogues. My dad had taught me all of it.

At the time, I'd been grateful that we'd had him around, and that he had the skills and knowledge to protect us. It meant we'd been safe, and not an easy target for others to pick on when looking for trouble. Now I wish he'd never learnt it. I wish he'd never learnt any of it.

The second, smaller door to the cage hadn't opened yet, leaving my dad standing in the metal corridor as he stared unwavering at Xavier, his next opponent, through the metal fence.

"This sure is a treat for us all tonight folks, not only is this wolf the father of the Rogue Killer's mate, but we also know a tiny little detail from his past which we think will make this an unforgettable fight," the man announced.

What was he talking about?

"Rogue killer... You were given that title because of your quest to hunt down and kill every rogue who was involved in the attack that killed your parents and little sister all those years ago. Well you now have the opportunity to add one more name to that list."

As soon as the words left his lips my stomach dropped. He couldn't seriously mean what I thought he meant... could he? I mean yes, my dad worked with some rogues sometimes to get enough money for us to live off when the money from my uncle didn't come through, but he would have never gone so far as to invade a pack's territory... would he?

I looked over at Xavier to see his reaction. I couldn't even begin to imagine what he must be feeling right now, but I knew it couldn't be good. I was counting on the fact that Xavier would maybe just knock my dad out somehow and not kill him, but with this new bit of information and the way I know Xavier reacts to people talking about his family, I knew this couldn't end well.

Xavier stood stock still as he stared ahead at my dad. His fists were clenched by his sides and were shaking ever so slightly with the will to stay in his human form for as long as possible.

Before I could even blink, the gate separating the two opened and the battle between two of the most important people in my life began.

Xavier had shifted at the last possible second, before darting out of the way of my dad's first attack on him. I was torn between wanting to look away from the bloody battle that was taking place right before my eyes and not being able to tear my eyes from the two wolves as they both tried to lock their jaws round the other's throat. I stared as silent tears streamed down my face, these monsters knew the exact way to get into Xavier's head. They knew if they presented my dad as his fight partner, he wouldn't put up much of a fight, but with the new information these people had just supplied him with, it was enough to poke the bear and get a reaction out of him. The man Xavier was fighting was no longer my father to him, he was someone involved in the murder of his entire family.

I once again wrestled with the man holding me back as the sounds of growls and snarls filled the room. Thankfully, my capture was so engrossed in the ongoing fight he didn't realise what I was doing, because all it took was a swift kick to the guy's shin and an elbow to his nose for him to release me.

I didn't waste a second as I kneed him in the head and elbowed him in the back of the neck, leaving him face down and unconscious on the floor.

My movements seemed to grab the attention of the guy standing next to me but there wasn't much he could do to stop me seeing as he had a thrashing Anna to deal with, who had decided to take a page out of my book and try to escape. I quickly dealt with him the same way I dealt with my own bodyguard and before long we were both free and heading for the secret tunnel.

"Jax is mad we didn't wait for him," Anna panted as we continued our sprint down the dimly lit hallway.

"Well tell him to get *himself* out of danger, we don't have much time," I shouted as we came to the fork in the road.

"Blaine follow me," Anna yelled behind her as she ran down the opposite tunnel to the one we'd previously gone down. "Trust me."

I did, with my life.

I quickly followed her as the sounds of cheers and snarls were quickly replaced with the echoes of our feet slapping against the dust covered floor and our laboured breathing as we continued to run at full speed.

"Where are we *going*?" I whispered. I wasn't sure why I was trying to keep my voice at a low volume, we weren't exactly doing anything to keep our approach a secret.

"Here," Anna suddenly exclaimed as she pointed to a gap in the wall.

I slowed down to a stop and hugged the wall with my back, hoping to peer in and get a look at what we were working with, but before I could peer my head around Anna ran past me straight into the room.

"Anna what the-" I hissed as I followed after her into the room. My words were cut short however as I came face to face with screen upon screen littering the walls of the cave and members from our pack running around the room like headless chickens. It was clear we were in some form of control room, there were security cameras covering an entire wall whilst the other was littered with wires and circuit boards. Apart from that I had no idea what I was looking at, thankfully it seemed some of the pack members did.

Two of them were sitting in front of the desk, each frantically tapping away at the keyboard in front of them as their eyes never wavered from the computer screens they were working on. My eyes caught a screen displaying the fight between my dad and Xavier, but I quickly looked away, unable to bring myself to witness it.

"Anna what's going on?" I asked as I turned to her. I had interrupted her talking to two other pack members as they finished binding some unknown and unconscious people to a chair.

"They're trying to break into the main server, that way we can control all the electrical functions of this place including the automatic doors, the cell doors and the collars around the wolves' necks," she explains. "We believe they're not only electrocuting them when they make too much noise, but also stopping them from shifting back into their human form. Our hope is that as soon as their collar is released, they'll turn back into their human form and along with it get their human emotions back."

I shivered at the thought of being forced to remain in my wolf form for any stretch of time. Don't get me wrong, I love being in my wolf form, the freedom you feel when you release her and just run for the sake of running. But being in your wolf form for too long could do serious harm to you, both physically and mentally.

A wolf's brain couldn't cope with the complex number of emotions that a human brain felt. Going through something like forced shifts could cause the human side of you to go dormant or even disappear altogether.

"That was why Julie didn't recognise me, if what you're saying is true then she's been forced to be in her wolf form for over two years," I exclaimed, worry lacing my tone.

Anna just nodded at me grimly as she walked over to me and pulled me in for a hug. "It'll be okay Blaine," she reassured me as she rubbed my back up and down in soothing circles.

"How could it though? My mate and dad are at each other's throats, literally! My brother and sister may never remember who they are, and we haven't even *found* my mum yet, how could everything be alright?"

252

"It just has to be," she said with determination as she looked into my eyes.

I was just about to respond, when we were both interrupted by one of the girls working on the computer.

"We're in."

Chapter Thirty-Three
Blaine's POV

Everything happened so quickly.

Anna instantly gave the order to override the system and with a push of a button everything seemed to happen at once.

It seemed that not only were the collars and doors controlled by this system, but so was everything else. The feed from the security cameras instantly died, causing the once clear picture to become black and white lines of static flickering across the screen. The almost too bright artificial lights significantly dimmed and were replaced with a red hue, signalling that their electronic systems had all failed.

I could also hear barking and snarling coming from down the corridor, meaning the collars had been deactivated, and I just hoped that the wolves figured out that they could shift so that they didn't attack each other in a bid to escape.

The one thing that really had me on edge though was the fact that I couldn't see what was going on in the main room anymore, or more specifically the fight that was no doubt still going on between my dad and Xavier.

"Anna I've got to get back, I need to make sure my Dad and Xavier don't kill each other," I shouted at her over the alarms that were blaring from the ceiling. I didn't wait for her reply as I turned on my heel and sprinted out the door and back down the hallway towards the fight ring. I could hear yelling and screaming in the distance, but I didn't let that deter me as I continued my advance, my mind solely focused on breaking up the fight that was currently going on between two of the most important people in my life. I knew that if I lost either of them, I wouldn't survive. I needed to make sure they were okay.

I rounded the corner where the fork in the road was but skidded to a stop when I came face to face with a wolf that made me instantly well up. My Mum.

"Mum?"

At the sound of my voice her hackles instantly raised as she turned around to face me, her teeth bared, and her head held down in an aggressive stance. I could see that the collar was no longer around her neck, having fallen off with the loss of power to them, but that didn't instantly make her shift back into her human form.

"Mum it's me," I whispered as I held my hands out in front of me, trying to look as least threatening as I could. Mum continued to advance on me, slowly taking one step at a time, as she backed me into the cave's wall, the jagged rocks cutting into my shoulder blades.

I had no idea what to do, no idea how to break her out of this lifestyle she had been forced to live in for so long, as I continued to stare pleadingly into her eyes. How do I explain to her that she was no longer a pawn in someone else's sick games and that she was free to leave and shift at will? To see her family whole again for the first time in years.

An idea popped into my head, but it was risky. It could either trigger her to attack me, or it could free her from whatever spell that was currently locking her into her wolf form. God, I hoped it was the latter.

I somehow had to free the human side of her brain from being trapped inside her wolf form, kind of like waking my mum up so that she could take control over her body again and remember who she was as a *person* and not just as an *animal*.

One of the strongest senses we had as a wolf was our sense of smell, and through that we could tell nearly everything about another wolf. Whether it was pack or rogue, friend or foe… or even family. If our scent was strongest when we were in our wolf form, then maybe I had to be *in* my wolf form for my scent to be strong enough for my mum to recognise me and help wake her up from wherever she was lying dormant.

"Don't attack me," I repeatedly pleaded in a whisper, as I shrugged off my jacket. "Remember Mum," I breathed as I felt the shift start to overtake me. "Remember who you are and who I am to you," I begged before collapsing onto the ground and welcomed the shift.

It was one of the slowest shifts I'd ever done, and the slower the shift the more it took its toll. It was as if fighting the shift used up more energy than accepting it, and after it was over, I lay panting and exhausted on the floor. Even though I was drained, I remained as alert as I possibly could, my ears pricked up high and my nose twitching as it took in the smells around me to make sure I was aware of my Mum's exact movements. I had no idea what she was about to do, she could just as easily attack me as she could accept me, and I had to be ready for any outcome. I just hoped that she wasn't too far gone to recognise me.

I slowly stood up on shaky legs, once I was sure that she wasn't going to attack me, keeping my movements slow and as least threatening as I possibly could to keep my mum at ease.

Looking over at her now I could tell that she was more confused and inquisitive than frightened. It was extremely out of character for a wolf to shift in the way that I just did, so slow and open. It left you vulnerable, and for someone who had lived in a world where vulnerability meant certain death, there was no doubt why she was so confused.

I used that confusion to my advantage, slowly inched my way towards her, inch by inch, so that my scent could reach her and she could understand who I was.

When she didn't openly reject my advances and I didn't see any threatening body language from her, I took another few steps forward and whined, allowing my desperation to seep through as I stared into her eyes. *Come on mum, recognise me.*

I froze as she took a hesitant step towards me, making sure she knew that *she* was in control of the situation, and with a few more calculated steps forward from her we were finally nose to nose. I looked into her eyes, hoping to see some form of change in them as recognition slowly started to seep in.

At first nothing happened, she just stared at me with blank golden eyes, but as time passed the tension around us started to shift. Her eyes started to swirl different colours and before I could blink, I was staring into the chocolate-coloured eyes of my mother.

I almost howled with happiness as I watched her bones slowly start to crack and shift. It took a few seconds for her to shift back, seeing as she'd been forced into the one form for so long, but eventually she had completely shifted and was back into her human form.

She was lying in a tense ball on the floor, sweat and dirt streaked across her skin, and I quickly walked over to my open rucksack so that I could grab a T-shirt from the pile. I had originally brought the spare sets of clothes for me, just in case I accidently shifted and shredded the clothes I was wearing, but looking at my mum now I could tell that she was in no state to shift back any time soon. She was as thin as a twig and panting heavily at the strain her body had just gone through.

As grimy and sweaty as she was, I couldn't help but walk over to her and lick her cheek, hoping that she understood just how grateful I was to see her right now.

"Blaine?" My mum whispered, her voice quiet and croaky through years of not using it.

I whined a small confirmation as I lay the button up top over her body. It would swamp her as the shirt was actually Xavier's, and she was so tiny and thin I thought she'd break under her own body weight, but it would do its job.

"You found us," she sobbed as she looked up at me, eyes full of pride and gratitude.

I hated the fact that I couldn't communicate with her, the downsides of creating the mated link with Xavier, but I hoped that she could see just how happy and proud I was of her for fighting against her instinct to stay hidden in her mind and to come out and fight.

Just then a loud bark and whine sounded from behind me, and I looked back to find my sister standing there with a huge wolf grin on her face and her tongue flopping out the side of her mouth. It seems like she had no trouble finding her way back into her body and remembering who we were.

I ran over to her and rested my head on her shoulder whilst she did the same to me, our form of a hug as we basked in each other's company. I breathed in her scent, and even under the blood and dirt, I could smell the calming scent of my little sister.

We stood there for a second, me savouring the feeling that I had finally gotten my family back, before I reluctantly raised my head and looked back down the hallway towards the main room where I knew dad and Xavier would be. I knew they both needed my help, needed me to break them up and show them that they no longer needed to be at each other's throats, but at the same time I didn't want to leave my mum and sister here alone and vulnerable.

"We've got them Blaine!" I heard Anna yell from down the hallway. "Go and save your mate and dad from each other."

I nodded my head over at my mum and sister, letting them know that Anna could be trusted, before turning around and sprinting off.

I just hoped I wasn't too late.

...

When I finally made it back into the main cave I was met with chaos. People were running in every direction, whether it be from the recently released wolves or from the guards waving around their tranquiliser guns trying to recapture the ones who had escaped. At least I hoped they were tranquiliser guns.

I ignored it all as I kept my eyes locked on the fighting cage. I didn't know where the rest of our pack were, whether they had gone back to help their Luna or whether they were helping the crowd escape, but I couldn't see a single familiar face as I weaved my way through the crowd.

Up ahead I could tell that the battle between my dad and Xavier was still raging on. Both appeared to be injured, but neither seemed to be showing any sign of surrendering as they continued to circle each other with their hackles raised and their teeth showing. I noticed the door to the fight ring had sprung open in the electrical surge and without hesitation I sprinted towards it, jumping over obstacles and darting around people in my attempt to reach them.

When I got within reaching distance, I jumped onto the slightly raised ring and stood in the doorway as I waited for an opportunity to come between them. I was no idiot; it would be near suicidal to get in between a fight like this when they were both more focused on ripping each others throat out than the environment around them. Even if they were my mate and dad, logic and awareness go out the window when you're locked in a battle like this one.

They were both snarling at each other as my dad swiped at Xavier's front paws, trying to knock him down so that my dad had the height advantage. It didn't work as Xav quickly dodged my dad's claws at the last second, jumping out of the way and out of my dad's reach, making sure he never gave my dad his back.

'Xavier?' I tried to yell at him through the link, hoping that I could gain his attention, but it did nothing because the next second Xavier was on my dad's back

and trying to roll him over so that he could get to his soft underbelly.

They were both so evenly matched, they were more likely to kill each other over fatigue than skill, and my heart thundered in my chest as I watched them claw at each other's fur. They had already been fighting for a solid ten to fifteen minutes, so I knew they were both exhausted, but both refused to show it as that would portray weakness to their opponent.

I stared on, feeling helpless that I couldn't do anything, as I watched the two wolves fight. This wasn't like a fight where there was a goodie and a baddie, if I jumped in and helped one person and not the other I could risk injuring one of them or getting injured myself seeing as I couldn't defend myself against them. What I really needed was more people by my side. With more of us we could distract each fighter, making sure our back was covered so that we didn't risk getting attacked from behind.

Just when I was about to jump in, throwing caution to the wind, I felt a presence behind me.

I turned around, ready to attack if I needed to as I knew it wasn't someone from my pack, but froze when I spotted the wolf that was in front of me.

My brother had found his way to us.

Chapter Thirty-Four
Xavier's POV

I had been ready to sacrifice myself when I had seen Blaine's dad emerge for the newly opened door. She had been looking for him for so long and she thought so highly of him that I knew I couldn't bring myself to hurt him. Hurting him meant hurting my mate, and that was something my wolf refused to do.

That was until the announcer had opened his mouth.

Upon learning that Blaine's dad had been involved in the attack that killed my whole family I saw red. All those years I had been seeking revenge for them, I had never truly known whether the rogue I was fighting had been directly involved in the attack or not. I had always just gone on the principle that a rogue was a rogue and needed to be dealt with.

Thankfully Blaine had opened my eyes to how prejudice that thought process had been and I had learned that not all rogues were evil. That knowledge was tucked into the far corners of my brain now, so far out of reach I couldn't grab onto it even if I wanted to.

I had one goal in mind, kill the man who had lent a hand in murdering my family.

It was an evenly matched fight, each of us giving as good as we got, but neither of us let up as we continued our battle in a blind rage. I ached all over, feeling the pulls and tugs of my muscles as I continued to force them into action even as they screamed for relief and a chance to rest. My skin felt itchy and hot where the rogue had gotten some lucky shots, his claws cutting through my protective fur and sinking into my skin as it tore it open.

I needed to end this, end the pain I carried with me every time something reminded me of my family. If I could kill this rogue, end his miserable life, then it would be one less rogue for me to worry about, one less splinter in my side. Maybe if I killed him, my pain would lessen.

That wasn't the case with every other life you've taken a voice whispered in my head and I had to shake my head from the thought as I narrowly missed a swiping claw to my front legs. *Think about what you're doing Xavier* the voice continued and I darted backwards swiftly so that I wouldn't take a hit in my distracted state. Who was that voice? It wasn't mine, or anyone else in my packs. It wasn't even Blaine's. This voice was softer somehow, almost breathy as it breezed through my head and embedded itself into my brain.

As the voice rolled around in my head, I suddenly became more and more aware of what I was doing and who I was fighting. This wasn't just any rogue, this was Blaine's father, this was my mate's dad, and I was currently doing everything I could to try and kill him.

What was I doing?

This wasn't me, this wasn't who I *wanted* to be.

I suddenly became aware of what I was doing as I pounced on Blaine's dad's back and rolled him over so that I could get to the underside of his belly. My wolf, who had taken control of my body throughout this entire fight, finally decided to retract his hold on me and I had enough sense to pull my claw away at the last second so that I didn't catch my opponent's sensitive flesh and kill him.

I jumped away from Blaine's dad as he lay shocked on the floor, his belly still exposed, and looked around, trying to find out what had drawn my attention enough for me to lose focus in the middle of a fight, and was instantly surprised at the chaos that was going on around us. How had I not noticed this before?

There were people and wolves running around everywhere, some screaming in terror as they ran away whilst others letting out battle cries as they chased someone down. What the hell happened?

A growl suddenly sounded from behind me, and I looked over to find Blaine standing in the ring with a wolf towering over her. She didn't show fear when facing off with the wolf, but she didn't exactly seem comfortable in his presence either, and that's when I recognised who he was. He was the wolf who had been involved in the fight as we'd walked in, the one who had *killed* his opponent.

I watched on in fear as I saw him crouch slightly, preparing himself to spring into action, and just when I was about to jump in between them I clocked movement in the corner of my eye, Blaine's dad.

He ran towards me at full speed, not taking his eyes off what was going on behind me and just when I was about to tense, readying myself for impact, he sailed over me and knocked over the unknown wolf who had been staring Blaine down. I swiftly spun around and got in between Blaine and her father, wanting to protect her just in case he still wasn't himself.

"It's alright Xavier," Blaine linked me as she nudged me slightly from behind. *"Look into his eyes, they're clear like yours and mine, not frosted over slightly with the absence of his human form. He remembers me,"* she linked as I suddenly felt a massive crash of relief through the mate bond.

Blaine went to take a step around me, but I growled a warning at her to stay behind me. This man had been in captivity for over two years, being forced to do God knows what to other wolves and that wasn't even taking into consideration his past before coming here. I didn't trust him at all, and I'd be damned if I was going to let him anywhere near my mate.

"Xav what are you doing? He's my father, he won't hurt me," she muttered as she tried to step around me again, but I just moved with her so she couldn't find an opening, my eyes never leaving her father or the other wolf who was now slowly trying to stand up after the massive hit he'd just taken.

"I don't care who he is to you Blaine, he just tried to kill me and I'm not going to risk him doing that to you too," I growled.

"Don't act all high and mighty Xavier, you just tried to kill him too and I'm not holding that against you, am I?"

"I had every reason to, he helped murder my family. Did you really think I was going to just let him get away with that? After everything you know about me?"

"And do you really think that I'm going to let you harm him in any way, after everything you've learnt

about me?' She replied as she once again tried to dodge out from behind me.

This time she was more successful, and before I knew it she was standing in front of me and resting her head on her dad's shoulder, the only form of hug we could do whilst in wolf form. I watched closely as I took note of every minute movement her dad made. I didn't trust him. Yes, it may have everything to do with his involvement in my family's death, but why shouldn't it. It took a certain type of someone to invade a pack's land and kill for the sake of killing.

I was just about to get in between them again, feeling uneasy with him being so close to Blaine, when I spotted movement in my peripheral vision. The strange wolf had recovered enough to figure out that his attacker was standing right here and decided to seek some form of revenge. Too bad he thought *I* was the wolf who had originally knocked him down.

I shifted so that I was in between him and Blaine, but before the attacker could even get close to us, Blaine's dad jumped in the way so that he took the full force of the blow.

I stood there for a second, shocked that he had put himself between me and the angry rogue, as I watched them circle each other in the fighting ring.

"Xavier, that's my brother, Daniel," Blaine sobbed as she watched her dad and brother leap towards each other.

That was her brother? *"Then why the* hell *is he attacking us if he's your family?"*

"I-I don't know, maybe his human side hasn't re-emerged after we'd managed to remove the shock collars. To him this is probably just another random fight

that he was being forced into by those monsters that took him," she explained, her eyes fixated in front of her. *"It probably doesn't help that we're in the ring right now. If his brain has been conditioned to fight to survive, the ring is more than likely triggering his fight instincts. I have to help them in some way, make sure they don't kill each other,"* she stated as she started to take a few steps towards the brawling wolves.

I was just about to stop her, yell at her to get back so she wouldn't get hurt, when her dad managed to hold Daniel and pin him down so he couldn't move. That took some serious strength to do, and I hated to admit that I was secretly impressed by him. What he managed to do next though was something I don't think I'd ever seen in my life.

Whilst her dad continued to pin Daniel down, using his body weight and paws to keep him immobile, he slowly started to shift back into his human form. I stared in amazement as I watched him partially shift without ever letting up his hold on his son.

"Blaine get... get out of here," he panted as he looked over at his daughter. "I'll deal with him; you get your mum and sister out of here-."

I could tell he wanted to say more but before he could he lost his grip on Daniel and slipped back into his wolf form so that he could defend himself. I honestly wasn't sure how he was still staying upright. Between the fight with me, the partial shift, restraining Daniel and being as malnourished as he was, I'd be on the floor by now if I were him.

My dad had always told me that you'd found strength where you never thought possible when it was to save your family and the ones you loved. I guess that was what his drive was, the fight to save his wife and children from this life that they'd been forced to live for so long.

"You heard the man Blaine, let's go before he can't hold him any longer," I told her as I nudged her slightly with my head towards the door.

"Jax, any news on Blaine's mum and sister?" I linked him and I continued to nudge a reluctant Blaine out of the cage and back into the semi chaos of the people around us. The crowds had started to empty out by now, but there were still people running around as they tried to escape the teeth and claws of the shifted wolves along with the barrels of guns that were swinging around.

"Annabelle has them hidden in the woods with a few pack members, she's treating their wounds and giving them some food and water. How about you? Are you all good?" he asked.

I nodded before remembering he couldn't see me and quickly responded to him. *"Yep we're both good, just trying to get Blaine out of here,"* I informed him as I gave her another gentle nudge.

I could understand her hesitation, she didn't want to leave her brother and father in the state that they were in after only just finding them, but we had to get ourselves out of here. Most of the wolves who had escaped were now gone, running off into the forest so as not to be re-captured. It was amazing news, knowing that we had helped free countless wolves from the captured lifestyle of illegal fighting, but on the other hand it was bad news for us, because the guys working for this fight club now had no one to shoot at, no one except us.

I spotted a guy trying to sneak up on us, gun in hand, as he aimed it straight at Blaine's head, but I shoved her out of the way before the bullet could reach its target. She spun on me, obviously not understanding why I had pushed her, but when she finally spotted the guy holding a gun, she quickly changed targets and ran right at him, knocking the gun out of his hand before hitting him over the head with her paw.

I smiled over at her as I watched her take the guy down before turning my back on her so that we could each watch the others six. The room had nearly emptied out by now, and from what I could tell there were only three or four pack members in here with the odd human scattered about who hadn't yet managed to find an escape route. The thing that grabbed my attention though was the amount of biker gang style guys that were around us, all sporting guns and all of them pointing in our direction.

"Umm Jax? I think we're going to need a hand over here after all," I stated through the pack link as I watched more and more guns getting pointed in our direction.

"I'm here, I'll watch on from my position and take them out one at a time whilst you draw their attention," he informed me and it wasn't till now that I spotted his wolf stalk around in the shadows, using the darkness as his camouflage as he took care of one biker guy after the other. Sometimes it paid to be the Alpha and have a jet-black coat to conceal him in the shadows.

"Blaine, Anna has your mum and sister safe outside, we just need to focus on getting out of here alive, okay?" I linked her as I walked backwards until I felt her tail touch mine. *"Jax is taking them out one by one, so we need to stall them until then."*

"And how do you suppose we do that?' She asked. *'We're both in wolf form so can't exactly talk our way out,"* she huffed.

"Well, I have to give you credit where credits due," a voice suddenly said as a figure appeared amongst the group of gun happy people. "It takes some serious skill to break up this type of organisation," the voice continued to say as the figure finally stepped out of the group and made himself known. "Oh, the name is Benjamin by the way, Benny for short," he smiled as he ran his hand through his beard.

Chapter Thirty-Five
Xavier's POV

"Blaine, any idea who this guy is?" I asked her, not taking my eyes off the ringleader.

"No idea" she replied as she too kept her eyes locked onto the man in front of us.

"Oh don't act like that," the man laughed as he looked over at Blaine. "After all, if it wasn't for your sorry excuse of a father we could have been *family*," he chuckled, his laugh bouncing off the stone cave walls. Even though he laughed through his statement there was an evil glint in his eyes that told me to watch him, to not relax.

I heard Blaine growl next to me and I stepped in front of her slightly, whether it was to protect her or him though I didn't know. She could give as good as she got in a fight, and while I would pay to see her rip this guy's throat out, I didn't want to see what his little goonies would do after their boss had been killed.

"Oh come on Blaine, it's not every day you get to meet the man who should have been your *father*."

By now I was beyond confused. Not only was his science way off when thinking that genetically he could be her father, but also how twisted his brain was in thinking that he could ever have been with her mum after she had already found her mate.

"Blaine, do you know what the hell he's talking about?"

"I can make a wild guess yeah," she sighed. *"He's probably the Alpha my mum was promised to back before she met my dad. Remember? She'd gone to his pack to meet the new Alpha and to be married off to him, but found my father there instead?"*

"And he left his pack stranded purely because he didn't get what he wanted?" I asked, shocked that an Alpha would ever do anything so selfish.

"Either that or the pack somehow crumbled," she grimaced.

"Get them some clothes someone," Benjamin suddenly yelled as he pointed at a random guy. "Them talking through their link is really started to piss me off," he growled.

The man scurried off in the hunt for some spare clothes and was gone only a few short seconds before he came running back in, a T-shirt and two pairs of shorts clutched in his hands.

"Put those on, not being able to see your facial reactions is grating on me."

I wasn't sure I liked the idea of us shifting out of our wolf form, but it wasn't like we had much of a choice in the matter. With a number of guns pointed in our direction and the main man staring us down with his arms crossed and a smirk on his face, I held my chin up as I began to shift.

"Blaine wait until I've finished and then hide behind me so that these freaks do get a show," I told her, hoping for once that she'd do as she was told.

I quickly slipped the pair of cut off jean shorts on and turned around so that I could hold the top up for Blaine to hide behind.

"Come on love... give us a glimpse," one of the creeps hollered whilst others around us wolf whistled.

I could feel my eyes swirl gold at the disrespect they were showing my mate but managed to keep a hold on my wolf long enough until Blaine had managed to tug the top over her head and pull the draw strings of the trackies they had given her. I growled when I got a whiff of another man's scent on the clothes but didn't act on my anger as we both turned round to face Benjamin, me standing slightly ahead of Blaine just in case anything went down.

"Better," was all he said as he looked over at both of us.

"What the hell do you want with us?" I demanded as I stared the guy straight in the eye. "You said so yourself, your little *business* is over, so why keep us here?"

"But where's the fun in letting you go?" he laughed as he looked around at the men surrounding him. "You see, we've been real nice to our wolves, making sure they had enough food and water so that they wouldn't starve... just about anyway," he laughed. "But now the fighting ring has collapsed, and we have no reason to keep them alive, we may as well have a little fun and games with the wolves we have left, don't you think?" he smirked, looking Blaine straight in the eye as he did so.

I tensed, not liking what this guy was implying as I took a step closer to Blaine, taking her hand in mine. *"Blaine when I say run, you run okay?"* I linked her as I squeezed her hand tightly.

"But what about you?" She questioned as her head shifted from side to side, taking in all our options.

"Just do it okay?" I begged before closing off the link so that I could talk to Jax.

"Any time now man, these guys aren't going to stand around chatting for much longer," I told him as I tried to spot him in the shadows.

"I've got you man, whenever you're ready," he replied.

Benjamin suddenly took a step forward making us take a step back, wanting to keep the same distance between us.

"And Blaine," Benjamin continued. "We've got *a lot* of catching up to do," he almost sang as he stared her down. "Over two years of it," he growled as he took another two steps towards us.

"NOW!" I yelled as I let go of Blaine's hand and lunged for Benjamin.

Gunshots rang in the air as the guards tried to shoot us down, but apart from a bullet grazing my left arm they all went wide. The wound stung but I didn't let it faze me as I leapt onto Benjamin and tackled him to the ground, hoping that if I had him in a compromised position the gunshots would stop, and it could give Blaine enough time to escape.

Unfortunately, I hadn't been fast enough as right at the last second Benjamin turned and dodged my attack, his Alpha blood assisting him in moving just that little bit faster and stronger than me. Damn it.

I looked beside me to find Blaine battling against four of her own rogues, all having dropped their weapons and shifted into their wolf form. Before I could do anything to help her, Benjamin stood back up and stared me down.

"Come on then Beta, let's see what kind of fight you've got in you in human form," he smirked before sailing a punch in my direction, making it land with a crunch straight on my cheek bone.

My vision blurred for a second, the punch having rattled my brain, but I forced my eyes to focus just in time to duck the second punch coming my way. Benjamin missing his target made him stumble slightly forward off balance, and before he had time to correct himself, I swiftly kneed him in the gut before elbowing him the back of his neck. It wouldn't knock him out, but it would slow him down long enough for me to get in another hit or two.

Jax had also now joined the fight, taking on a few of his own opponents as they tried to battle taking on an Alpha. They may have had the numbers against us, but we definitely had the skill. Half of them were only human and were fairly easy to handle, leaving just four rogue's left, one for Blaine and three for Jax.

I had the pleasure of going head-to-head against Benjamin, the man who'd kidnapped Blaine's family and caused her so much pain in the last few years.

We had each gotten a few solid hits in, but thanks to Blaine's training I knew what to look for and how best to beat this guy. He may have been an Alpha, but he was still a rogue, and they were always hot headed and tire easily without a pack to help back them up.

I was just about to deliver the final blow of the fight, knowing that he wouldn't get up after the last kick I'd landed to his ribs, when I heard a yelp come from behind me, making me lose my balance and stumble forwards into him.

The yelp had come from Blaine as she limped away from her opponent, a bite mark clearly visible on her back leg. I turned to run to her, planning on helping her, when I was dragged backwards by the hair on the crown of my head and slammed onto the floor making my head bounce against the stone beneath me. That was going to leave a mark.

I groaned as I began to see stars and held the back of my head where I could feel blood slowly oozing out. I looked up at Benjamin through half lidded eyes as he smirked down at me, blood covering his teeth from a split lip I had given him.

"It seems like your bark was a bit too big for your bite there *Rogue killer,*" he chuckled as he looked over to where Blaine was being held at gunpoint.

I scrambled to get up, hoping to get to her in time before the trigger was pulled, but was pushed down with Benjamin's foot on my chest as he forced me not to move. "These women can really distract us right? I mean before her mother I had it all. I was the future Alpha of my pack, and I had any girl I could have ever wanted," he chuckled. "But now…"

"Then why did you leave?" I asked, wheezing through the pressure he continued to put on my rib cage.

He shrugged and looked over at Blaine with a smirk, "I wanted what I couldn't have," he explained. "And her mother made it very clear that she was definitely something I could never have."

"So you left your pack and started all this just because you couldn't have *one girl*? A girl that wasn't even your mate to begin with?"

276

"What can I say," he shrugged as he finally looked down at me. "I'm someone who holds a grudge," he almost hissed out as he grinned down at me.

"Take her to my room, I'll deal with her later," Benjamin growled at the guy holding Blaine at gunpoint.

"NOOO!" I screamed as I tried to force his foot off my chest, failing miserably as the stars behind my eyes danced.

"Well... as fun as this has been, your services are no longer required," Benjamin smirked down at me as he pointed a gun at my face. "Just think, now you get to be with your family," he laughed as he loaded a round into the chamber.

I continued to struggle my way out from under his boot, hoping that I could somehow dislodge it enough for me to slip out and kick the back of his knee in or something. I looked around for anything that could somehow help me, but I saw nothing, no rocks that I could smash his shin in with and no nearby guns to point back at him. Jax wasn't even able to help me, he was still fighting his own opponents. Even if he had taken one of them out, he still had two snapping at his throat and clawing at his face.

I took one last look at Blaine as I watched her being forcibly dragged away from me and muttered a quick *"I love you,"* through the bond before looking back up at Benjamin dead in the eye. If I was going to go down today, then the least I could do was stare my killer in the eye and show no fear as I watch him pull the trigger.

"Bye bye little Rogue Killer," Benjamin almost sang as he squeezed the trigger, causing a loud bang to echo throughout the stone cave.

But... how was it that I could hear the echo if I was supposed to be dead?

Chapter Thirty-Six
Blaine's POV

"Nooo!" I screamed through the mate link as I heard the gun go off. It was like that was the trigger that gave me another burst of energy. I could feel the adrenaline surging through my veins as my heart pumped blood around my body at an abnormally high rate.

I turned on my captor with a new sense of purpose, aiming to free myself from the hand holding onto the scruff of my neck as my brain flooded with images of Xavier. It was a difficult task, the man holding me back was a wolf himself and knew exactly where to stand so that my teeth and claws couldn't make contact with his human skin. He also knew that by twisting the fur that he had in his hand he could force my head to turn in another direction because of the pain it caused me.

I fought through it, determined to get to my mate and help him anyway I could. After a few kicks and swipes of my paws, most of them unsuccessful, I finally managed to make contact with his left ankle. He screamed in agony as the bone snapped in two at the blow and I sighed in relief when he released his hold on my scruff, my eyes watering from the pain of my fur being pulled out.

I quickly shook it off and turned to where I knew Benjamin would be, my mind focused solely on seeking revenge for him taking my Xavier away from me.

What I saw though made me pause in confusion. Xavier was lying on the floor, coughing and cringing in pain as his right hand held onto his shoulder, the gun lying useless at his feet, but he was alive.

He was alive!

My mind was so focused on the fact that Xavier hadn't been killed, having been shot in the shoulder and not the chest like Benjamin had originally intended to, I didn't notice what was going on just to the right of me.

Jax had finally managed to shake his attackers, just long enough to tackle Benjamin to the ground, resulting in him losing his balance and missing his target on Xavier's chest. I sighed in relief as I silently thanked him, before running over to Xavier to see the extent of his injury.

Xavier was groaning and hissing in pain by the time I got to him, his body convulsing as a small amount of foamy pink blood trickled out of his mouth and down the side of his cheek. I frowned in confusion as I watched his body shake, his wolf trying to come through, to try and heal him, but unable to due to the bullet still lodged in his skin.

Being shot in the shoulder was bad for us, don't get me wrong, there were many arteries and nerves that could get nicked or severed from the bullet entering our body, but it shouldn't cause this type of reaction. He should be bleeding yes but not foaming at the mouth and convulsing uncontrollably.

I tried to talk to him through the bond, asking him what was wrong so that I could somehow help him, but he didn't respond, in too much pain to even try and reply.

I whined as I stared on helplessly, feeling useless as to what I could do for him. I took a step forward and placed my nose near his wound and inhaled deeply, trying to figure out why his skin was starting to bubble and blister around the entry wound where the bullet had gone. I coughed and flinched backwards as the scent hit the back of my nostrils, the intensity causing me to retch as I felt a burning sensation travel through my head and down into my lungs.

Wolfsbane.

This was bad, wolfsbane was poisonous to us. It acted a little bit like acid, burning away at our flesh and killing tissue as it travels throughout our blood stream. We needed to get him out of here and wash the wound out somehow, if the wolfsbane stayed in there for too long it could do irreversible amounts of damage to him. It could even kill him.

I shifted out of my wolf and scoured the floor for scraps of clothing, hoping to find *anything* to mop up as much of the poisonous liquid as I could, and sighed as I found the top I had been given by one of the guards. I also found a flannel shirt lying not too far away, completely in tact. My guess was that it was wrapped around one of the audience's waists and had come loose during the panic.

I slipped the flannel shirt on before collecting the scraps of my old top and ran over so that I could press them down on Xavier's wound. The wolfsbane soaked through the fabric and onto my skin but I ignored the pain as I focused on my task at hand.

I cried silently as I watched him scream in agony every time the fabric made contact with his skin, but I grit my teeth and carried on with what I was doing.

"It's going to be fine Xavier," I muttered as my tears fell from my chin and landed on his chest. "It's all going to be just fine," I repeated. "Just hang in there and once we get you out of here we can make it all better," I sobbed as I continued my task.

Xavier's eyes locked onto mine for a split second as I stared down at him, but I could tell he wasn't really seeing me. His eyes were unfocused and glazed over as he seemed to look through me rather than at me. His skin tone was a horrible white grey colour, and his veins protruded from his skin in an unhealthy dark green, almost black colour, making it painfully obvious that he was in serious trouble from wolfsbane poisoning.

I cried as I watched his eyes close for a second and quickly shook him awake, not allowing him to slip into unconsciousness.

"Xavier you stay with me," I demanded as I threw the fabric coated in wolfsbane as far from us as I could, having soaked up all that I could from his skin.

I was so focused on Xavier that I hadn't realised one of the rogues had escaped Jax and was running in my direction. It wasn't until I heard a furious growl from off in the distance that I turned around with just enough time to duck as a rogue wolf sailed over our bodies, landing just in front of us with a sneer on his lips.

I tensed as I stared at the wolf in front of me, daring him to attack, but before I could so much as blink another wolf flew over me and landed in between us and the rogue, growling at the rogue in a defensive manner.

My brother was here.

I looked over to where I knew Jax was still fighting and noticed that my dad had joined him, tackling Benjamin as he tried to go for Jax's neck. There were only two rogues left now, not including Benjamin, and I sighed as I realised we now had help.

I shifted my focus back to Xavier and stared as I watched the poison travel through his skin. We needed to get him out of here, and seeing as I was the only one free I knew it was up to me.

I wiped my hands on the fabric of my borrowed top, trying to wipe off the wolfsbane that I knew was on there, blistering my palms, and hooked my arms under Xavier's armpits. I knew I wouldn't be strong enough to pick him up, so I just had to try and drag him across the floor and towards the exit, leaving a trail of blood behind us as we went.

At the start Xavier had screamed in agony, the action of me moving him causing him too much pain to remain quiet, but that only lasted a few minutes before he passed out in my arms. I could tell he was still alive, I could still hear his heartbeat, but it was slow and out of rhythm.

I collapsed on the floor a couple of times as the weight of Xavier grew too much for me, but quickly shook off my tiredness and picked him up again. "There is no way... that I am letting you... die on my Xavier... do you hear me?" I panted as I tugged him with all my might. "I will... get us out of here... just you watch," I sobbed and panted as I looked down at his past-out body. After everything we've been through, I wasn't going to let some crazy Alpha with a grudge on my family kill him.

I looked back up at the fighting wolves and stalled as I watched Benjamin pin my father to the ground, him having shifted into his wolf during the scuffle. My mind was torn, on the one hand I knew I needed to get Xavier out of here, but on the other I wanted to help my dad.

It was like I was back in the cage again, not knowing who to defend for fear that it would cause the other more injury. Thankfully though the choice was made for me. As if my dad knew that I was looking at him he glanced up at me and motioned with his head for me to leave him.

I cried but nodded my head, the only thing making me listen to him was the fact that he had Jax and my brother by his side to help him. I continued to try and drag Xavier out, but by now my body was exhausted. It had gone through more shifts in such a short period of time than I'd ever gone through in my life, plus fighting with the rogue and then the hike here in the first place, my body had given in. But we were so close, *so close*.

I cried as I looked down at my unconscious mate, not yet able to admit that I had failed him. I needed to get him out of here, even if it killed me. I shoved my hands underneath his arms and pulled with all my might as I tried to get him out of here, and after what felt like hours, we were finally out of the main arena.

I lay on the ground, panting, but stood up in a defensive stance when I heard footsteps running towards us at an alarming rate. I tensed, ready for whoever came round the corner, but sighed when I saw Jax. He was in his human form, and I blushed slightly when I realised he wasn't wearing any clothes, but quickly pushed that aside as I realised my dad and brother weren't following him.

"Where's the others?" I panted as I watched him crouch down and take Xavier's wrist in his, checking to see how irregular his heartbeat was.

"They told me to run on ahead," he explained as he started to inspect Xavier's bullet wound.

"What do you mean run on ahead?" I yelled in alarm. "You left them?"

"I had no choice Blaine, we need to get Xavier out of there and your father knew you wouldn't just leave your mate here, so he told me to make sure you left this place no matter what. If that means picking you up and dragging you out I will," he stated.

I stared at him for a second as he carefully picked Xavier up off the ground, making sure his wound didn't touch Jax's skin anywhere. "But Jax they're my family," I muttered as I started walking back in the direction I had just come from.

"Blaine stop... look at yourself," he exclaimed, "You can barely stand upright, let alone get in between four fighting wolves and hope to help in some way. If you go there you'll be putting your life and the lives of your family in danger," he explained as he took my wrist in his to stop me going any further. "Just do as your father says and get out of here," he stated as he started to drag me out of the tunnel and towards the main exit.

I started to struggle for a second, not bearing the idea of leaving two of my family members behind, but before I could argue any further my vision started to blur and my body started to slowly shut down against my will, no longer able to handle the stress it had been put under.

The last thing I heard was the sound of a wolf crying in pain as it echoed off the cave walls. I could only pray that it wasn't my dad or Daniel.

Chapter Thirty-Seven
Blaine's POV

When I eventually came around I instantly knew something was missing.

We were no longer in the cave, not even in the forest or outside, but back in the pack lands. I looked around me as I tried to figure out where I was, but quickly realised as I recognised the smell of antiseptic. I was in a hospital, lying on a bed and hooked up to multiple different wires and tubes, as they measured my heart rate and pumped a milky looking fluid into my system.

That wasn't what woke me up though, what had stirred me awake was the sudden empty hole I was experiencing deep in my chest. It was as if someone had ripped my heart out and replaced it with a mechanical device. It was doing everything it should be doing, but it felt unnatural somehow, like it wasn't my own.

I frowned as I held my hand against my chest, feeling the beating that confirmed it *was* in fact there, but still not fully believing it. I stared down at my hand as it moved with every thump, trying to convince my brain that my heart was still intact, but as I slowly looked back up and through the window to my left, I instantly understood why I was feeling so empty inside.

In the room over from mine, just a sheet of glass and an open blind separating us, was Xavier. He was hooked up to multiple wires and tubes, similar to my own, but he looked so much worse. His cheeks were sunken in, and his skin had a sickening grey colour to it that made him look more dead than alive.

I felt my heart rate slowly incline as I took more and more of him in, the heart monitor I was attached to screaming as it hit an unhealthy rate. I paid it no attention, unable to peel my eyes away from the man I had promised to love and protect for the rest of my life.

I needed to get to him.

My body had a mind of its own, and before I could consider what I was doing, I pulled all the needles and wires out from my skin which were keeping me chained to my bed, then slowly stood with the help of my bed rail. The palms of my hands burned as I applied pressure to them, the raw skin blistered and red from being in contact with wolfsbane poison, but I ignored it. I needed to get to Xavier.

I took slow and calculated steps towards his room, ignoring the two nurses who had run over to me and tried to get me to sit back down in bed. But with one look at my gold swirling eyes they backed off, knowing not to get in between a wolf and her injured mate.

I stepped through the threshold to Xavier's hospital room and nearly collapsed to the floor as a sob escaped my lips, rumbling in my chest as I held both my hands to my face, unable to believe that this was my Xavier. He looked even worse than when I first saw him through the window. He looked fragile, like if I touched him his skin would disappear and crack beneath my fingertips.

"Xavier?" I whispered as I came and stood next to him, one hand still covering my mouth whilst the other hovered over his body, not knowing where I could touch him or if I was even allowed to.

"It's okay Blaine, you can touch him," a voice whispered from the corner of the room.

I startled, not realising that someone was in here with me, but relaxed when I saw that it was just Anna. She was slouched in an old armchair in the corner of the room, looking like she hadn't caught a wink of sleep in weeks. Her hair was piled up on top of her head and looked like it could do with a good wash, her eyes were red and puffy, and judging by the amount of tissues that sat next to her I could only assume she had been crying all night.

"Anna what...?" I started to ask before trailing off, unable to figure out how to voice the many questions that were running through my mind.

She smiled up at me slightly before gesturing for me to take the seat next to her, probably seeing my legs wobble as they tried to hold me up.

"Once Jax had gotten both you and Xavier out of that place we ran like a bat out of hell, knowing both you and Xavier didn't have much time thanks to the contact you both had with the wolfsbane. It was touch and go, we had to revive Xavier at least twice on the trek back. We washed off as much as we could in a nearby river, but it didn't do much good, it had already gotten into your blood streams," she explained as she ran a hand down her face.

"Thankfully we got here just in time, Xavier coded again but the medical team managed to get him back, we're now just waiting to see if the fluids will work in flushing out the toxins from his body." She looked over at Xav as he lay motionless on his bed, looking heartbroken that her friend was in this position.

"Thankfully you had very minor amounts of it in your system, so we knew you'd be alright after some rest and fluids, but Xavier... he had a lot of exposure," she sighed, continuing to rub her eyes with the heel of her hand.

"Anna," I whispered as I forced my eyes away from my dying mate and looked over at my friend. "I can't... I mean the bond is..." I stuttered as I frowned, looking down at my hands that were clasped together and shaking in my lap.

"You can't feel it can you?" She asks as she reaches over and cautiously placed her hand on my wrist, not wanting to touch my hand for fear that it might hurt me.

I shook my head as the tears welled in my eyes again "I'm not sure I can survive without him Anna," I explained as I wiped my cheeks. "I mean the pain and emptiness I'm feeling now is almost unbearable," I sobbed. "What am I going to be like if he doesn't make it?"

"Now don't you think like that," Anna demanded, trying to keep her voice strong even when it threatened to wobble. "Xavier is strong, he'll make it through," she said as she nodded her head. "His wolf is just taking some time off to heal... that's all," Anna continued to nod as her eyes remained unwavering on mine. "Once he gets better, you'll be able to feel it again."

I sighed before nodding with her, needing to feel as much positivity as I could right now so as not to break down further. "What about my family? Are they okay?" I asked, needing to distract my brain.

"Well... your mum and sister are doing well; both are resting in a nearby house that we use as a rehabilitation centre," she explained as she smiled up at me.

"And my brother? My dad?"

"They umm... well they didn't..." She stuttered as she struggled to form words to explain what happened to them.

"They didn't make it," I murmured, my voice emotionless as I thought of all the ways I could have tried to help them.

"Now we don't know that for certain," she stated as she held a finger out to me. "We ran ahead, knowing we had to get you both the help you needed. Without the doctors help you and Xavier would have died in less than a day," she explained as she held her hands back in her lap.

"After Jax placed both you and Xavier on the floor, explaining that you were suffering from wolfsbane poisoning, he went to go back in and help them. Your mother stopped him, saying that your dad would never forgive himself if you died trying to help him. She said he would want us to run ahead and get you the help you needed," Anna explained as she looked up at me, worried at what my reaction would be. "She said you'd understand why," she whispered.

I sighed as I brought my knees up to my chest. As much as I wanted to hate everyone for leaving my dad and Daniel behind I couldn't, it had always been our contingency plan.

Years ago, back when we were all still rogues and living together, my dad had decided to make a plan. I thought it had been ridiculous at first, the idea that us kids should run if ever we were ambushed, but dad had been insistent on it. He said, well more like demanded, if the family ever got into trouble, more trouble than he could handle, we should run ahead and leave him there to deal with it. I was never sure if it was pride or something else that made him say it, but his mind had been made up.

He and my mum had a massive argument that night, stating that there was no way she would be leaving her mate behind to fight when there was something she could do to help. He had eventually broken down in tears, shocking us all as we'd never seen him cry before. He had said that he could never forgive himself if he survived something when one of us didn't, that he would rather die than have to bury one of us.

We didn't know where the outburst had come from, but after watching my dad cry, the strongest man I'd known, I knew we would do as he asked. Turns out I was right; dad got his wish after all.

We both stayed in silence after that, just listening to the constant sound of the *beep beep* of Xavier's heart monitor as it slowly lulled me to sleep.

...

It was dark by the time I woke up again. I frowned as I tried to figure out what it was that had disturbed me when I heard hushed voices on the other side of Xavier's door.

"Look I'm sorry okay? I truly am sorry," Anna whispered, sounding more offensive than apologetic.

291

"I don't understand why you can't just heal him," the other voice, Hannah, said.

"I just can't alright? If I could I would, but at the moment it's impossible for me to do so," Anna replied, sounding irritated at Hannah's words.

"But you did it to Jax," Hannah whisper yelled back, "You managed to heal him when that witch had cut his belly with her knife. I really don't see how this is any different," she growled.

"That wasn't me who healed him, and you know it. That was the Goddess when she took over my body," Anna replied as I watched the arms of her shadow flail about slightly.

"So do that again, let the Goddess take over your body so that she can heal him," Hannah pleaded, almost sounding like she was talking to a child, not her Luna and her brother's mate.

"I-I can't," Anna sighed, sounding more defeated than I'd ever heard her before.

"What the hell do you mean you can't?!" Hannah yelled, her voice suddenly rising in volume as she became more irritated.

"I mean I physically can't Hannah, doing that and allowing her to take over my body like that takes an extreme amount of energy on my part, not to mention the amount of pressure it would put on my body."

"But wouldn't it all be worth it?" Hannah pleaded, her voice cracking slightly as it lost its strength. "Xavier is like a brother to us and he's put his life on the line for this pack more times than I care to mention. Do you not think he at least deserves us to *try*?"

I sat up in my seat as I waited for Anna to reply, not believing that she'd had a way to save him this whole time and she wasn't going to do it.

"Trust me, I would do it in a heartbeat if I could... you *know* I would Hannah," Anna sighed. "But when I say I can't, I really mean it. I *physically can't.*"

The two remained silent for a moment, obviously allowing what Anna had just said to sink into Hannah's mind. Eventually though I saw the two connect in a hug as their shadows blurred together.

"Does Jax know?" Hannah quietly asked, the previous frustration I heard in her voice now vanished into something sounding almost guilty and sympathetic.

"No," Anna muttered as her voice broke again. "I was going to wait until we had gotten Blaine's family back," she explained. "You know he'd never let me go if he knew," she chuckled, but it lacked any real humour.

They remained silent again for a while before both slowly stepping back into Xavier's room but froze when they saw me wide awake and looking furious between the two.

"Blaine just let me explain," Anna said hesitantly, her hands held out in front of her.

"Explain what?" I yelled, not even trying to hide my hurt and frustration. "Explain why you refuse to heal him?" I continued to yell as I stood up, all my emotions from the last few days bubbling to the surface.

"No Blaine it's not like that," Anna stuttered as she tried to get a word in.

"Then what is it? Is he just not important enough for you to even *try*? Will it make you a little bit too *tired,*" I screamed as I took a step in her direction. "And you call yourself his friend," I spat as I turned around to look at Xavier, hoping he would calm me in some way by just looking at him.

"Blaine, I understand why you are hurt and frustrated with me right now but if you would just li-."

"Save it Anna," I mumbled as I cautiously took his hand in mine.

"I'm pregnant," she suddenly rushed out as her shoulders dropped in defeat. "I can't heal him because neither my body nor my baby would survive the Goddesses touch," she sighed as tears leaked from her eyes. "If there was anything I could do for him, *anything,* I would do it, but I just... can't," she cried as she collapsed onto the floor, the fight leaving her body as her tears and guilt consumed her.

I stared down at her as I watched her curl into a ball in the corner of the room, instantly regretting the hateful words I had just spat at her. She had risked a lot for me, without her not only would I most likely be dead by the hands of her own mate, but I also never would have found my family and gotten my mother and sister back. Not to mention the fact that I never would have managed to get to know Xavier on the level that I did without her forcing us together.

A tear slipped down my cheek but for once it wasn't for Xavier, it was for the person I called a friend who I'd just hurt with my cruel words. I released Xavier's hand and walked over to where Anna was, slightly nervous that she would push me away but knowing I needed to at least try to apologise to her and show her that I regretted my actions.

Hannah looked up from where she sat on the floor, hugging Anna as best she could to try and console her the only way she knew how. Upon seeing me there she scowled up at me, clearly showing that she wasn't happy with what I had just said. Once she saw the look of regret and guilt in my eyes, she could tell I was trying to make amends because she got up and sat in the armchair I had previously been sitting in without a word.

With my back against the wall to use as a support, I slowly slid down the wall until I was sitting next to a still sobbing Anna, taking Hannah's place as I awkwardly wrapped my arm around her.

"Anna I'm sorry," I muttered as I stared ahead at the wheels attached to Xavier's bed. "I didn't mean what I said, I just have a lot of emotions running through my head right now and I took them out on you. It-it was wrong of me and I apologise," I whisper as I continued my staring contest with the wheel.

"I will forever be in your dept for what you have done for me and for what you've put on the line for me. You've saved my family, saved *me*, and introduced me to the most amazing mate a person could ever ask for, and all I did was yell at you for not doing more," I sighed as I finally broke my stare with the wheel and looked down at her.

She had calmed down significantly by now, only releasing the odd sniff or hiccup here and there as I continued my apology.

"It's just that with finding out my dad and Daniel may not have survived, feeling an overwhelming amount of guilt because I couldn't save them, as well as knowing Xavier's wolf is *right there* but unable to connect with him or the bond because he's too weak, I'm on edge and confused," I sighed.

"You what?" Anna whispered as she lifted her head up from her knees. Her cheeks were streaked with tears and her eyes were all puffy from crying, but her eyebrows were drawn into a V, staring confused up at me.

"I'm trying to say I'm sorry Anna," I frowned back at her, had she only now started paying attention?

"No I got that, you're forgiven by the way, what did you just say about feeling his wolf but unable to connect with him?" She asked, a spark of hope back in her eyes.

"Oh umm..." I muttered, confused why she was suddenly so focused on that piece of information when only five seconds ago she had been crying her eyes out. I looked up at Hannah for help, but she just shrugged and rolled her eyes, mouthing the word *hormones* to me.

I lifted an eyebrow up at that and looked back down at Anna who was still staring up at me with a small smile on her face. Did hormones really make someone this mood swingy, especially this early on in the pregnancy? I always thought the mood swings came on later.

"I just mean that when I tried to communicate with him through the link earlier, I could feel him trying to respond back but his wolf was too weak," I shrugged.

I flinched when Anna shot up from her place on the floor and walked over to Xavier, taking his hand in hers as she closed her eyes.

I struggled to get up with her, confused why this piece of information had her so excited, in the end needing Hannah's help to get me to my feet before we both walked over to Xavier on the other side of the bed from where Anna stood, her head bowed down in concentration.

"Anna, what are you doing?" I muttered, but I got no answer from her as she remained frozen in her position.

When she finally looked up at us, her eyes were glowing a bright pearlescent white as she stared at us through her wolfs eyes.

"I can feel him," she muttered, looking almost bewildered at the fact that she could feel Xavier's wolf. "I mean I have to really concentrate and use a bit of the Goddesses touch, but I can just about feel him," she whispered as she smiled over the bed at me. "I have an idea Blaine, it won't be easy, and it may not work, but it may just save him," she whispered as she stared into my eyes, her facial expression showing the smallest sign of relief, of hope.

My heart rate skipped slightly, happiness and adrenaline filling my veins at the prospect that I could get my Xavier back. "What do we need to do," I asked with conviction as I stared into her eyes, showing her that I was willing to do whatever it took to save him from this slow and painful death as the wolfsbane continued to eat away at his flesh.

. . .

A few hours later we were all gathered around a table in the hospital waiting room. Seeing as I technically wasn't discharged yet the doctors stated I had to remain nearby just in case I passed out again from some unseen side effect from the wolfsbane poisoning. Ridiculous if you asked me, apart from feeling a little weak I felt fine.

I humoured them though and agreed to stay here for now, but that was mainly because Xavier was here and I didn't want to leave his side.

We all sat in silence as we waited for Anna to start explaining. I was sitting with my legs curled up to my chest, hooked back up to the IV drip that I'd ripped out earlier, as my eyes kept wandering to the door to Xavier's room, feeling uneasy at having to leave his side. Jax was also here sitting next to Anna with a protective hand resting over her shoulder.

He hadn't been too happy to find out that Anna had hidden the pregnancy from him just so that she could come with us on the rescue mission. In fact saying that he *'wasn't happy'* was an understatement, but he'd quickly gotten over his anger after it had sunk in that he was going to be a dad again. He'd brought her in for a massive hug and refused to let her go ever since the news broke.

Other than Jax, Anna and me sitting here Hannah had also joined us along with Jax's dad Jackson and Xavier's doctor Dr Walters. Jax's mum, Emily, was still at their house looking after JJ, but was insistent on being kept in the loop through the link between her and Jackson.

"So what's this amazing plan you have for us Anna?" Hannah asked as she, like the rest of us, stared over at her expectantly.

"Well I thought of it when Blaine said that she could feel Xavier's wolf, but he was too weak to respond to any form of communication we tried to have with him. I was thinking that maybe if we bring his wolf out using the connection Blaine has to him, the blood bond, then maybe his wolf could heal Xavier quicker and stop the effects of the poisoning from progressing before it's too late," she explained as she looked over all of us.

I frowned along with everyone else as we thought over her plan. "But Anna," Jackson muttered as he looked over at her. "We have no way of being able to reach out to him with you being unable to host the Goddess. Not to mention if we try and force his wolf to do something faster than he is able to then it could kill not only Xavier's wolf but him as well," he explained.

"But every second we leave him the wolfsbane is doing further damage, we need to do this now before it's too late and he's too far gone for us to help," Anna argued back as she looked over at Xavier's doctor, hoping that he would back her up in some way.

"We aren't disagreeing with the facts Anna, we all know what happens to a wolf who continues to suffer from long term exposure, but we just don't have the knowledge or resources to achieve it," the doctor explained with a sigh. "Not to mention we have no idea what kind of strain that would put on Blaine."

Everyone looked over at me, but I ignored them as I looked over at Anna, assessing just how sure she was of her plan. "What would I need to do?" I asked her, ignoring the faces around me as they tried to silently protest.

"With your mate bond, a blood bond, you have a stronger connection to him than any of us combined. I'm suggesting that I feed the energy from the Goddess from me and into you so that you have the power to penetrate his mind and re-energise his wolf," she explained as she leaned forward. "That way my body is safe from feeling the full effects of Her Touch, but Xavier can still get the help he needs."

"But Blaine is still healing from her own encounter from the wolfsbane, is there someone else that could possibly do it, your mum maybe? Someone stronger? I mean I'm his Alpha and his best friend, that type of connection must count for something right?" Jax asked as he looked down at his mate.

She sighed before shaking her head, "the connection isn't strong enough," she explained. "The blood bond is the strongest bond two wolves can share and I don't even know if that would be enough," she shrugs as she looks over at me. "I don't know if this will work, but it's the only thing I can think of to try and help save Xavier," she muttered.

"It's worth a shot," I nodded as I looked over at everyone who had gathered in the small waiting room. "You've all done so much for me, let me do this one thing for you, for all of us," I said with my shoulders set firm and my chin held high. "Besides this may not even work in the first place so there really is no point in stressing over the what ifs just yet," I muttered as I stood up with the help of the arm rest.

"Blaine, are you sure about this?" Anna asked as we all walked back over to Xavier's room, the wheels of my IV stand ricketing beside me as I used it to help me walk. "Something like this has never been attempted before, and we have no idea how this could affect you in the short or long run," she explained as she took my hand in hers.

"I want him back just as much as you do Anna," I smiled as I squeezed her hand in mine. "And I'm going to do everything in my power to get him back to me, to all of us," I stated as we walked into his room.

"What first Anna?" I asked as I stood next to Xavier who was still lying flat on his bed, unmoved from when I last saw him.

"Okay so get up on the bed with Xavier and take his hand in yours," she explained as she pointed to the small space that was available next to him.

With some wiggling and manoeuvring, I was finally up on the bed next to him, holding back tears as I noticed the lack of tingles I felt when I took his hand in mine.

"Okay so Blaine I am going to take your other hand and use it as a channel to feed a small amount of the Goddesses Touch through me and into you. It's more than likely you'll pass out from the strength of it, just don't fight it and focus on your blood link with Xavier and his wolf." She explained as she looked down at me. "We will all be here monitoring everything so just relax and focus on the task at hand alright?" She asked as she took my free hand in hers.

"Well it's now or never," I muttered as I closed my eyes and waited.

"Best of luck Blaine," someone muttered to my right, but I didn't have time to respond. Before I could even think of forming a single syllable a blinding pain shot through my arm and began to weave its way through my body.

I screamed in agony as my wolf came through, causing my eyes to shift colour and my claws and teeth to extend. This pain was so much worse than anything I could possibly imagine, worse than the wolfsbane and worse than even the first shift.

"Fight the shift Blaine," I heard someone yell at me, but it sounded so in the distance it was almost a whisper. "Fight the shift," they screamed again but before I could respond blackness consumed me and I was pulled into sleep.

Chapter Thirty-Eight
Xavier's POV

It was so peaceful here... wherever *here* was.

I felt like I was floating in a lake of blackness surrounded by more blackness. It was the first time in I don't remember how long, I felt completely at peace with everything that was around me. I didn't have the worry of Blaine leaving me, the grief of losing my family or the paranoia of when the next threat would hit our pack. I felt... free... safe.

I sighed as I breathed in another deep breath of air, but froze when the oxygen started to cause a tingling in my lungs and shoulder. It wasn't a nice tingle, like the telling signs of a mate link, but more unpleasant like being electrocuted as it continued to spread throughout my body. It was like a small voltage of electricity was being shocked through my system and the more time went on, the more powerful it became.

I flinched away from the feeling, craving the blissful nothingness of the black waters that had previously surrounded me, but the more I fought the feeling the stronger it seemed to become. The fingers of electricity gripped onto my flesh and bones as I felt it tugging me in different directions, screaming in agony as I fort against it.

Just when I was about to blackout, not being able to stand the force of the currents, they suddenly ceased their movement. I could still feel them, rippling away under the surface of my skin, but they were no longer forcing me to go somewhere I didn't want to be. I sighed and sagged in relief, glad that I was able to return to my peaceful nothingness, but when I lay down to go back to sleep, I frowned. The tugging may have stopped, but for some reason the sense of calm I had previously experienced didn't return.

I looked around at the nothingness that surrounded me and frowned as I felt a shift in me, I no longer felt safe here. Before the blackness was like a calming balm to my emotions, soothing me so that I felt nothing, but now it was like a horror movie. I had no idea where I was and no idea what was lurking in the darkness just over my shoulder.

I was craving the electricity pulls again, wanting them to pull me to safety so that I could feel calm again, but they did nothing, just sat bubbling under my skin as if waiting to be told what to do.

The outline of a body suddenly started to materialise in front of me and I froze, not knowing where to go or what to do. The body shimmered in a golden glow, forming the only source of light around us, but it did little to brighten up my surroundings, the darkness around us sucking the light from the figure in front of me.

I started to stand from my position on the floor, not knowing where to go but feeling like I needed to go... somewhere, the figure sifteded and before I could blink, I saw my mum standing in front of me.

She looked as beautiful as I remembered, maybe even more so, as she stared down at me with the constant love and happiness I always felt whenever she held me in her arms as a child.

Gone was the blood and tears covering her body that always seemed to plague my memory whenever I thought about her, and what replaced them was gold and sequins as they emitted their own light all over her dress and skin, causing her to almost glow in the non-existent light.

"Mum?" I whispered, unable to believe that she was here, right in front of me.

She continued to stand there with her hands clasped in front of her, looking down at me as if assessing my every body part. She used to do this a lot when I was a kid, whenever I came home from school or if she'd known I'd been in some form of scuffle, she'd run her eyes over me to make sure that I wasn't damaged or in pain before she laid into me. I had always complained about it when I was younger, telling her that I was fine and that she needed to stop treating me like a child. Now though I craved it, craved the normality of it and the wave of nostalgia that followed.

"Hi Xavier," she whispered as she held her arms out to me with a soft smile on her face.

I sat there for a second, not believing that she was truly in front of me, before scrambling to my feet and engulfing her in a hug.

The hug felt weird, I could feel her in my arms as her own looped around my shoulders, holding me close to her, but at the same time it was like I was hugging a ghost. She was there but at the same time, she wasn't.

"I don't... how are you...?" I stuttered but couldn't finish my question. I was so happy to see her after so many years of missing her, but at the same time I was sad, because I knew what it meant.

"I-I'm never going to see them again, am I?" I questioned as my heart ached for the loss of Blaine, the loss of my friends and the loss of my pack.

"That's completely up to you Xavier, I've been brought here to help guide you through towards the Moon Goddesses Garden, but your mate and family are working tirelessly to try and save you. It is up to you whether you allow their efforts to be in vain or not," she explained as she held her hands in mine.

Just then I heard muffled voices coming from somewhere I couldn't quite distinguish. They were quiet, too quiet for me to understand what they were saying, but it didn't take me long to figure out it was Anna yelling something to someone.

I turned around, looking for the voice, but when I couldn't find anything but the blackness I turned back towards my mum and took a step closer. "But you're my family," I muttered as I took a few more steps towards her. With every step I took Anna's voice grew further and further away, until I could no longer hear it.

"They are your family too Xavier," she soothed. "Just because they aren't blood related, doesn't mean that they care and love you any less than we do," she whispered as she ran her thumb along my cheekbone.

It was then that I felt an invisible finger brush against my hand, it was the smallest of touches, but it caused the electricity to reawaken within me and I was suddenly being forced backwards again, away from my mum and my family.

306

"MUM!" I screamed as I held my hand out for her to take, hoping she would reach out for me and help me stay, but she didn't move.

"It's your choice Xavier, stay with us and I will bring you to the garden where your father and Louise are waiting, or go on and live your life with that beautiful mate of yours," she smiled.

"Help me decide!" I yelled, my hair and clothing having a mind of their own as if I were in a wind tunnel, the breeze pushing me backwards with every second.

"I can't help you decide this Xavier," she whispered with a shake of her head, her quiet voice piercing through the rushing of the wind with ease. "Just know that your dad and I are incredibly proud of you, and if you decide to live your life the way it should be then the three of us will be here, watching over you and smiling down on you until your time comes," she reassured me.

Anna's voice suddenly piped up again, screaming at someone to stay with her and to stay alive. At first I thought she was talking about me, pleading with me to choose life and not enter the garden with my mum, but when I heard another voice scream Blaine's name I turned. Blaine was in danger?

"Your mate can't hold this up much longer Xavier, make your decision or it won't be just you I'll be leading to the garden," she smiled as she took a step closer to me, the wind causing the gap between us to grow.

"Mum," I almost sobbed as the voices became clearer.

"We will always be right here and waiting for you when it's your time," she whispered as she reached out and again stroked her fingers down my cheek with a loving look in her eyes.

A tear escaped my eye as I looked into hers, her irises shining bright gold against her pale skin.

"I love you," I whispered with a sob as I held her hand against my cheek.

"We love you too," she replied with a smile just as I heard Anna scream that rogues had been spotted at the border.

The finger that had just brushed against my hand suddenly gripped onto mine tightly, linking our fingers together as the electricity increased to almost painful measures.

"Bye mum," I muttered as I watched her light slowly fade into the darkness and disappear.

The pressure on my hand slowly increased and before I could blink, it was dragging me out of the darkness and towards a soft glow that I hadn't noticed before. It was different from the light that was glowing around my mum, this one was a bright white colour instead of a soft golden glow, and the more the hand dragged me towards it the more pain I was in.

My shoulder was on fire and my hand had deep gashes in it as the blood trickled down my fingers and dripped onto the floor beneath me. My skin started to look a sickly grey colour and the muscle definition I once had was slowly deteriorating with every passing second.

I tried to shake the hand off of me, not liking where it was bringing me or what it was doing to me, but it was no use. I had made my decision to stay and live.

"We're losing her!" A voice yelled from in the distance.

"Someone bring in the crash cart!" Another voice shouted as a sound almost like a squeaking wheel rang through my ears.

"Someone separate them," I recognised Jax voice as I felt another hand brush against my skin. I screamed in pain as blood continued to ooze from my hands, but the pain lessened when I heard Anna yell at him to stop.

"Don't break the connection, if you do that we could lose both of them," she whispered. Her voice sounded pained and worn out, almost as if she was suffering through as much pain as I was.

"Annabelle, if we don't break the connection now, you and Xavier will be shocked and we could lose all three of you, including the baby... I won't do that," Jax growled.

"Just wait two seconds," she pleaded. "We've got him, but we just need to make sure-," Anna muttered but before she could finish a small whimper escaped her lips.

"Starting CPR," the original voice yelled, but I ignored it as I focused on Anna's voice, needing something to grip onto to find my way back.

A few seconds later I felt a blinding pain spread throughout my body before falling onto a hard surface with a thump. I tried to breath, but it felt like something was down my throat causing me to gag and splutter.

"Get that Intubate tube out of him!" A voice called before I felt the object being pulled up and out of my lungs so that I could finally breathe easier.

"Break the connection... get the crash cart in place... 1 2 3 CLEAR!"

There was so much noise around me, and the room was almost too bright for me to see as I tried to prise my eyes open. I recognised the smell of the hospital and the fact that I was lying down, but other than that I was confused and lost. Weren't we just in the caves fighting

Benjamin? How am I suddenly in a hospital bed and being shook awake.

"No response... charging again... clear... we have a rhythm... get that other bed in here stat!"

"wha...?" I tried to mumble but instantly cringed at the scratching of my voice. I tried to lift my arm up, wanting to rub my eyes to try and help them refocus, but frowned when it was tugged back by something.

"Careful Xavier, you're connected to a lot of leads right now so just stay still and we'll sort you out when we can," a voice, Hannah, muttered close to my ear.

I just nodded as I tuned out the craziness that was going on around me, happy in the knowledge that I had made the right decision and I was back where I belonged. My mum was right, they may not be family by blood, but they were still my family.

Chapter Thirty-Nine
Xavier's POV

When I woke back up it was dark out. At first, I thought I had dreamt fighting back to the living world as I was surrounded in the familiar darkness, but after I calmed myself down and started to take note of what was around me I realised that it was just dark outside and I hadn't slipped back into the *in-between realm*. I had no idea what time it was or even what day it was, but I was just glad that I was finally awake.

I lifted my head up slightly to see if I could find Blaine anywhere, but frowned when I couldn't find her. Hadn't she been just next to me not long ago?

I pressed the call button to get someone's attention and sighed when Hannah and a nurse walked in, both looking tired and dishevelled.

"Xavier you're awake," Hannah sighed in relief as she took a seat next to me. The nurse just offered me a small smile and a nod before checking my vitals and quietly leaving.

"What... what happened?" I asked as I cringed at the pain of using my voice.

Hannah didn't respond at first, she just offered me a small plastic cup of water with a straw in it to help ease the raspiness in my voice. Finally, she looked up and offered me a small smile. "Anna and Blaine managed to get you back, but it wasn't easy. It took a lot of energy on both their parts to achieve what they did," she muttered as she ran a hand through her messed up hair.

"Hannah... what happened?" I asked again, needing to know what happened to my mate and my Luna.

"Well after they managed to bring you back Anna collapsed on the floor, the strain of the Goddesses Touch too much for her to cope in the current state she's in. She's doing fine now though, both her and the baby are okay, they're just resting in a room a few doors down from you," Hannah nodded as she looked to her right, as if she could see Anna through the walls.

"And Blaine?" I prodded, my heart rate picking up and my palms beginning to sweat as a small dose of fear trickled down my spine.

"She... she umm... lost a lot of energy, too much energy for her body to handle, causing her heart to stop beating," she stuttered as she looked up at me.

I shot up into a sitting position but quickly collapsed back onto the bed as the bullet wound in my shoulder screamed in pain. "I h-have to see h-her," I managed to get out as I tried once again to sit up, groaning as the stabbing pain intensified.

"Oh no you don't," Hannah stated as she stood up and placed her hands on my shoulders, gently forcing me back down onto my bed. "Xavier, listen to me, we got her back, she's fine. She's currently unconscious and sleeping in the room next to yours," she explained as she walked over to the blinds on my left and pulled them up so that I could see into the room next to mine. "She's drained but the doctors are confident that she'll make a full recovery in a couple of days," she reassured me as she looked me over, making sure that I was staying put.

My eyes didn't waver from Blaine's figure lying motionless on the bed, as I watched her sleep through the glass wall. She looked so peaceful I would have almost guessed she was sleeping and hadn't just died trying to save my life.

"How did they...?" I muttered as I ran my eyes over her blanket covered body.

"It wasn't easy," Hannah sighed as she came and sat back down next to me. "The wolfsbane in your system was causing your body and wolf to deteriorate with every passing second. Your wolf was too weak to help heal you and without him we all knew you'd die," she sighed as she held her head in her hands. "Anna came up with an idea to use her gift to channel Blaine into your head and try and search out your wolf, offering him her energy so that he could resurface and heal you.

"At first it seemed alright, after the initial shock on Blaine's part she calmed down and fell into some form of trance-like state. She had semi shifted though, hence the fresh wounds on your hand where her claws attached themselves to you," she explained.

It was only then that I realised my left hand was all bandaged up and in a soft cast type thing. So the hand I was feeling was Blaine's and the electricity that had been running through me was energy as it passed from Anna into Blaine and then into me. "So what happened after?"

"Well, it all seemed to happen so fast after that," she sighed. "We thought it was working, Anna even confirmed as much as she said Blaine had found you and was transferring the energy. We're not sure what happened though, not long after Blaine found you, the energy transfer seemed to stop, causing it to build up in Blaine at an unhealthy rate. There was nothing we could do, Anna said that breaking the bond between the three of you could cause irreversible damage to not just you, but them as well." She paused for a second as her eyes unfocused, looking as if she was reliving the experience over and over.

I thought back to my time in the darkness, back to when I had forced the electricity to stop so that I could talk to my mum for just that little bit longer and froze. I had done that. I had put my mate and Luna in danger by being selfish and blocking their help.

"The energy eventually started to flow again though," Hannah sighed as she continued to stare off into space, "but because of the build-up, Blaine's body released too much of it at once and caused her heart to stop," she muttered.

She snapped out of her trance and looked back at me with a small smile, "like I said, it all worked out and everyone just needs a good rest before you're all back to normal again," she nodded.

I looked up at her and noticed a forced smile on her face, almost as if she was being overly positive not only to convince me but herself as well.

"Thank you for telling me Hannah," I sighed as I looked down at my hands.

We stayed silent for a moment as we both got lost in our thoughts. I had nearly killed my mate, all because I had been selfish enough to want an extra few minutes with my mum.

"It wasn't your fault you know," Hannah whispered next to me, breaking our comfortable silence.

I looked over to her in confusion, acting as if I didn't know what she was talking about, but sighed and dropped the act when she gave me a pointed look. "How'd you know?"

"I've known you my whole life Xavier, I know you'd never do something that would intentionally harm any of us," she smiled as she took my hand in hers.

"But it *is* my fault," I muttered, hating myself for it. "*I* was the reason the energy stopped flowing," I explained as I looked down into my lap. "I... I saw my mum and I think I unconsciously knew what the electricity thing was trying to do to me, and I just wanted to stop it so that I could spend more time with her," I sighed.

"You saw her?" Hannah asked in bewilderment as she squeezed my hand.

I smiled slightly as I thought back to my brief encounter with her. "Yeah, it was amazing," I sighed as I squeezed her hand back.

"I'm glad the Goddess allowed you to have those moments with her," Hannah whispered as she squeezed my hand again. "But there really is no reason to feel guilty over something that wasn't your fault. You had no idea what was happening, all you wanted was to see your mum and I think everyone can understand and sympathise with that. Besides nobody got hurt so there really is nothing to feel guilty over," she smiled down at me.

I gave her a pointed look before looking over at my still sleeping mate.

"Okay... nobody *died*," she said as she rolled her eyes at me.

I gave her another pointed look before looking back at Blaine again.

"Oh for the love of everything Xavier I'm trying to remain positive here for the both of us and you're really not helping," Hannah sighed as she crossed her arms over her chest.

"There's the Hannah I know and love," I chuckled as I smiled up at her slightly. I had always loved winding her up, even as a little girl.

She just stuck her tongue out at me and huffed before slouching back in her chair, obviously not impressed with my teasing.

"Oh did I hear something about rogues at some point?" I asked, changing the topic in the hopes she won't be grumpy anymore.

"Oh yeah!" Hannah quickly sat up with a big grin on her face. "You'll never guess who decided to show up," she smiled, almost jumping in her seat.

"Who?" I questioned, confused as to why she was jumping in her seat so much for a rogue.

"Well, we were supposed to keep it a secret for when Blaine wakes up, but whilst we were trying to save you we got a link saying that the border patrol had spotted two rogues trying to get into our territory. Jax told them to put them in the cells until he was available to question them and when he finally got down there, he realised that it was Blaine's dad and brother!" She squealed, rushing it all out in one breath.

My eyes widened at the information, "I didn't even know they hadn't made it out of the cave," I muttered as I looked back at Blaine again.

"Oh yeah apparently they stayed back to deal with Benjamin and the others so that Jax could get you and

Blaine out to safety. We had all thought they hadn't made it, but apparently, they did!" She squealed.

I smiled at her excitement, not taking my eyes off my mate. She had her whole family back and safe, just as it should be.

Hannah left shortly after that, claiming that she still had a whole hospital full of people to visit and that I needed to get some more rest so that my wolf could continue to do his thing and heal me. I lay back in bed and smiled at the realisation that I had seen my mum and that she was safe.

I had always pictured in my head her, my dad and Louise all looking like they did when they were killed, sitting in an empty darkness not dissimilar to what I was in. Now I knew though that they were happy and safe as they looked down on me from the Goddesses Garden, smiling away and waiting for when it was my time to join them.

I stared at my beautiful mate's face and sighed as I realised the weight of their death had been lifted from my shoulders. I couldn't wait to join them in The Garden, but I couldn't help but hope that it wouldn't be for a very long time, until I was old and wrinkly with a still smiling and feisty Blaine at my side.

Chapter Forty
Xavier's POV

It had been nearly two weeks since Blaine and Anna had risked their lives to save me, and I was *finally* being released from hospital.

Anna was the first to be released, thankfully all she needed was a bit of TLC and an IV drip and she was walking out of here with a smile on her face and a skip in her step, much to Jax's annoyance. He'd wanted her to stay in hospital for a few extra days just to 'be on the safe side', but after Anna and two separate doctors reassured him that her and the baby were perfectly fine and healthy he relented.

I'd laughed as I watched them constantly bicker, either in the hallway or in my room as they kept me company. Jax was constantly fussing about her safety and about how she shouldn't be doing anything, to help protect the baby, and Anna would always state that she was a grown ass woman and could choose what she could and couldn't do. She knew this was coming through, Jax had been bad when he found out she was pregnant with JJ, but now that he's found out she's pregnant with baby number two he's ramped up his overprotectiveness tenfold, especially as she'd kept it from him for so long.

Blaine was released next. It took a lot longer for her body to completely heal after coding. She was mainly kept in for fluids and observation though, the doctors wanting to keep an eye on her energy levels and nutrition input to help build her strength back up. Not only was she healing from the energy shift, but she was also dealing with wolfsbane poisoning on top of that, something I didn't know about until Jax had informed me.

Apparently, she had put her own life at risk by trying to get the excess wolfsbane off my skin as best she could, resulting in it getting on the palms of her hands when it had soaked through the fabric of whatever she had been using. I was stunned into silence at that, not knowing many people who would willingly put themselves at risk of wolfsbane poisoning for fear of what it would do to them in the long run. It was a known fact that coming into contact with wolfsbane targets your wolf, causing it to weaken and eventually die just like it had been doing to me before I was saved.

I would be forever grateful for my strong and beautiful mate who had put her own life at risk for the sake of my own, and I was going to do everything in my power to make it up to her, even if it took the rest of our lives.

I think the biggest thing that's changed since I've woken up was the fact that Blaine's family is all now here and safe. We had decided to wait until Blaine was awake and a bit more alert before telling her that her dad and brother had survived the fight with Benjamin. Her energy levels had been so low we were worried that one hit of adrenaline would wipe her out all over again and it was something the doctors wouldn't risk.

It had been amazing to watch her face light up when the two of them had finally been allowed to walk through the door, well her brother walked and her dad kind of hobbled due to a shattered leg which had been damaged during the fight. At first she had been speechless, just staring at them standing in the doorway to her room. But when her mum had kissed her on the head and confirmed that they were here and she wasn't dreaming she'd burst into tears, crying into the crook of her elbow whilst constantly muttering stuff under her breath, too low for any of us to hear.

Her family were doing well, for the most part, they said they found it weird being out of their wolf form and not having to be in constant fear of being put into the ring or abused by anyone. They all had some form of injury that needed looking at by the doctors but over all they had nothing that would have caused them serious long-term damage, just a few scars.

The only person that was finding it difficult to adjust was Daniel, he had been The Rings lead fighter and so had seen stuff and done stuff that most of the others couldn't even imagine. He refused to talk about it, saying he'd prefer to leave it all behind him and forget about it, but I do worry that one day he's just going to crack and not be able to handle the memories and the strain that they inevitably brought.

What surprised us all the most though was the fact that he and Hannah were mates. Hannah had been over the moon at the discovery, claiming that she couldn't be happier that she had finally found her one true love to be with for the rest of her life. I think she had come on a bit strong though, just by looking at his reaction to her I could tell that Daniel was a bit of a flight risk and wasn't quite mentally prepared to have a mate, especially someone like Hannah, who was completely the opposite to him. Where he was quiet and broody, preferring to sit in the background and just people watch, Hannah was the life and soul of the party, always wanting to be social and constantly talking.

We'd all decided to leave it alone and stay out of their business. It was already too complicated with just the two of them trying to figure their situation out, let alone having multiple people butt into their business and offering up their own opinion and advice as to what they should do. I just hoped that Daniel adjusts and manages to accept the fact that Hannah is his mate and that he's now safe and away from those monsters. I'm not sure if Hannah could cope if he doesn't.

"Are you ready to go?" Blaine asked as she popped her head into my hospital room.

I was currently packing up the last of the stuff I'd been brought whilst sitting in this hospital room. Even though our hospital was better than your average human one, the food was half decent and the rooms were all private and big enough to fit a whole family, it was still a hospital, and I couldn't wait to get out and go home.

"Yeah just packing the last few bits," I smiled over to her as I held up the small teddy bear that Blaine had given me. She'd done it as a joke, claiming she'd seen everyone do it in one of those Romcom movies Anna had forced her to watch. I'd found it adorable though and to her complete horror I'd given the stuffed toy a permanent seat on my bedside table, front and centre for everyone to see.

"Ugh do we really have to bring that?" She groaned as she leant against the door, crossing her arms over her chest. She was pretending that she hated the thing, but I knew she secretly loved the fact that I loved it so much.

"You know it," I chuckled as I walked over to her with my now packed bag in hand. I dropped it on the floor at her feet and wrapped my non-injured arm around her shoulders and brought her into my chest, kissing her forehead as I did. "That little toy is going up on the living room mantel for everyone to see," I chuckled as I heard her gasp in horror. "I want everyone who walks into our house to know that you '*wuve me*'," I laughed as I quoted the word that was embroidered on the teddies t-shirt.

"I hate you," she muttered into the crook of my neck.

"You love it," I laughed as I reached down to pick my bag up with my good hand and offered my strapped-up elbow for her to take with my other. I was being forced to wear a sling for another two weeks to make sure the joint was fully healed, safe to say I was definitely not a fan.

"I'll compromise and say it can go in our bedroom," she bargained as she smiled up at me. I knew that if I didn't relent she'd steal the bear from me when I wasn't looking so I just sighed and nodded my head, agreeing with her demands.

"Good... now everyone has said they're coming round ours to celebrate your release tonight for dinner so I'm just thinking about wacking out the barbeque and having it all buffet style? With the amount of people coming round it'd just be way too stressful to try and organise a sit-down meal whilst trying to keep everything warm, don't you think?" She asked as we walked out the hospital and towards my car which Blaine had been driving whilst I'd been bed bound.

I smiled down at her as she continued to plan our spur of the moment dinner party, but I couldn't help but zone out as I watched the sun peek through the clouds and hit her face. Her freckles had come out in the last few days due to the warm weather and her ginger curls had lightened slightly causing natural highlights to run through her locks. She was the most gorgeous person I had ever laid eyes on, and I still couldn't believe that this strong, feisty, loving, caring and independent woman was all mine.

"Are you listening to me?" She questioned with a raised eyebrow as she looked up at me, already knowing full well that I definitely wasn't.

"I'm sorry... I just got distracted by your beauty," I stated in an over sappy voice, causing her to laugh and roll her eyes.

"Whatever prince charming, just make sure everything is all set for tonight, there is no way I am letting this first dinner with everyone be a flop. Anna is doing most of the indoor cooking with the help of all the mum's and Will, preparing the potato salads and breads and things like that. I need you to man the grill with Jax and make sure nothing is burnt or raw. If someone gets food poisoning, I'm blaming it on you," she stated as she pointed up at me.

"And what will you be doing miss commander in chief?" I laughed.

"I'll be running around like a headless chicken making sure everyone is happy and topping up drinks. This is a dinner for fifteen Xavier, it needs to run smoothly," she stated in a very *duh* tone of voice causing me to laugh.

I pulled her to a stop once we'd made it to my car, boxing her against the passenger door as best I could with only one arm. She looked up at me with raised eyebrows, amusement clear in her eyes as she took in our position.

"I love you... you know that?" I smiled as I pressed my forehead against her, looking deep into her bright green eyes.

She smiled up at me as she placed her hands on my cheeks, the palms feeling bumpy due to the scarring from the wolfsbane. Her battle scars which in my opinion make her ten times more sexy. "I *wuve* you too," she chuckled before raising onto her tiptoes and sealing her lips against mine.

Electricity tingled its way through my body and I couldn't help but lean my body against hers as I dropped my bag on the floor and wrapped my unstrapped hand around her waist, pulling her as close as physically possible to me.

I didn't know what our lives would bring or what was going to happen next for us, but as long as I had her by my side, I knew we could accomplish anything.

She was my mate, and I would love her until the end of time.

THE END

Epilogue
Blaine's POV

"Blaine come on, she'll be fine," Xavier chuckled as I continued to stare at my little bundle of joy through the window of my parents' house.

"I know that," I grumbled as I brushed my curly hair from off my forehead, the fringe already starting to fall out of my updo. "Just because I know she'll be alright doesn't mean I'm not allowed to worry about her," I defended. "This is the first time since she's been born that I've been away from her for an entire night."

He smiled over at me as he brought me into his arms, kissing the side of my head as he drew me into his chest. "I know, but I also trust your mum and dad to protect our little girl with their lives. You and I both know that she's safer here than anywhere else, especially with your dad around," he stated as he tried to calm my nerves.

Tonight was the night of the ball, the one that Anna had been organising for months in the hopes that wolves from across the country could come into a neutral zone and meet their mates. I had been hoping that we didn't have to go, that I could skip out on it and spend an evening with my little girl, but as the Beta female of the pack who's hosting it, I was expected to attend. All I had to do was show my face, have a few conversations with other pack members, shove some food into my mouth, then I could leave and come back for her.

"Fine let's go," I sighed as I took Xavier's hand in mine and lifted my floor length dress with the other so that I didn't stand on it and trash the hem. Anna would not be happy with me if I ruined the dress she'd spent hours picking out for me.

I don't honestly know how she does it. With two kids and juggling all the responsibilities of not only being Alpha female but also the Moon Goddesses Messenger, she still manages to find time to come dress shopping with me and Julie. I secretly think she gets it all done by not sleeping and living off caffeine and sugar.

"You look gorgeous by the way," Xavier smiled as he walked over to the passenger's side of the car and opened the door for me.

"You don't look so bad yourself," I smirked as I looked him up and down. "You should wear a suit more often."

"If it gets you to look at me like that I just might," he whispered into my ear as he pressed up against me, the silk of my dress feeling cool against my heated skin. After all this time being with him, I still reacted like a hormonal teenage girl whenever he so much as looked at me. I blamed the blood bond, but if I was being honest, I wouldn't have it any other way.

Xavier looked down at me with heat in his eyes as a small flicker of gold swirled in his irises, obviously feeling my emotions through the link we shared. I reached up onto the tips of my toes, which wasn't much further due to the heels Julie had forced me to wear, intent on pressing my lips against his, when Anna contacted us through the link.

"I know what you two are up to and we don't have time for that. Get your butts over here now, people have already started to arrive, and you were supposed to be here before them."

"I'm going to be so happy when this is all over and she goes back to her normal self," I sighed as I retracted myself from Xavier's arms and got in the car as he did the same. "She's been driving me mad all month with fabric samples and menu choices, she's almost as bad as humans get on the run up to their wedding day."

Xavier laughed beside me but otherwise didn't comment, he knew what I'd been dealing with the past few weeks and knew better than to encourage my complaining and put me in a bad mood.

"Just think," he smiled over at me as he took my hand in his free one. "Come tomorrow morning we'll be waking up to an empty house. No Anna messaging us at stupid hours of the day and no cute little baby Charlotte to wake us up with her screams, demanding us to sing her a song to get her back to sleep," he smirked.

I did have to admit, I liked the sound of having a morning with just me and him, we hadn't been alone since Charlotte's birth. Not that I would change anything for the world, she was my little angel and I loved everything about her, but I would like just one night to be with my mate and enjoy some alone time together.

"I like the sound of that," I murmured as I brought out joint hands up so that I could kiss his knuckles. "Do you know what I'm most looking forward to though?" I smirked as I looked over at him.

"I have an idea," he grinned back at me before moving his eyes back to the road.

"A lie in," I exclaimed as I closed my eyes, already picturing what it would be like to wake up feeling rested and when the sun was already up high in the sky. Charlotte wasn't much of a sleeper; she was so active and aware of everything around her it was almost comical. She was only seven months, but she sometimes seemed so much older than that as you watched her eyes assess everything.

"You read my mind," Xavier almost groaned next to me and I couldn't help but chuckle at his reaction to a possible lie in.

We drove for another few minutes and before long we arrived at the field where the party was taking place. I took in the marquee that Anna had hired and couldn't help but marvel at the size of it. I had been wondering how she was going to find something big enough to house everyone who had RSVP'd yes, but now I see how. She hadn't just hired a standard marquee; she'd pretty much hired a festival tent.

"She really goes all out for these things doesn't she," I whistled as we parked where all the other cars had started parking.

"Yeah I know," Xavier laughed as he took the key out of the ignition and got out of the car, quickly coming around to my side so that he could open my door and help me out. "The last one we hosted was such a success that even more people decided to come this year. I had been helping her out with planning it and helped her find the company that hired out the biggest tents we could find," he chuckled.

"And then I came along," I chuckled as I took his elbow in mine.

"And then you came along," he laughed as he kissed the side of my head.

We walked into the tent and were instantly handed a flute of champagne each. We had decided to hire a human company to help cater the event so that everyone was available to attend the event if they wished to. We made the other attendees aware of this and were all under strict instruction not to show any signs of what we were just in case we were outed to the human population.

I smiled gratefully to the server before taking a small sip and walked further into the tent, feeling the bubbles tingle against my tongue.

"She's definitely outdone herself," I muttered as I took everything in. The inside of the tent had been completely covered with hanging fabric, draping across the ceiling and down the walls in different colours of whites and beiges with fairy lights strung amongst them. On one side of the tent was the food and drink section, a large bar stretched the entire width of the tent serving every form of drink you could think of. There was also a hot and cold buffet with tables set up for people to sit and eat if they so wished.

The other side was left nearly empty, aside from a small stage where I knew a band would begin playing all different types of music. The first half of the night would be more civilised, playing orchestral music whilst we all chatted amongst each other. By the later stage of the evening it would all change, the band would switch up their type of music and the whole place would come alive with lights as we danced the night away and had a laugh at each other's moves.

That part was mainly put in for the younger wolves, knowing that they probably wouldn't attend if it was just some stuck up ball where everyone had to eat delicate finger sandwiches and ballroom dance. To be honest I don't think *I* would have even attended if it was like that, and I was friends with the person who organised it.

Whilst we waited for Anna and Jax to become available so that we could quickly chat to them and show that we had finally arrived, I linked my parents. I had demanded that they give us, well me, hourly updates on how Charlotte was doing. This was the first time I wouldn't be there to sing her a goodnight song and I was worried she wouldn't sleep because of it.

Upon hearing from my mum that she was doing fine and was having her evening bottle so that they could put her to bed, I closed the link back down. Not before demanding another update in an hour and to remind them to message me if they needed *anything*.

"So how's she doing?" Xavier asked as he whispered in my ear. He could laugh all he wanted about me being an overprotective mum, but I knew that he was secretly feeling just as anxious about leaving her as I was.

"She's fine," nodded as I took another sip of champagne. I watched as Anna and Jax said goodbye to the couple they had just been talking to and made their way over to us.

"That's one pairing already found," Anna sang smugly as she walked over and pulled me in for a hug.

"Already? That has to be some kind of record, right?" I exclaimed as I watched the couple as they walked over to the bar to get a drink.

"They actually met in the hotel last night," she laughed as she released me and pulled Xavier in for a hug. "The place they are staying in accidently booked their room out twice. James was showering when Elaine walked in and screamed her lungs out at finding a naked man in her shower. The screaming didn't last long though when they realised they were mates. Apparently, they didn't even bother with complaining to the hotel and just stayed in the room together," she laughed.

I couldn't help but laugh with her, finding it too funny for it to be real. "That's something you'd see happen in a movie or something," I laughed as I thought about all the Romcoms I've watched over the years.

"I know right!" Anna laughed harder before looking up at Jax and leaning into his side.

"So how's it all looking?" Xavier asked as he took a sip of his own drink.

"Good," Jax and Anna replied at the same time, both nodding as they looked around to take everything in.

"Although there is one thing I'd like to talk to you about before-" Anna started but was interrupted as a man and woman walked over to us, both looking a little tense as they stared at me and Xavier.

"Hello," the man spoke as he held his hand out for me to shake, then Xavier. He offered Anna and Jax a small bow in acknowledgment but otherwise didn't say anything as both him and his mate stared over at us.

"May we help you?" I asked as I looked them over. I couldn't figure it out, but he seemed almost familiar somehow.

"Beta Blaine, Beta Xavier it's lovely to meet you both," the woman suddenly piped up as she took a slight step towards us. "My name is Linda, and this is my mate

Simon, we are the Alpha and Luna of the Moon Lake pack," she explained as she took her mate's hand in hers. "I hope you don't mind, but we decided to come and talk to you in person when we heard about what happened to your family and thought I'd be best to talk in a neutral setting," she continued to say as she looked around the tent.

"So what can we do for you?" I asked as I tried to hold my nerve. The news of Benjamin's fighting ring had spread like wildfire, no one could believe that an Alpha in line could have done something like that to their own people. We'd heard some reports of the captured finding their way back home and reuniting with their packs and families, a lot are still missing though. We helped out as much as we could, but there wasn't much we could do besides talk to my family to see if they remembered seeing any specific people.

"Well..." she muttered as she looked back up at her mate, I could tell they were both silently communicating about something, and it wasn't long before Alpha Simon sighed and nodded a small nod at his mate.

"I hope you don't mind me bringing it up but... my brother..." Alpha Simon sighed as he rubbed the back of his neck.

That's when I realised what he was trying to tell me and why he looked so familiar to me. "Your brother was Benjamin," I confirmed, saying it as a statement rather than a question.

Alpha Simon sighed before nodding his head in confirmation.

I thought I'd feel something when I eventually came face to face with his family, that I'd feel some form of anger or disgust at having to talk to the people who were related to the monster who kidnapped and harmed my family for so long. I waited for the telling signs, for the inevitable feelings of anger to bubble up to the surface, but was surprised when nothing happened. If anything, I just felt sorry for the man who obviously felt such remorse and guilt for what his brother had done.

I felt Xavier tense next to me, preparing himself for how I was going to react, but he quickly relaxed when he felt nothing but acceptance through our mate link.

"Thank you for coming to talk to me Alpha Simon, I really appreciate it," I nodded as I smiled over at him. His brother may have been the reason for me living on my own for over two years and the countless deaths of many wolves over the course of his fighting days, but that was just it. It wasn't him that had been responsible for those crimes, it was his brother, and it would be unfair for me to hold him accountable for his brother's actions.

Alpha Simon's shoulders sagged slightly, clearly relieved that I wasn't going to cause a scene and hold him accountable. "I just wanted to come on my family's behalf and apologise to you in person for everything that Benjamin put you through," he explained as his eyes flicked between the four of us. "And also to thank you for stopping him before he could harm any more people," he continued. "We never knew he was capable of doing anything like that, and if we did you have my word that we would have stopped him long before he could have hurt anyone."

"You are forgiven Alpha Simon," I smiled at him as I held my hand out for him to shake.

He looked down at my outstretched palm for a second, staring at the scars that the wolfsbane had left, before taking my hand firmly in his.

"Truce?" I asked, my eyebrows raised and an amused smile on my face.

"Truce," he nodded back at me with a small smile before releasing my hand and moving to shake Xavier's. "I'm glad you managed to survive the wolfsbane Beta Xavier," he nodded to my mate before moving on to talk to Jax and Anna. "If it is alright with you both, I would like to take over the search for the missing wolves, it's the least I can do to try and help redeem my family name."

Anna smiled up at him before looking over at Jax, waiting to hear his verdict. We all knew he was going to say yes though.

...

The rest of the evening went by in a blur. The whole event was a success, and even though not everyone found their mates, not even half of them, it was still seen as the highlight of their year. Anna had outdone herself, and it wasn't long before we were all stumbling into taxi's and getting lifts home thanks to the ridiculous amounts of alcohol we had all consumed.

Xavier and I all but fell into the house at gone one in the morning, both of us laughing at the fact that neither of us couldn't get the key in the door on our first attempt. It was a good job I hadn't insisted Charlotte and my parents stay the night here, with the amount of noise we were making I knew we would have woken them up.

"So you're definitely okay?" Xavier asked me. It had been the hundredth time he'd asked since we'd met Linda and Simon and every time I sighed and rolled my eyes.

"Yes," I exclaimed as I downed a pint glass of water. "Is it really so shocking that I wouldn't run around guns blazing after finding out who he was?"

Xavier smirked at me as he took the glass from my hand, refilled it and downed it himself. "Honestly? Yes," he laughed as he placed the glass in the open dishwasher. "You're like my little firecracker," he chuckled as he scooped me in his arms.

"I'm not that bad," I tried to defend myself as I playfully hit him on the shoulder. "Besides, he seemed like a nice guy," I shrugged. "Not many people would have the courage to step into our territory during an event in front of hundreds of wolves and admit to what his brother did. That took guts, even for an Alpha," I stated as I stared up into his eyes.

"Mmmhmm," he smirked as he kissed my forehead before trailing his kisses down until they landed at the base of my neck. "Come on, let's see if I can bring that firecracker out of you again," he whispered against my skin before lifting me up so that my legs were around his waist.

"Sounds like a fun challenge to me," I breathed against his lips before reaching forward so that they were pressed firmly against mine.

Acknowledgements

About four years ago I picked up my iPad and sat down to write the first chapter for the first book in this series. Fast forward two years and I'd just finished my second book of this series during the first lockdown in the COVID-19 pandemic. Never in a million years did I believe that either of my books were good enough to do anything with other than put them on a free writing platform called Wattpad. But thanks to all the love and support from all my readers I decided earlier this year to take the plunge and publish my first book, The Alpha and his mate, onto Amazon to see how it would do. To my amazement and astonishment, it has gone above and beyond anything I could have possibly dreamed, helping me build my deposit ready to buy a house next year, I know scary! Without the support of those amazing people on Wattpad I never would have dreamt that this would have been my reality, being able to make money from my overactive imagination, and for that I want to say a massive THANK YOU! That's not to say I haven't had friends and family cheering me on. My mum being one of my top cheerleaders and announcing my first book publication to anyone who would listen, whether they wanted to hear about it or not. Since publishing my first book I have also opened up massively to my friends about the world that I have created, and they couldn't have been more supportive and encouraging. To them I want to say a huge thank you. Lastly, I'd like to thank my boyfriend Alex, for just being his amazing self. I love you and I can't wait until you've finished your book as well so we can live in the self-publishing world together.

About the author

Bryony Wakeford is a wig maker by trade working in the hustle and bustle of theatre life. When she isn't buried in her laptop writing or in the pages of her current read drinking tea she can be found in her home town in East Sussex, England walking her dog Otis and enjoying the country air.

To keep up to date with all things books and her life follow her on Instagram @authorbryonywakeford

Printed by Amazon Italia Logistica S.r.l.
Torrazza Piemonte (TO), Italy

51956700R00197